CRY FOR ME

R SULLINS

To request permissions, contact the author at rsullinsauthor@gmail.com

ISBN: 9798530228605

Cover by
Love Drunk Premades

DEDICATION

To all the ladies that are more than a few years out of high school but still enjoy reading about it... same, girl, same.

SUMMARY

Paige

Loner
Outcast
Charity case
Orphan

I was all those things.
Years after my parents died, I was still being bullied, and it was all led by my cousins.
They hated me for years as children, and moving into their house didn't make them change their minds about me.
I was counting down the days until I could finally get away from every single person in this town.
Until there was one person I wasn't so sure I wanted to leave.

Reid

My life since age 7 revolved around football and what it would take for me to get into the NFL.

I didn't have time for girls or parties.
I had never been tempted by anything that could take my mind away from the sport.
Until I walked into my new school on the first day of senior year.

It wasn't long before we both realized that someone didn't like that we had found each other.

CHAPTER 1

Paige

I reached over and blindly slapped my hand around on my nightstand for my phone, needing to turn off the most annoying sound on the planet. I moaned when the sound of my phone hitting the plush carpet reached my ears over the squawking alarm. I finally cracked my eyes open to peer over the side of my twin-sized bed to follow the sound to locate my phone. Of course, it somehow managed to make it under the fucking bed.

I leaned over as far as I could without actually falling over the edge of the mattress. I swept my hand back and forth until I felt the edge of the phone case and pinched it as well as I could between my fingers and dragged it up to me, right before I fumbled it... and it fell back down to the floor.

"Ugh fuck me!" I groaned low because even though my aunt and uncle weren't on this end of the huge house, that didn't mean that either of my cousins wouldn't hear me. Either of them would report it at the first opportunity they came across-even if their language was decidedly more colorful than mine ever was.

I sat up and swung my legs over the side of my bed, bent down to pick up my fallen phone, and finally hit the dismiss button for the alarm. Normally I would hit snooze and try to get another few minutes of sleep in, but that dream ended now that I had worked so hard to turn off the alarm. I was too wide awake to try and close my eyes again.

I looked at the time, disgusted to see that I was awake too early, but if I didn't give myself plenty of snooze time to wake up slowly, I would feel like a zombie until I managed to wake up fully.

There was the distinct sound of a foot kicking my closed and locked bedroom door. "Thanks for waking up the whole house, bitch!" Jason was less of a morning person than I was, though it could be said that he was never exactly cordial with me no matter the time of day. He hated me almost as much as his twin sister, Jessica, hated me.

My cousins pretty much always went above and beyond to show how they felt about my presence in their home and in their lives. I've had to live with them now going on four years. Just after the start of my freshman year, my parents had been in a car accident. They had been driving home from a dinner date when a drunk driver crossed the yellow line and hit them straight on. Seeing as they had been traveling over a bridge at the time, my father had no room to swerve to avoid the accident.

I was told that when they were cut from the inside of the car, my dad had been wrapped around my mom, trying to protect her. And her arms had been wrapped around her stomach where my baby sister had been. My mother had been six months pregnant at the time of the car accident. Everyone had been so excited when she had ended up pregnant again. I had been a surprise baby; my mother had been told that her uterus was too hostile to carry a fetus to full term, so when she managed to defeat the odds a second time 13 years later it was a very, very happy surprise.

I lost so much in a single moment in time.

Almost immediately, my aunt and uncle had shown up to claim me and brought me 1000 miles away from the home I had lived in my entire life to their home in Texas. And to their adorable twins. My cousins.

The cousins that hated me for being alive.

It wasn't as if my dad's brother had really cared so much about me that he felt the overwhelming need to swoop in and tuck his only brother's child under his wing. Nope. He did it out of duty. It had been made pretty clear from our first conversation when they had picked me up from the temporary foster home that I had been in for four days. They hadn't been mean about it. It's just that they had virtually no warmth in them at all. Well, my aunt was cold as ice, and my uncle was stern and a workaholic.

My cousins, though? They had been as welcoming as a den of vipers.

From the second I was ushered through the front door of their large house, I had been sneered at. That was the nicest thing they had done. There was a reason I kept my door locked and even put my desk chair under my doorknob at night. I was finally able to sleep a bit better once I installed a deadbolt.

Jason did it because he sided with his precious sister no matter what. If she hated someone, then so did he. If she wanted to show her hatred by bullying them at every turn, then by god, he was going to show her how much he supported her by bullying them twice as much. I guess there was much to be said for that kind of loyalty.

I couldn't understand why they had such instant hatred towards me for the longest time. We didn't know each other that well and had only seen each other a handful of times. They had visited our house for Christmas the previous year and had seemed nice, if not super friendly. They had practically hung off my parents the whole time they were there, gushing compliments and begging for attention. Being here in their house this time, I had started to understand. They were utterly and ridiculously jealous.

My dad had been a little bit richer than their dad. My parents were warmer than their parents, who seemed more content to sit around talking with the adults and drinking wine than to spend time playing board games or baking cookies with their kids.

My mom had been the perfect mom. She always knew who my friends were, made sure she knew my friend's parents. She taught me to cook by letting me help her in the kitchen. Mom had been on the PTA. And she had been so amazingly beautiful.

Sometimes I still sit in front of my mirror and look at all my features just so I could bring her face to life in my memories. I had been told practically since I was born that I looked exactly like my mother, and I would love to believe that since she was everything to me, her and my dad. But sharing something with my mother, it made her seem so much more a part of me. In a way, I could keep her memory alive.

We had the same thick golden blond hair, the kind of thick that required me to use two hair bands to hold it in a ponytail. We had the same small, straight nose with just the barest hint of a slope at the end. The same heart-shaped face. The same lips that were just a little too full, lips that caused me no end of embarrassment from the catcalling and names that the immature jerks at school seemed to favor.

The only thing I got from my dad when it came to my features were my eyes, though I loved having a part of him, too. My mom had the softest green eyes. I had always thought they looked like the soft moss that I'd seen growing on the trees in the forest. But my dad had bright blue eyes, the kind of blue that reminded me of pictures of tropical waters, a little more aqua than blue.

I had also inherited my mother's body structure, and as I've matured, I've kind of wished I hadn't. I was of average height and small-boned, which would have been fine if my boobs had gotten the memo. They weren't giant, but on my smaller frame, they might as well be. My dad had told me that when he met my mother in college, he'd had to get in fistfights almost every day, having to fight the guys away from my mom. He might have been exaggerating, but I had no doubt my beautiful mother had admirers.

So, yeah. My cousins were jealous assholes. Jessica especially. They were jealous of the fact that I had better parents, a better house, and Jessica was jealous that I was prettier than her. While that may actually be true, I never tried to do anything at all to enhance my looks since even leaving my hair down seemed to throw her into fits of rage. But Jessica was extremely beautiful in her own right.

She was tall and willowy, the type of tall and willowy that you would see on a runway. She also had deep brown hair with natural red highlights. At least, I thought they were all-natural; it wasn't as if I had ever been invited to go to the salon with her. Her eyes were a clear baby blue, and the contrast of her hair and eyes was striking. She turned heads everywhere she went, and she could easily get a job as a model anywhere if she wanted to. Whereas the only modeling I would likely ever get invited to do was for Victoria's Secret.

It killed me that they were still so jealous of my parents. I had great parents, yes. The best even. But they were gone. I would never get another hug from my father, and my mother would never sing me to sleep or teach me how to make her famous pumpkin pancakes.

They were jealous of my ghosts.

It could also be that my parent's estate was being held in a trust for me until I turned 21 years old, provided I went to a four-year college and graduated. Otherwise, I would have to wait until I turned 28. The house, their cars, their bank accounts would all be turned over to me. Currently, any funds I needed were accessed by my uncle, along with a small team of lawyers. He had to request the funds and valid reason why he needed them; the lawyers would decide if the reasons were good enough and release the funds.

The millions in the bank were accruing interest faster than my uncle would have ever been able to request it. Though, it had to be said, as far as I knew, my uncle had been doing right by me when it came to my parent's estate. He could have been trying to siphon money off of it, but he wasn't. Honestly, it wasn't as if he needed to anyway; they were rich with their own millions.

To try to curb my cousin's jealousy, I had convinced my uncle that I didn't want a fancy new car for my 16th birthday like the two of them had gotten. Instead, I asked for a Jeep. It was still plenty nice, but it wasn't Porsche Cayenne nice. I liked to keep the top and doors off as much as possible because it would make it harder for them to try to put something nasty in it. Well, actually, they could put something nasty in it, but the worst things they could think of wouldn't stay. No thanks, spiders and snakes, not today.

My bright red Jeep was cute and fun, Jessica's baby blue Porsche was, without a doubt, glamorous and sexy. But when she drove it, she made it look obnoxious. I wasn't the only person that she treated like pond scum. It wasn't uncommon to see other students have to run or even dive out of the way of her speeding car while she raced through the student parking lot. Her entitled ass acted like she was the only one that mattered. Of course, she was the head cheerleader. I mean, why not finish the whole cliché? She couldn't date the quarterback though, that would have been incestuous.

Jason was the typical jock douche with the raised truck that a girl would need a ladder to climb up into -or a hand on her ass, giving her a boost. He was good at football, no doubt, but there was no way he would make it into the pros. He wasn't dedicated enough. He spent all his free time partying and screwing all the girls in the school that he considered worthy. Luckily for me, he had been spending more and more time away from the house since he got his shiny black truck almost two years ago, than spend time at home finding new ways to torment me.

I IGNORED the kick to my bedroom door and opened up my favorite social media account. I never posted much, but it was a great way to keep apprised of our school's comings and goings. If someone split up, it would be on the internet. If someone were planning on beating someone up, it would be there, too.

What I hadn't expected to see were at least twenty posts about the new guy. I had completely forgotten that we were getting a new student this year. I honestly didn't know how I could have let it slip my mind since Jessica had done nothing but squeal about him on her phone to all her friends for weeks. Apparently, he had arrived over the summer and started football camp with the rest of the guys.

The word on the street was that his dad asked for a transfer to our town because he wanted to make sure his son had a better opportunity for a football scholarship than the one he'd had in California. Admittedly, our school was one of the best in the state, even with our shitty quarterback. Of course, I might just be biased. Or bitter, whichever.

Jessica had taken one look at him from across the football field when she had been in cheerleader camp and had fallen, unfortunately not literally, head over heels.

I heard her swear to anyone who would listen to her squealing that she was already in love with him and would have him in her bed by Homecoming. Honestly, it probably wouldn't take much at all. Jessica, as I said, was gorgeous. Most teenage boys had zero problems ignoring the attitudes that came from pretty girls as long as said pretty girls had no problems spreading their legs. I didn't think Jessica was promiscuous, but I also knew for a fact that she was no virgin. We shared a bedroom wall, and, as I said, her parent's room was on the other side of the house.

I stopped my scrolling dead in its tracks when I spotted the boy, no, the man that someone had taken a candid picture of. He was holding a football while wearing a practice jersey. His helmet was off and, even though he was covered in sweat from the high Texas heat, and his hair was plastered to his forehead from the helmet, he looked amazing. He was the most gorgeous man I had ever seen. Oh, I knew that he was still in high school, so technically, he was a boy, but I could tell from the simple picture that he was lightyears ahead of the rest of the guys.

He was taller, broader. His dark, sweaty hair looked like it was definitely on the longer side, reaching his shoulders and wavy. His eyes were blue, his jaw square. I felt my heart thump a little harder and faster. God, if this was the new guy, I was just going to give up on life. Jessica would have her claws in him, and it would have to take the jaws of life to detach her from his body. It was a goddamn shame that she had claimed him. She would have him ruined in no time. There was no way that her type of toxicity wasn't contagious.

I took one more long, lingering look at the picture and clicked my phone off, then tossed it behind me on the bed. I squeezed my eyes shut and rubbed the heels of my hands over them. I wanted to scream as loud as I could at the unfairness of the world.

CHAPTER 2

Paige

I rolled into the student parking lot and pulled into my favored spot. As usual, nobody acknowledged me; I was the invisible girl around here. You'd think that would bother me but, trust me...it was a relief not to be noticed since most acknowledgments from this crowd involved snickers at best and heckling with a side of being pelted with nasty food items at worst.

I unbelted myself and reached behind me onto the back seat floorboard for my backpack that was safe from flying out if I had to turn a corner too fast, don't ask me how I knew that. I heard loud pipes rumbling in the distance. Hearing motorcycles wasn't entirely uncommon; it was Texas, after all, even rich guys liked to ride on the weekends sometimes. But it wasn't normal to hear them so close to the school that it sounded like they were coming *on* to the school.

My head turned to follow the sound and my eyes caught on to the sight of a large guy riding a pretty red bike. He turned into the student parking lot and slowed down until he found an empty spot to back into. I could no longer see him from my seat, and when he disappeared from view, it broke whatever spell had taken over me. I looked around to see if anyone had noticed me staring like an idiot, only to realize that literally everyone else in the parking lot were all turned and had their eyes glued to the guy.

I did a mental shrug and slipped down out of my Jeep, pocketing my keys, and slinging my backpack over my shoulder. I walked quickly while everyone was distracted to the side entrance, grateful that I didn't have to confront any Jessica followers, for now at least. I turned back to look with one hand on the open door, trying to see who had been riding the motorcycle since I didn't think anyone that went to the school would, but there were too many admirers around the rider to see who it was.

Out of the corner of my eye, I saw Jessica zooming into the parking lot, going her usual speed of just under mach one, and shook my head before turning to enter the building. No way was I going to be a witness to her killing someone. Likely I would be the only one to tell the truth, and everyone else would point the finger at me instead in order to save their precious queen bee.

I walked down the crowded, noisy halls until I reached my locker in the Senior wing and quickly put in the code that I had memorized the last few days in anticipation of today. The halls were typically noisy, but today they were louder than usual. Everyone was either excited about the first day of the school year, or the newest boy band had just agreed to play for us during lunch.

"Hey, bitch!" Someone slammed their palm against the locker next to mine while I was emptying my backpack and replacing what I needed for my next couple of classes. I jumped and turned, my hands already raising to cover my face defensively until I saw my best friend's contrite look. "I'm so sorry. I didn't mean to scare you like that. I mean, yeah, I did try to scare you, but I didn't think that you'd think it was one of the bully assholes from around here." She turned her head, long braids swinging, and glared at the general population of the students in the hallway.

"Hey, Lisa. No, it's okay, you just startled me, that's all." I gave her a half-smile while my heart rate returned to normal.

"Well, if people around here weren't such asshats, you wouldn't have to fear for your life." She put her middle finger up and waved it around until I quickly covered her finger with my hand and pushed it back down to her side.

"Seriously, what's gotten into you? Have you forgotten the status quo around here? Don't wave the red flag at the snorting bulls, alright? Not unless you are literally trying to kill me off. I promise you, I haven't written my will, so you won't inherit if I die."

She sighed heavily and pulled my arm through hers as she started leading me towards the office. "You're right, I guess I did kinda forget over the summer. I'll try to be more careful. I just hate how you're treated around here. I don't get how all these people don't understand what a wonderful girl you are and treat you right instead of trying to bully you just because your asshole cousins painted a target on your back almost four years ago. Why do they have to be such sheep? Baaaa."

"Because that's the way high school works. The kings and queens of the high schools dictate, and the rest of the school follows. It just so happens that they are following the two people that hate me most. No one wants to lose their social status by making the queen angry for nothing more than being nice to me." I bumped her shoulder with mine. "It's okay, really. Nine more months and all of this is over. I can go as far away as I want and never have to deal with them ever again."

"Yeah." She looked thoughtful as she stared at a football poster the cheerleaders had made. There was so much glitter on it you could hardly see the background of the poster board. "Have you seen the new guy yet?"

I gave her the side-eye. Since I knew she was in love with the same guy since middle school, I didn't get why she was asking. She couldn't have fallen under his spell, too?

"I really only looked at one picture on social media." I shrugged, ducking my head to hide my blush while trying to come off as nonchalant. "Why? Why are you asking?"

"Well, as you were saying, none of the students here want to shake up the status quo. But the new guy hasn't established his place here yet, has he? Maybe what you need is a boyfriend. One that has instant status, is already admired by the male populace and lusted after by the females. You would be protected by his umbrella. No one would try to hurt you without pissing him off."

I was shaking my head before she even finished. "Wrong, so much wrong. That wouldn't be saving me; that would be me building my own bonfire and lighting my own match. Jessica has already called dibs on the guy, and if she even caught me glancing in his direction, she would cut me." I took a deep breath and let it out noisily. "Nope."

She frowned. "You don't think he'd be able to protect you?"

"Maybe here in these halls, he could glare someone into thinking twice about putting peaches down my shirt or dropping tampons in my pudding, but you forget I live with the monster twins. I wouldn't make it back to school alive."

"Hmmm." She didn't sound as sure as I was that it was suicide to even consider.

We stopped outside the office, which was packed with students trying to get a last-minute class change. She gave me a tight squeeze and said, "Just don't give up completely yet, okay? I have a feeling things are going to change this year."

"Do you? You really have a feeling?" Lisa's feelings were notorious and not in a bad way. She once had a feeling that something terrible would happen if her boyfriend, Chad, went on a fishing trip with his dad and brother. They had fought over it, him accusing her of being jealous of his time, but in the end, Chad decided not to go. That weekend, his dad and brother had food poisoning so bad they had to go to the hospital. A few more instances like that, and I was a firm believer in her 'feelings'.

"Yeah, I really do. Don't turn him down, okay?" She squeezed my hand and walked off. I stood staring at her, playing her words over in my mind, until Chad grabbed her from behind, making her squeak and then jump into his arms. The embarrassing PDA that followed had me turning and pushing my way through the crowd and behind the counter, where my first period would be every day until the end of my senior year.

I pulled my lightweight cardigan around me as I took my seat at the front desk. It may be hot as hell outside, but here, at this school and surrounded by all the raging assholes that were my peers, wearing an extra layer of fabric felt like a layer of armor - even if it was only in my head.

This wasn't the first year I had been an office aid as an elective. I had started spending lunches in the office with Lisa during my freshman year since her mom was the school nurse and liked the atmosphere and the safety. I had gotten to know the office staff and decided they were good people and that it would be a great place to while away some of the required time I had to spend at school.

Luckily, I didn't have to interact with any of the idiots this morning, and they scattered like the roaches they were as soon as the registrar handed them their transfer slips. Once they were all gone and it was down to just the office staff and myself, I pulled my current read out of my bookbag.

Even though I had never had a boyfriend, and the only kiss I had ever received was a stolen one, one where the giver had won the prize of aching balls after being introduced to my knee, I loved romance novels. I mostly stuck with historicals since contemporary romances had too much reality in them. Life sucked enough as it was. I didn't need to spend quality escape time on possible real-life scenarios. Give me a pirate or a knight, and I would be a happy bunny. I wasn't jaded about love, but I was realistic enough to know that as long as I stayed in this town under my cousin's thumb, I would always be alone and miserable. She would do anything to make sure I wasn't happy.

I was caught up in a story about a woman posing as a cabin boy on a pirate ship, only to have the captain figure it out without letting her know when movement caught my attention. I turned to look up at the figure standing there.

The new guy. He was even hotter in person than he had been in that one picture I had allowed myself to look at this morning before getting out of bed. He was wearing a faded band t-shirt, well-worn jeans, and heavy black shoes. He was holding the strap of his backpack that was hanging over one shoulder. He had a wide, black leather cuff and a couple of black and gray beaded bracelets on his arm that was holding the strap. His hair was long, falling around his face and brushing the collar of his shirt. My fingers itched to brush it back out of his eyes. His blue eyes. His gorgeous blue eyes.

Shit. Blue eyes and dark hair. If he and Jessica were to have babies, they would probably be begged by every ad agency in the world to let them use their child as the face of their product.

I internally cringed at the memory that Jessica had claimed this guy for herself. If I even thought about kissing those lush lips that were slowly turning up while I was staring at him, Jessica would pluck me bald.

I closed my eyes in defeat.

CHAPTER 3

Reid

I t was going to take some getting used to being at this school.

Back home, I was known as the guy that was quiet and dedicated to school and football. I was friendly, had plenty of friends, really, but there was no denying that I was mostly a loner.

Keeping my own company didn't bother me. I'd rather study to make sure I got into a good college if my plans for playing professional football didn't work out than to go to parties. I watched both my parents work for what we had, knew that they weren't handed a trust fund, and though we had some of the best now, we hadn't always. I wanted to show them that they could be proud of the son they raised.

Girls hadn't been on my radar. Sure, I'd seen them and appreciated the beauty of the fairer sex, but I'd also noticed how much my parents loved each other. I wanted what I knew I would only find with that one special girl. My dad had assured me that I would know when I met her. She would be the first one that meant more than football, more than the drive I felt. She would also be the one that would appreciate my dreams and goals, just as I would hers.

When I backed my motorcycle into one of the available spaces that didn't have BMWs, Aston Martins, or Audis in it, I watched as some of the guys from the football team made their way over. When I took my helmet off and ran a hand through my admittedly too long, wavy hair, I saw that the rest of the kids hanging around the parking lot took their cues from the team and rushed over, too.

I knew being the new kid made me the oddity; being the new football player that was already being scouted just made me even more interesting. Girls were twirling their hair and pushing out their chests, hoping I would show interest. The guys were staring down the girls like it was a pussy buffet. I shook my head. They could have them; I still wasn't interested in what was being so blatantly offered. Nothing had changed for me from my old school to this one. I was still determined to focus on school.

Screeching tires caught everyone's attention. Almost as one, they turned to watch the light blue Porsche speed down the row of the parking lot. Some who hadn't crowded around my bike had to jump out of the way since the driver didn't slow until they reached an open spot right by the school entrance. I shook my head again, this time at the reckless stupidity of the driver. When the door opened, and a tall, leggy brunette stepped out, I almost groaned out loud.

The girl, Jessica, was turning out to be a menace. She was in my space more than I would have believed possible. All summer long, she had been working on getting on my dick even though there had never been a chance, and I never gave a single indication to her that I was up for it. After seeing her attitude in action over the last couple of months, that 'never' had changed to 'a cold fucking day in hell'. The head cheerleader and the queen bee of the school. I heard a lot about her in the locker room and heard stories that the others laughed about but made me cringe. She took entitlement to a new level.

Jessica decided who was popular and who was nothing. The social hierarchy was determined on her whim. The guys of the school wanted to be with her, and if the talk could be believed, the girls wanted to be her. She only had to crook her finger at a guy for him to puff his chest out in pride that the school princess had chosen them.

I had heard all about it from the guys that she'd 'allowed' to fuck her and the bitching from those she didn't. She only entertained the upper elite of the school. You had to be the richest or the best at something in order for her to show interest. It seemed that since I was arguably the best player on the team, it was my turn for her attention. I had been polite to her after the summer practices, but being aloof and disinterested hadn't slowed her down.

"Reid," she purred as she sauntered up to me where I had gotten off my bike and swung my backpack over my shoulder. "Just the hotty I was hoping to see this morning." She ran one long painted nail over my arm, and I had to repress a shudder at the revulsion. Sure, she was beautiful, but it was in an obvious, black widow kind of way. A man would have to cover his dick and hope she didn't swallow him whole - and not in a good way- if he displeased her. "I was hoping to welcome you to our school. Maybe show you around." Her words and the way she let them slip off her tongue sounded more like an invitation to show me the places that were hidden, the kind every student knew about but the adults always seemed oblivious to.

"Thanks, but I have an appointment in the office this morning. I don't want to keep you from your classes." I nodded at her and stepped away until her hand dropped from my arm.

Her mouth tightened, recognizing the dodge to her seduction efforts, but her smile brightened again before anyone else could see that she was unhappy at the slight. "Okay, well, you can find me in the cafeteria later. I'll save you a seat." She turned and grabbed the arm of one of the hair twirlers that had been surrounding the other football players and me. "Come on, Candace, we don't want to be late to class. This is our final year, and it needs to be perfect." She started walking away, swinging her hips in her tiny denim shorts that couldn't possibly be within the dress code regulations.

She turned to look over her shoulder, catching me looking at her shorts, and winked. I hadn't been checking her ass out, I had been wondering how she would get away with showing that much skin, but knowing her ego, she would be thinking she had my attention and admiration. I turned away, not wanting to encourage her any farther than I already had this morning.

"I'll see you guys later. I'm heading to the office."

John, one of the tight ends, started walking in step with me. "I'll walk with you. You're the current pussy magnet around here, and since you don't seem to be interested, I'll take advantage and offer to comfort the losers. I'll wipe their tears...after they choke on my cock in the bathroom." He grinned.

I shook my head again. If I weren't careful, I would give myself a neck injury from all the head shaking. "Seriously, man? Your mom must be so proud of you."

He chuckled, "Nah, mom's too busy with her boyfriends Pinot and Chardonnay to be proud of anyone. My dad, on the other hand? He'd be proud of me when he isn't banging his secretary."

Yeah, I had nothing to say to that.

"So you're heading to the office. I hear that DSL works there in the morning this year. Lucky you. Try not to show her too much interest, though, or Jessica will cut your balls off."

I scrunched my eyebrows together. "DSL?"

"Oh hell yeah. DSL - dick sucking lips. Every guy in the school wants a piece of that shit. But Jessica hates her guts. Anyone that is seen even looking at her gets cut off from all pussy in the school. No one has tried it yet, even though it might be worth it. That is the hottest chick on the planet."

"Okay, why does Jessica hate her?" I wasn't really interested but couldn't help the morbid fascination with the way Jessica managed to run the school. How could one teenage girl have so much power in one school?

"She's, like, Jessica's cousin. She moved here in her freshman year after her parents died."

"Her cousin?"

"Yeah, her uncle, Jessica's dad, took her in. Everyone knows that Jessica hates her because she's jealous, but she has too much power over the social scene, you know? What she says goes. So if Jessica says hands-off DSL unless it's to dump milk over her head, then it's hands-off."

What the fuck? It's like I landed in an alternate universe.

"That's not right. Her parents died, and Jessica is jealous?"

"Yep." He just grinned and kept walking down the hall, winking at girls. "Alright then, I'll see you later." He called out as he stopped at one girl's side and slipped his arm around her, bending her over his arm. I kept walking, ignoring the spectacle, and reached the front office just as the bell rang. The halls were clearing, but it was obvious that most were going to wait until the warning bell went off before heading to their prospective homerooms.

I grabbed the door before it could close after the last person left and walked inside the quiet office. It was a change from all the laughing and shouting ringing out from the busy hallways. I walked up to the desk past a few other students that were waiting and smiled at the receptionist.

"Hi, I'm Reid Johnson. I was told I needed to come in here for an orientation?"

The middle-aged woman looked over her glasses at me and then down at her computer screen. "Reid Johnson, the new student, yes. Just come in through that swinging door there and head to the counselor's office. It will be the third door on the right. He will make sure all your classes are good to go and give you a quick rundown of what is expected of you before I send you out with the office aide to show you where to go to get to your classes."

I smiled and thanked her before stepping over to the waist-high door. I pushed it open and walked down the hall. Finding the office marked Senior Counselor wasn't hard, but the room was empty. I went to one of the two plastic chairs sitting in front of the desk, swung my backpack off my shoulder, set it down in one chair, and sat in the other. I crossed my leg, ankle resting on my knee, and let my head drop back. I had only been at the school for about 15 minutes, and I was already mentally exhausted.

This school was nothing like my last one. It was nothing like I had ever expected any high school to be. There were too many weird hurdles to jump when it came to pleasing the social gods here. Or just the one god in particular. Why was it so hard to just show up, go to class, play football, and graduate so I could go to a good college and make something of my life that I could be proud of?

I heard someone enter behind me and sat up straighter, dropping my foot to the ground. The counselor walked around to the back of his desk and held his hand out.

"Mr. Johnson. It's good to meet you." He sat down after a firm handshake and picked up a file from his desk. "I was looking over your school records the other day. You have some excellent test scores, and your grades are very good. We are lucky to have you. I doubt you will be in the running for valedictorian here. Unfortunately, that honor will probably go to Paige, but you should definitely end up in the top ten percent, if not five. That will open up a lot of opportunities for scholarships and should give you a shot at your choice of colleges. Of course, with your football skills, you have those opportunities as well. It's rare that I see a student with such high academic marks as well as a strong athletic talent."

We talked for a few minutes about my goals and classes. I assured him that I wouldn't have any problems with a course load of AP classes and football at the same time. I'd already been doing it since my freshman year, though this year, I had 4 AP classes instead of the one or two I'd carried for the previous three years.

When we were done, he told me to head back into the main office where Paige would be able to show me the layout of the school and make sure I knew where to go.

"Paige? As in the possible valedictorian?"

He chuckled. "There's no possibility. Paige will definitely become valedictorian. She's the best student we have ever had under this roof."

I left his office and walked back out front. I came to a complete stop and just stared. The girl that had turned to look at me when I walked in took my breath away and made my heart speed up at the same time. She wasn't just beautiful. She was stunning in a way that few women could ever compare.

There was an innocent quality to her looks. She was golden blond and had eyes that were neither blue nor green. Her hair was pulled back in a bun, and she wasn't wearing any makeup that I could see.

She was perfect.

I finally understood what my dad was talking about when he said I'd know when I met the one.

CHAPTER 4

Paige

I could feel him move over to me but kept my eyes shut tight. If I couldn't see, then none of this would be real, right? Isn't that the way life worked? I snorted internally. I could only wish. If I couldn't see the one guy I just knew would have the ability to change my life but would be out of reach, then I didn't want to face him.

"Hey, are you alright?"

The deep voice that ran over me like hot fudge melting a bowl of ice cream had goosebumps popping up on my arms. I squeezed my eyes tighter and let out a small groan. Damn it. He looked like a young god, and his voice could melt me with a few words. What was a girl to do?

I opened my eyes and saw him standing right in front of me with his head cocked to the side, studying me. I shook my head. "I'm fine." I stood up and stuffed my paperback into my backpack. I expected him to step back, to give me some space, but he didn't move. It brought us so close that I could feel his body heat radiating off of him. He smelled like fresh citrus soap, Old Spice deodorant, and just a tiny hint of sweat from the already blazing heat outside.

I looked up and realized that he stood an entire head above me, my face even with his upper chest. I felt my face heat at the images that jumped into my mind of him wrapping me in his arms and resting his chin on my head as I snuggled my face into his chest. I cleared my throat.

"If you have your schedule, I can show you where all your classes are as well as the cafeteria and library. I'm sure you already know where the gym is since you've been going to football camp all summer."

He grinned. "Yeah, I've been in the gym and weight room a lot already. You know who I am?"

He still hadn't backed up, and I was starting to feel out of sorts. I didn't want to be rude since he hadn't given me any reason to be yet, but I was really starting to feel closed in. It wasn't a bad feeling. That was the problem. I crossed my arms over my chest and rolled my eyes at his question. "You're Reid. Everyone knows who you are. The guy that transferred here the summer before his senior year. The one that is going to take our football team to the playoffs, the one that is guaranteed a football scholarship to his choice of schools."

He shrugged and finally stepped back. He reached up and rubbed the back of his neck in a cute nervous gesture. His cheeks turned pink. It was adorable. "I guess everyone knows."

"Yep. And your place as Homecoming and Prom King is already secured if Jessica has anything to say about it." I started through the swinging gate to the office lobby and headed towards the glass door, looking out into the empty hall.

He was following right on my heels as we left the office, and I started towards the hallway where the majority of the senior classes were held.

"Yeah, about Jessica." He walked right next to me, his long legs having no trouble trying to keep up with my quick pace. "I have zero desire to have her on my arm in any capacity and definitely don't have any plans to make king for any dances."

I side-eyed him, turning down the hallway. "Why?"

"Why, what?"

I let out a big sigh and stopped, turning to face him. "Jessica is the most popular, most beautiful girl in the school. If you were 'on her arm' or she on yours, then you would be at the top of the school food chain. Kids would clear whatever table you wanted to sit at. You want a desk in the back - it's yours. You want the last slice of pizza? It's yours. You would bump Jason out as the current king."

"Is that important? Because all I am interested in is playing football, going to all my practices, doing my homework, maintaining a good GPA, and getting into a great college." He stared at me, intently. "I've never been into the social scene. I've never gone to parties or dances. I've never been interested in any of that stuff. My future is what's important to me, not high school social status."

I stared up at him, trying to determine if he was feeding me a line of bullshit. I hadn't known anyone else during this whole high school career of mine that hadn't either gone to or longed to go to the big parties that were thrown at some of the richer kid's houses whose parents were more gone than home most of the time. Even Lisa and Chad had gone to some of the parties, and both had gone to the prom last year.

"You don't date?" Was the only dumb thing that I could think of to say.

He grinned. "Nope. Never had any desire to." He paused, and his stare became more intense. "Until now."

I swallowed thickly and looked away. Did he mean that he was interested in me? God, if only he did. And if only my cousin wouldn't kill me in my sleep or cut my brake lines. Or burn my homework. Well, she might pay someone to do her dirty work. No way was she going to get down on the dirty ground- if she could even find my brake lines.

"Here, you go."

I looked back and saw the small piece of paper being held in the air between our bodies. It took me a good second to focus on what he was holding before realizing it was his class schedule. I took it with shaky fingers and tried to calm myself enough to read the page. When I finally focused enough, my mouth dropped.

"These are your classes?" I looked up in shock.

He shook his head and frowned. "I don't come across as a dumb jock, do I?"

I cleared my throat and looked back down at the sheet. "Umm, no. I'm sorry. I didn't mean to be rude. It's just that these are almost all the same classes I'm in, and, well," I grimaced and looked up at him through my eyelashes, "you have to be really smart to be able to take this many AP classes. And dedicated to your grades. I wouldn't have thought you'd have time with your football schedule." I gave him an apologetic look. I was being really judgy. But to be honest, I hadn't known many jocks that kept up their grades. I had tutored plenty of them just to help them keep their GPAs up high enough to stay on the team.

"Well, I told you school was important to me." He looked down at the paper and ran a large finger with a clean, neatly cut fingernail over the room numbers. "What you're telling me is that we have most of the same classes and that if I need a study buddy, you would be the perfect person to ask?" His finger trailed off the page and over my hand, stopping to rest on top of my thumb.

"Uh…"

"You will sit next to me in all my classes, right? I mean, I am the new kid, and you are one of the only other students I know at the school."

"The, uh, other football players…"

"Don't take the AP classes, according to you. That means you'll be the only one I know."

"That's true…"

"It's your job to show me around and help me get comfortable in my new school, right?"

"My job as the office TA…"

"Doesn't really end after one period, does it? What if I get lost?"

His puppy dog eyes and slightly pouting lip broke the spell I had been under, and I started laughing.

"Alright! That's enough!" I couldn't stop the laugh that spilled out at his ridiculousness. "You can sit by me, and I will be your study buddy." I poked a finger at his chest. "But that's it! School's important to me, too. I don't date or party either."

He grabbed my finger and flattened my hand against his chest with his own. I could feel the hardness of his pecs, could feel his strong heartbeat that felt like it was racing in tandem with mine. "I will accept. I will allow you to study with me and sit with you in your classes. We might have to eat lunch together every day, too."

My voice came out slightly breathless in a way I had never heard it before. "We do?"

His puppy dog eyes and lip came out again, making my lip twitch. "Unfortunately, yes. Football takes up so much of my time most evenings that I try to get as much studying done as I can during the day." He tapped my fingers with his. "So, you see, we have to spend lunch together studying."

"And when the football season is over?"

His grin was wide, showing all of his beautiful straight white teeth. "Well, by then, I will have had you fall deeply in love with me, and we will want to spend all our free time together anyway."

My breath caught, and my eyes widened. His grin dropped, and his eyes became serious. We stood there exactly like that until we heard a door open nearby. I started to pull my hand back, but Reid held me still, not breaking eye contact. He wanted me to fall in love with him by winter? Mission. Fucking. Accomplished.

"You're smooth, Casanova, I'll give you that. You've got great lines for someone that doesn't date." Maybe he just uses girls without making a commitment?

"Paige, I've never had any lines to use. You are literally the first girl I've ever wanted to get to know romantically. There's something about you…"

"Reid! What are you doing?" The angry screech had me pulling my hand away before he could stop me this time. I turned to see none other than Jessica storming up to us. Her eyes were blazing with fury, and her face was red. She swung her gaze to me, and I took a hasty step back, nearly tripping over my own two feet and probably would have stumbled if Reid hadn't put his arms around me and pulled me tight against his chest.

I looked up at him to tell him that it was in my best interest if he released me, but his eyes were still intently focused on me. I didn't think he even looked at her to acknowledge her presence at all. I swallowed the thickness in my throat. This was my fear coming to life. Jessica was going to annihilate me as soon as she could. It hadn't even been an entire day, and I was defying her, touching the man she considered hers.

"Reid, I think you should let me go," I whispered.

"Never." He whispered back.

"You don't understand."

"You're going to pay for this, you fucking tramp. Just wait until we get home. I. Will. Destroy. You!"

"Miss Anderson!" The principal's stern voice filled the hall, and I closed my eyes at the brief reprieve from Jessica's wrath. "My office." When Jessica continued to stand there glaring at me and took a step towards me, Reid pushed me behind him in a protective move, and Principal Nieves barked out, "Now!"

Jessica stomped her foot and stormed past us, slamming her shoulder against mine as she went. I winced because, damn, her shoulder was bonier than mine.

"Miss Anderson, Mr. Johnson?" Principal Nieves looked at the two of us with one eyebrow cocked, and her arms crossed over her chest.

I sighed and rubbed at my shoulder. "I'm sorry, Ms. Nieves. I was showing Reid his classes."

"Yes, that is your job. But that doesn't explain the...clinch I saw you two in." Her red lips tipped in the corners, betraying her amusement. I've known her my entire high school career since I was often hanging out in the office. She was always kind and had a welcoming smile, even to the troublemakers. Because I was her star pupil, though, she was always super friendly, and she knew me well enough to know I was level headed and not one to be boy crazy.

"Umm, well, you see..."

"I'm sorry, Ms. Nieves. It was my fault. I was laying on the charm, trying to get my study buddy here to hang out with me at lunch. I got carried away." His cheeks pinked up again. I sighed internally.

"I see. Well, study, yes. Intimate clinches in a public school hallway? No. Understand?" She raised an eyebrow and tried to maintain a stern look, but I could see the amusement dancing in her eyes.

"Yes, Ms. Nieves." We both spoke together in unison, making her drop the sternness.

"You better get back to your tour, Miss Anderson. You only have," she glanced at her delicate gold watch, "30 minutes until the pep rally starts." She started back down the hall she had come from, her heels clicking against the tiles, likely on her way to the office, and to discuss the scene she had walked in on with Jessica.

I sighed deeply and took another step back from Reid. "I'll be your study partner, Reid, but I can't be more. There are things you don't know, things that are complicated and maybe ridiculous, but until I can move away from here, I have to keep my head down."

Reid looked like he was fighting with himself. Or maybe he was fighting with what he wanted to say to me. The emotions flickered across his face as he battled with what he wanted to say. Anger was there, though I didn't feel like it was directed at me. There was a little bit of sadness, too. What was most prevalent, though, was determination, and that scared me. I didn't know if I'd be able to battle determination. If he let me have my say and respect my boundaries, I could probably keep Jessica off my ass, but if he tried to push the issue, tried to make us into the couple he'd suggested we became, then I needed to start shopping for coffins. I was thinking gray with a pretty teal satin lining.

I sighed again. "Reid-"

"I let you have your say, but it's my turn now. I have heard things, and you're right; I don't know the whole story. But, Paige, if you think I'm going to let some spoiled little princess try to dictate to me how my life will go for even one day, let alone an entire year of my life, both she *and* you are seriously mistaken. I've only known you for a handful of minutes, but I feel it in here." His fist thumped his chest where he had held my hand to him just a few minutes ago. "If you don't see it yet, that's okay. I will believe enough for both of us. And I will protect you. I promise." He held out his hand for mine, and I raised it, my fingers shaking with emotion. "Now, show me where my first period is."

He twined our fingers together, giving me a small squeeze as I lifted his class schedule back up to look at it.

CHAPTER 5

Paige

When we entered the gym where the pep rally/assembly was being held, I was so nervous I wanted to bolt in the other direction and leave this nightmare behind. Reid's firm grip on my hand was the only thing holding me in place. I gave a quick thought to kicking out the back of one of his knees but changed my mind when he looked down at me with a 'don't try it look'. I looked away, trying to paste an innocent look on my face.

His chuckle had me whipping my head back around to settle a stern glare on him. "Come on. It's an assembly, not a death march."

"That's easy for you to say," I grumbled as he pulled me through the crowd of students and up a few rows of bleachers until he found a satisfactory spot on one. He surprised me when he sat me down but didn't join me on the same seat. Instead, he sat in the one directly in front of me and leaned back against my knees.

"Really?" I asked wryly and lifted an eyebrow as he leaned his head back to give me an upside-down grin. He reached a hand behind him and wrapped his large hand around my ankle. Having this guy give me this kind of familiar attention caused butterflies to flutter around in my belly.

We had dropped our backpacks off at our lockers after I had shown him each of the classes he would be taking. Honestly, the school wasn't so large that he couldn't have found his way around by himself, but I had a good time with him chatting and flirting. I still wasn't too sure about his plan of being more than friends, though.

It wasn't that it wouldn't be worth it, but the headache it would cause dealing with the twins... I shook my head. God, I really hoped he'd be worth it.

I sat there on the uncomfortable metal seat, contemplating what kind of hell I would be in for with Jessica when I got home. I didn't know what, if any, trouble she might have gotten into when Ms. Nieves sent her to the office. If they called my aunt or uncle, chances were high that absolutely nothing would be done. Chances were even higher that it would be me that would be grounded. All the pretty pretty princess would have to do is whine to her mommy that I was being mean and I would be stuck with kitchen duty for the next month.

I was interrupted from my thoughts when a loud group of guys that I recognized as members of the football team stomped up the stairs laughing and carrying on. One of the guys shoved another, and he stumbled into me. I was saved from falling over into the person closest to me by Reid when he stood up and pushed the guy back away from me while keeping a steadying hand on my shoulder.

"Hey man, how's it hangin'?" The laughing jock, Roy, yelled out and clapped a hand on Reid's shoulder.

"Careful where you guys horse around. You almost knocked Paige over." Reid's words had a hint of anger, but his face only showed mild irritation. I watched him carefully. I didn't want to find out that he had an anger problem. I'd been around the monster twins long enough to absolutely despise people with anger problems. So far, he'd been really easy-going and friendly, but he seemed pretty upset that Roy had almost knocked me over. I wasn't sure if I should be pleased that he would stand up for me or worried that he had a short fuse on his temper.

Roy looked down at me as if he had just noticed I was sitting there. "Hey DSL, I didn't see you there. One of these fuckers pushed me. You didn't get hurt, did you? I could kiss it and make it feel better." He gave a big exaggerated wink and kissy lips at me.

I closed my eyes in mortification. DSL. That name had started up early freshman year, and by the end of the semester, nearly everyone had started calling me that. Luckily it had died down over the summer break, with only a handful still snickering it as they passed me in the halls. By the start of the junior year, only the jocks seemed to still say it instead of my name. Maybe it was that I kept my head down, I was a good student, or I had the ear of the Principal, but most of the students left me alone. It actually might have been because of Jessica. She was so jealous of me that she didn't even want me to have any attention, even if it was something so disgusting and derogatory.

I looked up to see Reid leaning in close to Roy and speaking in a low tone. I watched as Roy's eyes got rounder with each word.

"Dude, I won't say it again, I swear. But are you sure you want to do this? Jessica will have your balls, man, and not in a good way. If you piss her off like this, you won't ever be allowed to go after any pussy at the school. You won't be able to go to parties, or…"

Reid sat down sideways on the bench and draped an arm over my lap. "I don't know how many times I've told you all; I don't party, and I don't date. I don't care what Jessica has to say about it or what she will threaten me with. This is fucking high school, and she is just another student. She's not in charge here, no matter how much she thinks she is." He slid his arm off my lap and turned back towards the front, wrapping his hand around my ankle again and acting as if nothing had happened at all in the last few minutes.

"Whatever, it's your funeral, man." Roy slapped his hand on Reid's shoulder again before following his group up to the top of the bleachers.

I couldn't resist any longer and leaned forward to whisper in his ear. "What did you say to him?"

He turned his head, and before I could lean back, his face came so close that I could feel his breath and the heat of lips nearly touching mine. I swallowed hard, resisting the strong urge to lean forward that extra inch and finally get a taste of a real kiss. I shuddered and turned my head so he could talk into my ear, tamping down the disappointment in myself.

"I told him to spread the word that if I ever heard anyone call you that name again that I would destroy them on the field. You're my girl, and you deserve respect. Not because you're mine, just because you do."

I chose to ignore the 'my girl' comment and giggled. "You seriously told him you would beat them on the field?"

He grinned that huge grin of his. "Hey, I'd love to say I'd beat them up or break an arm, but I'm not really interested in going to jail when I have a future I'm looking forward to." He winked at me then and I finally understood at that moment what the heroines of my stories meant when they would swoon. A smile and a wink were just too much for my poor heart to handle.

I sat back and tried my hardest to wipe the stupid grin off my face.

I looked around and was startled to see most eyes were on us. Seeing so many pointing and whispering to their friends or just staring at us, wide-eyed managed to destroy the grin faster than a bucket of ice water. Shit. I looked around quicker, trying to find Jessica, to see if she had witnessed our interaction, and sighed with relief when I saw her hurrying through the door dressed in her cheer uniform. Come to think of it, that was probably why she was in the hall this morning- she had been on her way to change for the rally.

A waving hand caught my eye, and I smiled at Lisa, who was sitting with Chad, of course. I waved back and looked back towards the center of the gym floor where the cheerleaders were gathered, and Ms. Nieves was waiting with the Vice Principal. I watched as the girls surrounded Jessica and spoke animatedly, and pointed up to where we were sitting.

I closed my eyes and tried to pretend I was on an island far away, listening to the waves and the seagulls calling out. I felt Reid lightly squeeze my ankle. He probably felt the tension running through me. He wanted me to trust him, but he still didn't know the whole situation just yet. I bet he believed he did, but he really didn't. I needed to make him understand how dangerous it would be for us to see each other.

The music turned on and was so loud that I could feel the vibrations running from the floor, to the bleachers, and up my legs. The students started cheering loudly and stomped their feet, adding to the vibrations until the entire room was filled to the brim with frenetic energy.

I kept my eyes closed, wanting to ignore that my cousin was dancing in front of the crowd, showing everyone her amazing skills that she had been working on since she was three years old. I wasn't jealous of her, but I was woman enough to admit that I was insecure. Reid would be seeing what he was missing if he stayed away from her.

I felt him let go of my ankle and sighed in disappointment. I knew it was too good to be true. Jessica had so much more to offer someone like him than I ever could. They would be a perfect couple. It didn't take long for him to come to his sens-

I felt his hand cup my cheek, and it startled me from the depressing thoughts that were trying to pull me under. His thumb brushed over my bottom lip lightly, and my eyes slowly opened to see his bright blue eyes looking at me with a tenderness that took my breath. His words in his low timbre just barely made it to me over the music and screaming. "You are so beautiful. If we weren't in the middle of a crowded gym filled with screaming infants with body odor issues, I would kiss you right now. But when I kiss you, it's going to be private and just for us."

I blinked at him, absorbing his words. "How did you know?" I whispered the words too low for him to possibly hear, but he must have read the words on my lips.

"Because Jessica looked happy."

I nodded my head because, really, what more needed to be said. If she thought she was winning something over me, then that was all she needed to be absolutely thrilled. She had probably seen that I was upset, and Reid was looking at her instead of me.

He turned back around and relaxed back against my legs again. His hand went back around my ankle. This time his thumb swept a pattern back and forth, reminding me constantly that he was with me. I needed to get a hold of my emotions. I had never been down this road before, wondering if a boy actually liked me or not. I never knew what real jealousy was until today.

When I woke up this morning, it was to the same routine I had always had—school, studying, tutoring, disappearing into the background. Boys noticed me, but they weren't giving the kind of attention I'd ever want to encourage. They gave out childish taunts, leered at me while I passed in the halls. And they occasionally pulled pranks that could easily be considered bullying.

I hadn't been hurt physically. I was usually embarrassed or had food items dumped on me. No, the hard bullying happened at home. It was what had me the most concerned. If I dated Reid like he seemed to want, then I had to figure out how I would be able to protect myself. Locking and barricading my bedroom door worked most of the time, but I couldn't keep locked away for the next four months until my birthday rolled around and I could move into my own apartment.

It was impossible even to consider that I might make friends with Jessica to get her off my back. Too many years had gone by with too much animosity. Maybe I could ask my uncle if I could move into the pool house. It was separate from the house and private. I would have my own key, and I wouldn't have to speak to the monster twins again. Except when I was expected at the dinner table. My uncle and aunt always planned a family dinner every Sunday. It used to be Fridays, but Jason started going out, and then Jessica started dating. With them gone every Friday and Saturday, family dinner was relegated to Sundays.

Honestly, I rarely saw my uncle or aunt since they were always gone with work or whatever it is that my aunt did all day. Hang out with her country club clones, I supposed. If I could disappear for the rest of the time, it might be possible to stay safe. If I could talk with them, make them understand how unhappy the twins made me...

I broke out of my thoughts when the music finally cut off, and the cheers died down. I watched as the cheerleaders ran to a set of bleachers that had been roped off for them to use after their dance.

Ms. Nieves stepped up to the microphone that someone quickly brought over and set down in the middle of the gym floor. After a high pitch squeal from the feedback of the microphone, and everyone settled down from their laughing, Ms. Nieves began her annual speech about her expectations for the year. It was mostly the same each time- she wanted everyone to take their classes seriously, behave outside of class, no bullying allowed.

I could be thankful for Ms. Nieves' anti-bullying policy since I was sure that was the reason that my taunting had never been worse than it had been the last three years I had been at this school. Bullying was reported immediately by any staff that saw the incident. Any of the students involved were either given detention or suspended, depending on the severity. We hadn't had an incident that was so bad that it required expulsion at our school.

After her speech, the Vice Principal, Mr. Sullivan, a short, balding, but pretty nice guy, stepped up and reiterated some of what the Principal had already said. He then went on to brag about the sports teams with a heavy emphasis on the football team. It was easy to see in most of the student body the excitement for the football season. This was Texas. I didn't think there was a single school district in the state that wasn't big on football. It had been a huge change when I had come from California, where football was just another sport that had its fans, but the entire town didn't close their stores so they could all pack themselves into the stands on Friday nights.

As soon as Mr. Sullivan mentioned the possibility of going to the playoffs, everyone erupted into cheers louder than the ones they had given during the cheerleader's demonstration. I saw Jason on a different set of bleachers than we were sitting on, looking smug while he was surrounded by girls and a few of his team members. Being the quarterback and the team captain, he felt it was his due to receive all the praise for the team's accomplishments. We would have to see how that changed this year once Reid was officially running the ball for touchdowns this season. I didn't really involve myself in football, but it was pretty much impossible not to be aware of the team's standings in the league or whether they lost or won.

I reached out my hand and lightly set it on Reid's shoulder. I wanted him to know that I would support him and cheer him on. We had all heard about how amazing he was, and even Jason had talked about him over the summer during family dinner. For someone who was so arrogant and cocky, it had made an impact on me of how great the new wide receiver was. Apparently, Reid never dropped a ball. I didn't know how great Jason was at throwing passes, I was pretty biased against him in general, but he talked so much about how Reid could catch every throw. It seemed like an exaggeration to me. How could he catch *every* throw? For the first time since moving here, I was looking forward to going to a football game.

CHAPTER 6

Paige

As soon as the assembly ended we made our way to our 3rd period class. We both walked into AP English Lit together to immediate sounds of silence. I hadn't realized exactly how big of a deal it really would be to the rest of the students in this school. Seriously? They all had nothing better to do than make a huge deal out of the outcast and the football star?

I didn't say a word, but I held my head up high as I let Reid guide us through the desks and towards the back row. I usually sat in the front row of all my classes. It was just easier to pay attention during the entire class without letting my mind drift too much if the teacher happened to be a boring one. I'd learned that lesson early on. I may have always been a great student, but even I could fall asleep while listening to a mind-numbing lecture.

"Hi, Reid." Suzanne was another student that was in the top ten percent, according to the class rankings that I looked at this morning. Yeah, I'm competitive, sue me. Suzanne had her head down, her long black hair was hiding her like a curtain, and her cheeks were flaming. She was perpetually shy, barely ever said a word, but somehow even she was pulled into the gravity field that was Reid Johnson. I smiled at Suzanne as we passed. Reid just nodded his head politely with his face blank.

As soon as he guided me into one of the empty seats in the back row, he leaned over. "Do I know that girl?"

I giggled quietly while I carefully extracted my notebook, pencils, and textbook and lined them all up neatly on the desktop. "I told you, Reid, everyone knows you. You may not be aware of this, but the last time we got a new student here at Rocky Hills High was back in my sophomore year. The girl's family moved for a new job. She was instantly popular and instantly famous. Nearly every guy dated her. Unfortunately for her, her dad lost his job only a few months later, and they had to move back where they came from. I'm pretty sure she was from some town outside of Dallas." I shrugged my shoulders. "Honestly, I never really paid too much attention. But when it comes to new kids, you can't help but hear the news."

"So is that the real reason why everyone follows me or says 'hi'? Because, if so, I'll be glad when the newness wears off. I want to go back to being just another face in the crowd."

I turned in my chair to look at him. For being a young adult, he was already very masculine. Many other guys our age tended to still have that baby faced look to them with their slightly rounded cheeks and little to no facial hair. Reid didn't have any facial hair currently, but I was sure that it was thanks to a razor blade and not adolescence. It was easy to see where the hair would be once it grew in due to the faintest shading that was nowhere near a 5 o'clock shadow but had the potential to be there by this evening. His jaw was strong-looking, sharp, and square and would have made an excellent mold for a statue. He certainly didn't have rounded cheeks.

I couldn't resist reaching over the aisle to brush some of his hair away that was hanging down his forehead. "Reid, I already told you, you are the new football star. If you play half as good as people say you do, then not only will every single person in this school want to talk to you every day, but your face will probably be in the display cabinet at the front of the school, outside the office." I laughed when he grimaced. "But beside all that? The girls will never stop following you around simply because you're so hot." I rolled my eyes and sat back in my chair when the teacher stood up and closed the door announcing the start of class.

"Welcome to AP English Literature and Composition. My job as your teacher is ultimately to make sure that you are able to pass the AP test at the end of the year with a decent enough grade to earn you college credit. That will be one less class you have to take and one less class that Mommy and Daddy will have to pay for later. If, for whatever reason, you fail the AP test, hopefully, you pass the class with a decent grade. That will end up being the only credit you'll get. Though it does look good on your high school transcripts to take and pass an AP class."

Mr. Rhodes paused and looked over each of us, briefly pausing on me with a raised eyebrow. I just gave a little shrug of my shoulders in a 'what can you do?' gesture. He had to have been wondering why I was in the back row. "Anyone that passes the AP test will automatically receive an A in this class."

Several students looked relieved, while a couple of them looked even more nervous than they had before. It was always easy to tell the newbies to advanced classes.

Mr. Rhodes continued his speech on his expectations and assignments that would need to be completed throughout the year. He dropped a reading list off on each of our desks that we would be responsible for reading on our own time. "I will not be following behind you to make sure that you are completing these books since they are not required to pass my class."

He paused back at the front of the class. He looked around at each of us, noting the ones that were already beginning to freak out. "However, these books will be important to the AP test at the end of the year. So, wisen up, people, this is nothing to what you will have to face in college. That being said, each of you will be pairing off as a buddy system to make sure you don't fall behind. Think of it as the Marines -

No Man Left Behind. Your buddy is your accountability partner. So choose wisely."

Every single student in the class started looking around frantically, and all eyes ended up landing squarely on the back of the room, right at the pair of us sitting there silently watching. Before anyone could say a word, Reid took my hand in his and lifted our clasped hands together.

"I got my partner."

They all sighed in defeat and turned to each other to figure out who would be the best runner-up. A few gave sad eyes, some to me and some to Reid. I turned to him with a raised eyebrow.

"You didn't think I'd let someone else claim you, did you?" He leaned forward, erasing the bit of space that separated us between our desks. He brushed away a stray strand of hair that kept falling against my cheek and grinned. "We already had an agreement, remember? Buddy?"

I rolled my eyes and smiled before looking down at the recommended reading list, pleased to see that I had already read most of them. I was still looking over the list when I asked Reid if he'd read any of them yet. His answer had my jaw dropping and turning my head to face him so fast I nearly broke my neck.

"Bullshit!"

He leaned back in his chair and stretched out his legs as far as he could in his cramped space. "Not bullshit. I read them all over the last couple of years, but I read Crime and Punishment on the trip out here when we moved."

"Huh." I didn't want to admit it, but I was impressed. I thought I was always the biggest nerd in the room, but I may have just found some real competition.

The rest of class wrapped up quickly, and we headed towards the cafeteria after dropping our bags off at our lockers. By the time we made it, there was a decent sized line of students waiting to be served. I glanced at the calendar taped to the door.

"Looks like chicken nuggets, french fries, and green beans. Your choice of white or chocolate milk. Oh! Look! You also get a cookie today!"

Reid chuckled and took my hand, and began to lead us to the back of the line. He was stopped when a familiar girl with long dark hair and long legs walked into his path.

Jessica trailed a finger down the center of his chest, and I had to clench my teeth tight to keep myself from blurting out something that was likely to get my ass kicked. "Reid," she purred, "I'm glad you finally showed up to join me. I saved you a seat and got your tray all ready for you." I had never been a violent person, have never really thrown a punch. I usually covered myself with my hands and arms in a protective shield if Jessica or Jason became physical. But I could honestly say that I wouldn't mind breaking her perfect little nose with my fist.

Reid stepped back, taking me with him. "Jessica." He nodded. "I'm sorry you went through all that trouble for me." He looked sincere when he shook his head and gave an apologetic smile. "But we were just assigned our reading list for AP English Literature. My assigned accountability partner and I have to go over our strategy so we can make sure we pass the class. It's going to be a really tough class to get an A in." He smiled his big toothy grin. "You know how important school is! Maybe another time." Then he pulled me behind him and to the back of the line.

I wanted to, but I fought the urge to turn around to see her reaction. But I didn't have to wonder when I saw the look on a girl's face that was looking in Jessica's direction. The wince and the involuntary step back told me what I needed to know. Reid didn't let on that he was worried in the least.

I glared at his back. This was all his fault. He came to this town with his good looks and fantastic football skills, made half the female population fall in love with him...then he turned my world upside down by choosing *me*. Of course, the most popular girl was going to set her eyes on him. What did he expect? And because he wasn't giving her the time of day and chose her unwanted cousin instead...I was going to end up buried. I just hoped that someone writes something nice about me on my headstone. Maybe I should write my own epitaph?

Here lies Paige,
She was killed in a fit of rage.
Blame goes to Reid,
May his hairline early recede.

Nah, I'll keep working on it.

We finally managed to get our food and sat down at a table that was towards the side of the room. I couldn't say it was quiet, but it didn't have the yelling and carrying on that was going on towards the center of the room where Jessica sat. I worked on keeping my eyes carefully away from that area. I wondered if she realized yet that Reid and I were sitting here without any books?

She may not be the smartest girl in the school, but she wasn't stupid either. She knew that Reid had lied and made excuses to not have to sit with her. How she would continue to handle his rejections was something I wasn't looking forward to.

I felt Reid nudge my shoulder with his. "So, what are your plans for after school?" He popped a nugget into his mouth and watched me as I swiped a french fry through my puddle of ketchup.

"I usually go straight home and lock myself in my room to get homework done."

He frowned. "You lock yourself in every day?"

I gave a small shrug. "I mean, yeah. I told you it wasn't safe for me there. And now you've gone and pissed her off even more."

He rubbed a hand over his face and then ran it over the top of his head, gripping a handful of his hair. "Fuck. You're right. I should have listened to you. I don't want you in danger." He groaned long and loud. "Is there no way you can tell her parents that she is harassing you?"

I snorted. "Yeah, right." I swiped another fry through the dwindling puddle of ketchup and eyed his ketchup packets sitting on his tray. "My uncle is too busy working, and my aunt either doesn't care, or she's too disconnected to care. It's easier just to wait it out and leave the minute the clock strikes midnight on my birthday." I looked up at him. "My birthday is December 10th, when's yours?"

"Next month, actually." He still looked stressed, but he bit another chicken nugget in two.

"No kidding?"

He grinned. Luckily his food was all behind his teeth, so I didn't have to see any of it. "Yep. I'll be 18, and my parents said I could move into the apartment over the garage."

I moaned. "I am so jealous! I was thinking about asking my aunt and uncle permission to move into the pool house right now, but I doubt they will let me."

"Maybe they will let you move in with me?" He said it all nonchalant as if the words weren't crazy ridiculous. I just stared. I had nothing. Finally, my jaw started working, but no sound would come out even though it was moving up and down.

"Are you insane?" I screeched a little too loud if his wince and him sticking his pinky into his ear and wiggling it around gave any indication. "I will not even go into the million reasons why that idea is absolutely insane." I stopped and drew in several deep breaths until my heart rate lowered a bit. "All I will say is there's not a chance on this great big planet that I would ever be able to get permission to move in with a boy."

He looked down at his pile of fries and searched around for his missing ketchup packets before giving up and poking one of his fries in my ketchup puddle. He ignored my growl and grumbled, "It was just an idea."

CHAPTER 7

Reid

I put my arm around my little ketchup fiend and walked her from the noisy cafeteria back towards our lockers.

I knew she was worried. Well, sometimes she seemed actually scared, and that bothered me. The last thing I wanted to do was cause her any problems at home or school. But at the same time, this girl was going to mean something to me. I could feel it in my bones. My head and my heart were in agreement; we need to pursue this. If I let her have her way, she would make excuses and push me away. It may be the easiest way for both of us, but my mom always said nothing worth having ever comes easy.

I didn't want to be the guy who strong-arms his girl and pushes her past her comfort zone, but I could tell my girl is stubborn and scared. I would try to prod her gently. If she ends up resisting too much, then I would worry about pushing.

I listened to her talk about the English assignment we had due on

Friday and hummed in agreement when I needed to. I was definitely listening to her, but most of my brain was focused on her, the person.

When I saw her sitting in that chair in the office, my first impression was of a goddess or an angel. Her golden hair and turquoise eyes were a striking combination. Her whole face and body were in an incredible package that would make any guy my age stop and drool. What could I say? We were bundles of hormones held back by society's rules of behavior. Okay, that's a little harsh; we actually do have some self-restraint. But seeing such an amazing girl like Paige would make it hard not to react.

So, yeah, I was drawn in first by her beauty, not going to lie. And when she stood up, and I got to see her curves? Yeah, even though I was very firmly in the 'no girls for now' mindset, I fully planned to commit her to memory for later. But then we started talking, and she started showing her personality. She was everything I wasn't looking for - but everything I hoped to have. There was no way I could ever deny myself the chance to get to know her, to be the first one she would allow to be by her side, hold her hand. One day soon, I hoped to be the first one to kiss those truly amazing lips. I wondered if they were as soft and luscious as they seemed.

She was the total package: brains, beauty, and a personality that even my Nana would approve of. I couldn't let her slip away from me. So, yeah, I was going to fight for her- for us. I would use everything I had at my disposal not only to keep her as mine but to keep her safe. Everything about her was my first priority now. Football was still up there, but I wouldn't allow myself to put her second.

"So, I was trying to ask you what you were doing after school when we got sidetracked about your living situation." I felt the anger burning in my belly when I thought of her only feeling safe if she locked herself in her room.

She paused her thoughts about the English assignment, and I winced, realizing that I had stopped paying attention there for a minute or two. "Yeahhhh..." She drew the word out, her curiosity and bafflement showing in her tone.

"Well, I thought that maybe you could sit on the bleachers and do your homework or reading assignments while I'm at practice."

"Why would I do that when I have a perfectly good desk in my bedroom or even in the library here at school?" Well, when she put it that way...

"I was hoping you would sit there so I could see you. It would be harder to protect you while I am playing, but I wouldn't be able to protect you at all if I can't even see you."

We stopped in front of my locker, and she looked up at me, those big turquoise eyes shining, making me start to worry that I was causing her cry.

She reached up as if she was going to place her hand on my cheek but hesitated before making contact and ended up touching my arm instead. "Oh, Reid. You want to protect me?"

I took her hand off my arm and held it between my palms. Her hands looked almost like a child's, small and delicate, inside my own large ones. "Paige, I don't know if you understand this or not. I am extremely protective of you. You've told me that you are scared at home, and that is killing me. I want to solve your problems and make the danger go away, but I can't do that for another four months. What I *can* do is watch you when I can. I am still working out plans in my head for when you are at home."

She stared at me for several seconds before blinking, then looking down and covering my hands with her other. "I think I understand, Reid." She looked back up at me and then slowly swiped that damn lock of hair that was always falling over my forehead back behind my ear. My skin tingled where she had barely touched me, and I knew I never wanted to lose that feeling. "It's quick, isn't it?" She whispered.

"Yeah, I suppose it is." I nodded. "But, you know what? Some people search their entire lifetime for that one single person that makes them whole. We are new; we are still learning who we are to each other and even who we are ourselves. But, Paige, if we are right, and we found each other this early in our lives? That makes this more than special. We are both very intelligent people. Even for our young age, we both have good heads on our shoulders and make good decisions."

She giggled and ducked her head for a second before looking back up at me with her bright eyes. "That sounds like something the school counselor would say."

"And he'd be right." I winked before dropping my grin. "Paige, we'd be stupid to throw this away."

She nodded her head. "I know."

I blinked. "You do?"

"Yeah. I mean, I've never been interested in a boy before, you've never been interested in girls. We are both smart and in advanced classes together. We have personalities that seem to mesh well." She shrugged. "It's almost like karma brought us together. Who am I to tell the universe it's wrong?"

I smiled so big that my cheeks were starting to hurt. I didn't think I had ever been quite so happy in my life.

The warning bell for 5th period rang, and I looked around, just now noticing that the hall was filled. I was so wrapped up in Paige that I drowned out anything else besides her. "We have AP Stats next, right?"

"Yeah, I need to grab my bag from my locker." She started to step away, but I grabbed the back of her sweater and pulled her stumbling back to me. "Reid!"

"Give me time, buddy, yeah? I have to get used to this feeling of possessiveness. Plus, I am protective of you and don't want to let you get hurt. I can't protect you if you're not by my side.

She huffed but didn't really look mad. "How long will it take you to get over your," she raised her hands to make air quotes, "possessiveness?"

"I don't know, you'll have to let me ask my dad when he thinks it will start to let up for my mom."

"Well, this ought to be fun." She mumbled it under her breath but started to laugh when I poked her side.

"I heard that."

She quickly retrieved her backpack from her locker, and we practically ran back down the other end of the hall to make it to the class right when the final bell rang. She followed me to the back of the room and sat next to me, and I watched as she, once again, arranged her desk with the notebook and pencil perfectly lined up. I tugged the new notebook my mom bought me a few days ago and pulled a pencil out of the side pocket of my backpack, and double-checked to make sure the lead hadn't broken off. I wasn't as hyper-organized as she was, but I was still always prepared.

"We need to put all of your stuff in my locker. There is plenty of room." I said quietly while the teacher began taking roll call.

"Okay."

I glanced over at her, surprised at her easy capitulation. She rolled her eyes at me.

"Relax. I understand logic perfectly well. It makes sense. Your locker is in the middle, and it will be quicker to use one locker instead of running back and forth between two." She leaned over and patted my hand reassuringly. "Don't worry, big guy. There will be plenty of other things I will argue over."

"I guess I will just have to provide a reasonable and logical explanation as to why I am always right."

She giggled-snorted and covered her mouth with her hands, and turned red. It was adorable.

"Mr. Johnson, Miss Anderson. If you are ready, I can start the class off by explaining this year's syllabus?" The teacher stood at the front of the class with one bushy eyebrow arched.

"Yes, Mr. Wu," we said in unison.

CHAPTER 8

Paige

The rest of the school day flew by, not that there was much left to it. 6th period was the only other period that Reid and I had separately. I had choir and he had weight training which, come to think of it, really explained why he had the physique he did. Between football practice almost daily *and* weight training? Yeah, it was a good combination.

7th was AP Physics together and 8th period was our free period, which allowed us to either go to study hall or sign ourselves out early to go home. Since Reid wanted me to stay to hang out on the football field, I figured I'd go to study hall, so I didn't have to go home and then return an hour later.

Since it was the first day of school, There was little homework or studying to be done, so we found ourselves a quiet corner to talk. It was time to explain things to Reid. He knew a lot, but he still didn't really understand the dynamics and how they came to be.

"In my freshman year, I had to learn quickly how to protect myself while here at school. I switched my PE period to 8th, so I didn't have to shower and change. After I found my clothes in the showers a couple of times, I wisened up." I watched as Reid took my hand and started drawing on my palm while I spoke. "Jessica didn't have as much influence over the students nearly as much as she has now. As a freshman herself, she showed definite promise but didn't control the upperclassmen. At least, not until she started dating the Varsity Football Quarterback.

"That was when she first got a taste of the power she could wield." I took a deep breath and let it out. Watching him drawing was hypnotic and helped soothe my nerves as I recounted how the reign of terror began. "It was also when I learned that I needed to protect myself. All she had to do was whisper in her new boyfriend's ear, rub his cock, and I had an orange juice shower during lunch." Reid stopped drawing and frowned at me. I missed the soothing feeling immediately.

"She went from him to the best player on the baseball team once spring rolled around. With those two in her back pocket, a Homecoming princess and a Prom princess crown on her resumé, she had herself set up for the remaining three years."

"Wow." He bent his head to start working again. "I think she's a lot smarter than I gave her credit for." I hummed in agreement.

"She continued her reign by dating only the best or the richest. From what I understand, she doesn't put out with all of them. I think she is actually smart enough to know that she would only be able to maintain her power with a few of them by holding them off instead of giving in.

"Obviously, having her own brother as the current varsity football QB put a kink in her typical plans of 'date the most popular or best sports player' because her brother happens to be both of those things, ironically, it was thanks to riding on the caboose of his sister's popularity train. He would never have made it as big as he has if it weren't for Jessica." I snorted and shook my head.

"Anyway, I think that's where you come in, to be honest. Jessica was screwed, or actually, the opposite of screwed, when it came to her brother being QB, so when you showed up during the summer football camp and showed everyone what an amazing player you were, you were too much for Jessica to pass up." Looking at Reid, though, I knew that she liked what she saw, too. His looks were icing on the cake, while the real prize for her was his imminent popularity.

"I don't know if she only started on her campaign to be the Queen Bee of the school just so she could make my life miserable, or if it was just a fun little perk for her. But one thing I knew for certain, finding out that you and I had become an item before she managed to sink her talons into you? That is priceless. And some kind of karma, too."

I sat at the table with my English assignment in front of me, not really seeing the words. It wasn't due for a few days, so I wasn't going to stress too much over it. I planned on reading while Reid was at practice. I looked up at the clock and saw we had 30 minutes left to go. We didn't have to stay, but there was nowhere to go when we would just have to come right back. Maybe sometime we could head for a quick bite to eat or coffee or something.

"You still haven't told me what happens to you at home." He gently reminded me.

I sighed. "Being at home has been a nightmare. Most of the things they have done have been annoying. They steal my shit. They lock me out of the house. But one thing they did that broke my heart was when I had a betta fish for about a month before I found it lying on my bed when I got out of the shower."

Reid squeezed my hand and kissed the top of it. It was so sweet of him to comfort me.

"The night before my 14th birthday, I was woken up in the middle of the night. Someone was holding me down, and someone was cutting my hair. They never said a word, but it was beyond obvious who it was. They were also super careful not to cut too much. If I had told on them after they hacked at my hair like they'd done it with a weedwacker, even my uncle would have had to say something. So they cut it up to my chin." I ran my fingers over my bun.

"How long is your hair now?"

"It's almost to my waist."

He smiled. "I'd love to see that."

"Maybe someday, you will." I laughed.

"Why have they never cut your hair again?"

I smirked. "Because the next day, my aunt commented on me cutting it, and I cried that I hated it and I swore I would never cut my hair again. I made such a big deal about it that if the monster twins tried to cut it again, it would be obvious that I didn't choose to do it. Even though the things they did were awful, they always did them in a way that it would seem I was lying or did it myself, like with my fish. My bedroom door had been locked. Someone picked the lock somehow and locked it back up before I got out of the shower."

"So they haven't physically hurt you?" He sounded hesitant to ask. Either he didn't really want to hear that I had, or he didn't want to make it sound like what had been done wasn't that bad. All the little things really weren't too horrifying, but when you list them out and realize it had been going on for over three years, it was a little bit traumatizing.

"See this scar?" I pulled the back of my shirt collar down so he could see the thin line that went across my upper shoulders about three inches. "That is where she dug the scissors into me while she was cutting my hair off. I was pushed down the stairs more than once, and one of those times, I broke an ankle. Another time it was my wrist."

He looked furious and sad now, "I need to know if they have ever been punished."

I frowned and shook my head.

"Never? They've never been held accountable for all that shit they've done to you?"

"No, Reid. They are twins. The other one could kill someone, and they would provide an alibi without being asked. When I broke my arm falling down the stairs, both the twins swore that they had been playing a video game in the game room. My uncle took me to the hospital to get a cast and told me I needed to be more careful."

He sighed loudly. "I see why you are scared. Let me figure out what we can do."

I stared at the top of his head, bent over my hand. Seeing his long, wavy hair brushing the tops of his shoulders was too much to resist. I ran my fingers through the waves, loving the softness. No one had cared about my wellbeing in a long time, not since my parents died. Now, this gorgeous, smart, funny guy has come along and reminded me what it was like to have someone care. All day long, I have wondered if he was real or too good to be true, but he has seemed to be nothing but sincere. And then there were the words that Lisa had told me this morning. "Don't turn him down." I trusted her feelings. I had a choice to make, and I needed to make it soon.

"Okay," I whispered. I guess I made my choice. Huh.

The final bell rang, signaling the end of the first day of our senior year. It had been completely uneventful while at the same time thoroughly life-changing. What a weird day.

Reid sat up and lifted my palm so he could blow on it to dry the ink. His pale blue eyes stared straight into mine. The way he was looking at me was hypnotizing. I couldn't blink and didn't want to. Then he looked down at my palm and smiled, breaking the trance that he had me under.

I finally got my first look at what he had just spent the better part of the last 45 minutes drawing into the palm of my hand with an ink pen. It was the most adorable kitten, and of course, my first reaction was to say "Awwwwwww!" in the highest pitch that I was probably capable of. It was so cute and had incredible detail. I looked up at him while he gathered our things and put them away in our bags.

"You did all this with an ink pen? That's crazy impressive! What else can you do? Do you have a sketchbook I can look through?" I was still looking at my hand. How was I supposed to wash my hand now?

I heard Reid chuckle and looked back up to see him shouldering both of our bags onto his shoulders. "Yes, I have a sketchbook, dozens probably, and you can look through any of them you want to. The earlier ones aren't that great, but I've managed to improve over the years."

"Is that your first-period class?"

"Yep."

"I can't wait to see more!" I bounced next to him as we walked out of the library and made our way to the gym so he could change into his practice gear and get out onto the field.

"I hadn't noticed." He lightly bumped me with his elbow, and we stopped outside the boy's locker room. "I will be out in just a few minutes, okay?" I nodded. "Are you sure you want to stay?"

"Yeah, I'm sure."

He looked relieved like he was glad I chose wisely because he would have chosen for me if I'd chosen wrong. I was starting to see that possessive streak peek out a little. While he had his little inner battle about being too possessive, I was having a little internal struggle of my own, wondering if I should accept it or fight it. What I came up with is what my mom used to say to me all the time when I was a kid, and things upset me, or I didn't get my way - pick your battles. Mom was usually right. Somethings just weren't worth getting upset over, while other things definitely were.

I decided that there were some things that I would allow him to do or demand if they weren't that important, or they didn't affect my physical wellbeing in a negative way. If I were adamant about something, then I would just have to put my foot down. Another thing my mother always said nearly every single day - the most important key to maintaining any type of relationship was communication.

"I'll wait for you right here and then walk with you to the field."

He looked around as if assessing any dangers lurking. He sat our backpacks on the floor at my feet. We were standing inside the gym at the doors that led to the boy's locker rooms. He looked undecided, but it was either this, or I waited outside.

"Hey, I'll be okay. The twins are both getting changed for their own practices, right? Just hurry and change. We can figure something else out another time."

He grunted and ran his hand through his hair roughly before putting a hand around my waist and yanking my body hard into his. "Stay safe. I will be right out. Don't. Leave." He placed a kiss on my forehead, let me go, turned, and walked through the doors.

I sighed, picked up our heavy bags, and walked a few steps over to the bleachers that were still out from the assembly and the classes all day. Since it was the first day of school, there wouldn't have been any dressing out. The coaches would have had the classes fill the bleachers while they went over the year's expectations.

He hadn't been gone more than 5 minutes when the door banged open, and he was standing there panting, his hair sticking every which way and his t-shirt inside out. He was carrying his practice pads and jersey in one hand, and his other hand was on his hip as he took in a deep breath. I wanted to laugh, but the thought of him being that worried about me was a bit alarming.

I got up and rushed over to him. "Hey, it's fine, everything is fine."

"I can't help it. I keep picturing something happening to you. Them dragging you into an empty classroom or bathroom and hurting you. It keeps playing in my mind."

I sighed and picked up our bags from where I had been sitting. "I shouldn't have told you. I'm sorry. You wanted to know why I was scared, but I didn't think it would have freaked you out this bad."

He took my hand, twined our fingers, and pulled us towards the outer doors that would lead to the practice field. "No, I'm glad you told me. You needed to tell me so I would be aware." He bumped me with his elbow again and grinned at me. "Knowing is half the battle."

I groaned. "Okay, G.I. Joe, get out there and practice, I'll wait for you right here in plain site."

He stopped and cupped my cheek before placing a lingering kiss on my forehead again that was just as sweet as the last one. "Okay, buddy." he whispered and ran off onto the field.

CHAPTER 9

Paige

I sat on the metal bleachers looking over the practice field for a solid five minutes until my poor skin couldn't take the heat anymore. I fished around in my backpack and found my emergency umbrella down at the bottom. The shade from the umbrella didn't relieve much of the heat, but it was a decent way to keep the sun off me.

I read a good portion of my reading assignment for English class and was fairly engrossed in it when a shadow fell over me. I looked up, smiling, thinking it was Reid, but my smile dropped along with my stomach when I saw it was Jason standing in front of me, sweaty and drinking from a large squeeze bottle of water.

"Ah, cousin. You've been a bad little girl, haven't you." He smirked at me and squirted more water into his mouth. "You know..." He looked over towards the gym where the cheerleaders were likely practicing their routines. "I always thought you were the smart one. Straight A's, shoo-in for valedictorian..." He looked back at me, studying me. I swallowed hard. I didn't think the sweat that was rolling down the center of my back was entirely from the heat. He narrowed his eyes, and I could see the cold menace that was usually reserved for only me.

"Jessica can't call dibs on a human being, Jason. Reid didn't want-"

"Oh, little cousin. You know better than that." He gave me another hard look and started walking backwards to the field when the coach called his name. "We will continue this discussion at home. No interruptions there, right? I'm sure Jessica might have something she would like to say."

I looked over towards Reid as a shiver ran up my spine. He was standing with the coach with his hands on his hips. He was nodding his head as he listened while the coach was making broad gestures with his hands. But his eyes were on me and darting to Jason, where he was back at the water table, laughing with the other players. His eyes came right back to me, and it was easy to read the concern there in them.

This was a bad idea for so many reasons, not the least of which was the scorching sun. I gave Reid a weak smile and quickly closed my umbrella and stuffed my book into my bag. I pulled out my phone and sent him a quick text so he wouldn't worry.

Me: **I need to go**

Me: **I will talk to you later, okay?**

I GAVE a small wave and walked quickly away. I didn't want to see his disappointment. Anyway, it was probably for the best to get home before anyone else did and lock myself in my room where it was safe.

I jumped into my jeep and pulled out of the parking lot, only looking around enough to make sure I wasn't going to hit any body or any thing. My hands were shaking, so I gripped the wheel harder.

It had been a while since I got on the twin's bad sides. They had been pretty busy all summer. They both had summer camps and practices, which kept them busy during the day, and they spent the rest of the time going to parties and hanging out with their friends or significant others until Jessica broke up with her previous boyfriend a few weeks ago. In preparation for dating Reid.

Shit. Shit shit shit.

I couldn't think of what they might have planned to do to me tonight. They couldn't hurt me unless they could easily explain it away as an accident.

I wanted to scream in frustration. It was all bullshit.

Since I knew I wouldn't be leaving my room once I got to the house, I swung into a fast food drive thru and ordered some nuggets and fries. The sweet tea would be gone by the time I pulled into the driveway because, holy freaking crap, it was hot.

I drove up to the house and pulled into my designated parking space, grabbing my backpack and the bag of food after stuffing one of the nuggets into my mouth. I dropped the empty cup into the trashcan by the side door of the house. One thing about having a vehicle with no top or doors, bugs, especially ants, would easily find their way into my car if I left food in it longer than a minute.

I walked through the kitchen, not seeing any signs of life, and jogged up the stairs, eager to get in my room so I could barricade myself in.

I felt my head slam into the wall hard and slid to the carpet at the top of the stairs before I realized anything was wrong. I lay on the floor as my chicken nuggets and french fries tumbled down a few steps. I watched as one of the nuggets made it half-way down the stairs.

My head was ringing.

I slowly turned my head to see Jessica standing next to the alcove at the top of the stairs. Back when every house had multiple phones that plugged into the wall, the alcove was where a table and corded phone would have sat. As far as I knew, it had been empty for the last couple of years, ever since Jason and his friends were horsing around and broke the little table that used to sit there with a vase of flowers. None of us ever told my aunt; it wasn't as if she would ever come to our side of the house anyway.

Jessica was still wearing the clothes that she had gone to school in. She'd never changed into her practice clothes. Had never gone to practice at all. She must have parked somewhere else so I wouldn't see her car and be worried about an attack.

Jason had to have known that I would freak out and run straight home.

Jessica swung her tennis racket around like a baton.

"You're usually so predictable. School, lunch, study at the library, go home, lock yourself inside. Who knew that you would suddenly flip the script and become a man-stealing whore?"

I just laid there. I knew if I moved, she would just hit me again. I wouldn't get into my room quickly enough since I would have to unlock the deadbolt that I had installed two years ago. They hadn't tried to break through the lock yet, and I wasn't sure they would. My uncle wouldn't be pleased with me drilling the holes to install a deadbolt, but he would be pissed off if they actually damaged the door or doorframe.

My head throbbed where it had slammed into the wall. The lights that had flashed behind my eyes had finally faded, but the ache was still pounding inside my skull. I watched as her shoes stepped closer to me.

"This is what you're going to do, whore." She squatted down and grabbed my chin, her nails digging into my face. "You're going to tell Reid that you aren't interested. You are going to find a new little partner to study with. Maybe that guy with the red hair and zits? You two would be perfect together!" She laughed like she had said the most hilarious thing ever. She was talking about Tom. He moved away last year after begging his parents for years to take him away from this town. The principal didn't allow bullying on her campus, but there wasn't a damn thing she could do about whatever the kids did off school grounds.

She took her tennis racket and pressed the edge of the rounded end into my throat. She didn't press down hard. She didn't dig in. No, she just wanted to make sure I knew that she *could*. The intention was clear to see. I could call her bluff. I could report this attack to her parents, and I could call the police and have her charged with assault and battery. But I wouldn't because there wouldn't be any evidence.

Jessica and Jason were experts at not leaving behind any evidence.

Jessica pressed just the tiniest bit more into my throat. "Do you understand, whore?"

I wanted to push back, and I wanted to yell and scream. I wanted to stand up for myself and tell her no. Instead, I nodded my head as the first couple of tears slipped out to wet the hair at the side of my face.

"Awww, did I make the baby cry again? Poor, poor baby. You thought a guy was actually interested in you, huh?" She kept speaking in a baby voice, mocking my sadness and frustration as she always did. No matter how hard I tried to be strong, to not let her see that she affected me, I still ended up crying. And she always poured salt into my open wounds. "You'll *never* get a guy like Reid, baby whore. How could you ever think that a guy like him would want a girl like you?"

She stood up and smoothed her skirt down with one hand while she swung the racket loosely with the other. "See you later, little cuz." She turned and walked down the hall and into her bedroom. Before she shut the door, she looked back at me, still laying on the floor with my backpack by my side and my dinner laying across the steps of the stairs, and finger waved. I could hear her laugh until the door clicked shut, blocking out the sound.

I wanted to lay right where I was until the pain went away. Not the pain in my head, that would fade soon. No, the pain in my chest. It felt hard to breathe, like a boulder was sitting on me. But I knew she could come out at any time. I sat up slowly while my head spun a bit. I walked down to the middle of the stairs and quickly picked up every spilled nugget and fry that lay across the stairs. I stuffed them into the torn bag as I went. When I made it back to the top, I picked up my backpack and carried both bags to my room. I fished the key out of my pocket and let myself into my room.

I threw the fast-food bag into my garbage can and tossed my backpack onto my bed. I pulled my cellphone out of the side pocket and turned it off, not even looking at the messages or calls- if there even were any.

I went into my bathroom after double-checking that my lock was engaged and shoved my desk chair under the doorknob. I turned on the water to fill the bathtub, making sure to add some bath salts. Oatmeal and honey. It smelled good and usually helped lift my spirits. Today I just wanted to close my eyes and wait for tomorrow. Or the next day.

I picked up my headphones from my desk and turned on my favorite playlist after I undressed and kicked my clothes towards my hamper. I usually kept my room tidy, picking up after myself right away, but not today.

I gingerly stuck my toe into the bathtub water and was relieved that it wasn't so hot that I'd have to wait until I added enough cold water to make sure my skin didn't boil off. I slid all the way under the water and held myself there until my lungs couldn't take it, and then I held for a few seconds longer. When I popped back up and wiped my face with a washcloth, I reached down to the floor to pick up my headphones and put them over my head.

I closed my eyes and listened as Fix You by Coldplay started playing. No one was around to see me completely break as I listened to the words and hoped that there was a happy ending out there for me.

CHAPTER 10

Paige

I woke to the alarm on my phone, and for the second morning in a row, I didn't hit snooze or try to get more sleep. I lay back with my phone face down on my chest before finally sighing deeply and lifting the phone to my face.

I had been a coward last night. I hadn't looked at any of the messages that I knew had to be from Reid. There was so much to think about. I had also needed the night to wallow in my misery. The threat that the twins posed wouldn't be going away any time soon, and I spent most of the night crying over that fact. Today I needed to find my courage and strengthen my resolve.

Reid: **are you okay?**

Reid: **I asked Jason what he said to you, but he just**

laughed and said it was family business that Jessica wanted to talk to you about.

Reid: **Did she hurt you**

Reid: **I swear, I don't care if she's a female. I will destroy both her and her brother.**

Reid: **Buddy, please message me back so I'm not worried about you...as much**

I WAS MAKING my way through all the messages, thinking how sweet he was to be so concerned, when my phone started ringing in my hand. I accepted the call a split second before I realized the call coming through was a FaceTime call. A part of me wanted to squeal and throw the phone across the room in mortification. I was lying in bed after a long sleepless night of crying. There was no way I didn't look like an extra on a zombie movie set.

"Hey, Reid," I whispered. He looked amazing in his sleep rumpled state. I couldn't stop the heat from filling my cheeks when I realized he was shirtless.

"Paige!" He closed his eyes, and his whole body seemed to relax into his bed. Seeing him so relieved now that he finally got ahold of me made me feel terrible for worrying him.

"I'm so sorry. I know I should have answered your texts." I shrugged and picked at a loose string on my blanket, unable to meet his eyes. "I guess I'm not used to anyone caring about me except Lisa. She knows that I don't talk when I'm upset." I shrugged one shoulder helplessly. I looked back at the phone in my hand to see Reid moving his lips. It looked like he was counting?

"Paige, I'm going to let this one go. I get that you are used to being alone. But if you had any idea how absolutely worried I have been, you never would have let me stay like this for so long."

I bristled at his words. He barely knew me. How dare he lecture me?

I narrowed my eyes at him, and he sighed, seeing it. "I'm not trying to piss you off, Paige. Yeah, we just met, but every relationship started somewhere. If we are going to mean as much to each other as I am sure we will, then we need to start respecting each other and communicate now." He ran his hand over his face. "Fuck! I don't want to fuck this up already!" He let out a long groan that showed me just how frustrated he really was. He mumbled something under his hand that sounded like he didn't know how his dad did it.

Even though I was emotionally wrung out and so exhausted, it was unreal; seeing him flustered somehow managed to calm my nerves. Maybe it was because he always seemed so confident and sure of himself, since the moment we met, he had been determined to prove to the world that we were meant to be together. But dealing with me and my insecurities for less than 24 hours made him seem more human. Crap. Maybe being involved with me wasn't the good thing that he seemed to think it was. Not if I drove him crazy already.

He uncovered his face, and it was his turn to narrow his eyes when he caught the look on my face. He pointed his finger at me. "Now stop that. We are going to have to make a rule or something. No negative thoughts, only positive thinking when it comes to us. Got it?"

I just stared at him for a long minute. I could have sworn I heard him growl. "You're really that sure?"

His face softened, and he lowered his finger. "Buddy, I told you already how sure I am. But I'm patient. You take as long as you need to get used to the idea of you and me. Just as long as you do it with me by your side."

I took a deep, shuddering breath, determined not to cry again. Reid was stubborn as hell, but all that intensity and surety in us as a long-term couple did something to my insides that made me feel warm and gooey inside.

"You need to tell me what happened yesterday, Paige."

I took one more deep breath and started from the beginning. I watched his eyes change from irritated to pissed off to sad. His jaw was clenching so hard when I told him about the meeting with Jessica that I was afraid he was actually going to hurt himself.

"This happens all the time?"

I shook my head no. "It occasionally happens, yes. I think Jessica likes to remind me before I get too comfortable. But, honestly, after about six months living here, I figured it was just easier to give in than to always find myself under her shoe...literally."

He scowled. "That's really not funny."

"I didn't mean for it to be," I whispered, feeling the sadness trying to creep back in. I squirmed on my bed, finally noticing my bladder, and that made me remember how dreadful I probably looked at the moment. "I need to let you go, Reid." My face got warm, knowing he was seeing me look like a hot mess.

"Yeah, I need to go too. I had to try you as soon as I woke up." He sat up, and I watched his ab muscles bunch and flex, making me forget all about my swollen eyes and rat nest hair. I swallowed hard. I thought that if I had that as my view every morning, then maybe his prediction that we were meant to be together wasn't exactly a bad thing.

"We are going to talk more about this as soon as we have a few minutes alone, got me, Buddy?"

"Yeah, *Buddy,* I got you." I rolled my eyes. "You're going to have to do something about your bossiness."

He smirked, "I think you like my bossiness."

I smirked right back, "Just as long as you understand that I probably won't actually listen to you, then we will be perfectly fine."

"As long as you understand that we are a *we.*"

"I'm beginning to," I whispered and watched his eyes go soft. "Later, Reid."

"Later, Buddy." And my screen went black.

Gah! Him and that nickname. I wondered if I was going to stay Buddy for the rest of my life. The heat warming my veins at the thought definitely told me I didn't mind.

I jumped out of bed and glanced at the time. I was going to have to rush. Our conversation took a lot more time than I had realized. When I looked into the mirror, I sighed. There wasn't going to be much I could do about the swelling in my face. I always looked like that after a crying jag. I grabbed a washcloth and ran the water as cold as it could get. I wet and wrung out the cloth and pressed it against my eyes. My nose felt stuffy, too. I was so surprised that I had not turned off Reid.

I finished up in the bathroom after throwing my hair up into its usual bun and dabbed a bit of concealer under and around my eyes. Some mineral powder helped even out my complexion, while a couple of swipes of mascara and some tinted lip gloss made me feel a little more feminine.

Another look at the clock showed me that I would be seriously late if I didn't get out of the house within the next three minutes.

I heard Jessica walking down the hallway past my bedroom door. It sounded like she was on the phone with someone. Either that or Jason was there too. But if Jessica was heading out, then that meant I was out of time since she was the kind that always managed to pull into the parking lot with barely a minute to spare before the warning bell rang for the first period.

I grabbed a clean shirt from my closet and a pair of jeans from my drawer. I had a fresh pair of panties and bra on before I heard the front door close behind my cousin. I had my jeans and shirt on before she had her car completely backed out of the garage. And I had my feet slipping into a pair of ballet flats and my backpack over my shoulder before she cleared the driveway.

I rushed down the stairs so fast that I slid down the last two steps, nearly giving myself a heart attack. I ran through the kitchen to the inner garage door, having a feeling Jessica closed the garage door behind her, which would have made me even later if I had gone out the front door instead. I slapped the button for the garage rolling doors and jumped into my Jeep, jammed the key into the ignition, and was backing out before the door was completely open.

I drove around the fountain in the middle of the circular driveway and pulled through the gate and onto the road. It was always quiet on our street. Literally, nobody would be around here if they didn't have a reason to be. We lived at the end of a winding road with old, stately trees lined on either side. I had always loved the road. It was always beautiful, but in another couple of months, the colors would change, and that was when it was at its scenic best.

I passed the houses that started showing up after about a half-mile from our end of the street, and from there, I turned onto the main road that would lead me into the town. The town wasn't big, but its proximity to the large city was the perfect place for people to choose to live and commute from to raise their children in the slower, quieter setting.

When I pulled into the school parking lot, most of the other teens had already started filing into the large brick building that housed the only high school in town. The elementary school was down the road and started 15 minutes before ours did, probably to allow parents to drop off both kids without tardies, or most likely so that the students that drove could drop off little siblings before heading into their own school.

I grabbed my bag, hopped out of my Jeep, and wasn't surprised to see Reid waiting for me. I was even less surprised to see Jessica standing next to him. I could only guess what she was saying to him, but his body language told me that she was annoying him. He stood stiffly with his arms crossed over his chest. His face held boredom, but his eyes held barely concealed hostility. He knew she had hurt me the night before, and he wasn't going to pretend not to hate her.

He stepped back from her, the hand that she tried to place on his arm held in midair for a second before she pulled it back to her hip. I watched as she lifted her chin defiantly. She wasn't going to take rejection well. She undoubtedly had a plan to get closer to him regardless of what he was saying to her. I almost felt sorry for her. She had built herself a world where she was the queen, and no one ever said no. It had become her identity, and she would have a hard time accepting this change to her well-ordered plan.

Reid saw me, and his face softened, making Jessica turn to see what had his demeanor changing so quickly. Her scowl made her blue eyes narrow and her mouth twist. I could see her warning to me written on her face. I wanted to take a step back, years of programming, of me being scared to upset her was telling me to do what she said, but I looked back at Reid. He was encouraging me to trust him.

He held out his hand, and I walked forward a little reluctantly.

"Hey, Buddy. I'm glad you made it." He tugged me closer to his side and kissed my temple. The kiss took me by surprise, and I inhaled quickly. He just grinned at me and turned back to Jessica. "As I said before, I'm flattered, but I'm really not interested, Julie. I will be really busy with my study buddy here so we can keep up our grades and get into good colleges. We have a pretty heavy schedule with all our AP classes. You understand, right?"

Jessica ground her teeth and fairly snarled when she growled out, "Jessica." She turned to me and stared, expecting me to fold to her demands from last night, but I was frozen in place. I had never heard anyone, student or teacher, put her into place so easily and smoothly. He hadn't been mean or raised his voice.

When I didn't respond to her silent demand, she glared death at me, and I couldn't entirely hide my wince. It was a small triumph for her, but she seemed more than happy with it by the smile she suddenly produced. She turned back to Reid and said, "That's such a shame. But a boy can't do nothing but study, right? You'll have to come to the football parties and show you are part of the team. The cheerleaders are always there. I'll make sure you are never lonely." She winked and turned away. She took a couple of steps before stopping and looking back. "Oh! I almost forgot!" Her face was all smiles and joy, "The cheerleaders adopt a varsity football player. They make sure they have everything they need during away games and decorate their lockers, stuff like that. Guess who claimed you?" She winked and then strode away, all hips and swinging mahogany hair.

I closed my eyes and sighed. I should have seen it coming. Of course, there was another way for her to get her claws into Reid that I would never be able to. He didn't really have a say in it either.

He swung his arm around my shoulders and started leading me

into the school. "I'll walk you to the office. Don't worry about her. She can decorate my locker and bring me a water bottle all she wants. It doesn't mean I have to date her."

I didn't say anything. He was right, but knowing her, she would make his life hell if he fought her off much longer.

CHAPTER 11

Paige

Reid walked me to the office door before turning me to face him.

"You're okay?"

I smiled softly at the concern on his face. "I will be."

He tucked a stray wisp of hair that managed to escape my bun from the wind on my drive to school this morning. "You need to let me know if there is anything I can do." His look was stubborn, and he wasn't going to take no for an answer. Somehow I had gained a champion in my corner without ever looking for one.

"I will, Reid. I appreciate it, truly." I felt my nose sting from the urge to cry, but I had already done plenty of that, and I would never willingly show weakness inside these halls if I could help it. The majority of the students at this school were Jessica followers. She would know within seconds if they saw me cry. It would become more ammo, as if she didn't have enough already.

"You never need to thank me for looking out for you."

Okay, he was too sweet and too kind. I took a deep breath to control my emotions. He just watched me with a smile on his face. I had a feeling he knew exactly what he was doing to me.

I glared at him, and he just grinned wider.

"You'll get used to it." Now he was just being cocky.

I was about to say something snarky back, but the office door next to us flung open, and a loud cry rang out.

"Oh my god, Reid!" A girl that was about my same height with blond hair threw herself into Reid's arms and started talking so fast I could barely keep up. I was pushed back by the enthusiastic embrace and just kind of stood there with my mouth hanging open.

What the heck?

Reid pushed the girl back so he could look at her and then the biggest grin I'd ever seen him make spread across his face.

"Jenna? Holy shit! What are you doing here?"

The girl, I now recognized as Jenna Ivanov, was bouncing on her toes with her hands braced on his shoulders.

"Did you come for me? Oh my god, I always knew you'd come for me!"

Reid looked a little confused.

"What do you mean? Have you been here all this time?"

"Yes, my dad transferred here four years ago. I missed you so much." She sniffled, and he wiped a tear away.

I was starting to feel really uncomfortable. Reid had told me that he'd never had a girlfriend, but the girl that he was currently holding onto seemed pretty familiar with him. I had never felt jealousy over a guy before, but I was pretty sure that the spinning in my gut and the heat in my face were pretty good indicators that I was in a full-on jealous fit.

"Aww, Jenna, don't cry. I'm sorry we lost touch after you moved. How have you been?"

"I've been okay, and it's a nice school. But there hasn't been anyone special here for me, you know?" I winced at that. Jenna was on the cheerleader team with Jessica, and from what I had seen, she had been pretty 'special' with a few of the football players if their PDA at the cafeteria tables were any indication. I hoped Reid wasn't buying her act.

I started backing away, realizing that their reunion wasn't a spectator sport, and I really didn't want to see more anyway. In the short time we had known each other, Reid had convinced me that we were going to be something special together. I cringed at the thought. Jenna had just indicated that he was special or they were special together. Ugh. I needed to leave.

"Hang on, wait. Paige! Come here. I want you to meet someone." He reached out and grabbed my hand, and dragged me back over to their little huddle just as the warning bell rang. "Crap, we'll do this fast. Paige, this is Jenna. She was my next-door neighbor and friend growing up. Our dads also worked together, which I guess explains why we ended up in the same place again." He looked at her. "Small world, huh?"

"Oh, did your dad get transferred too?" She looked disappointed. I guessed she was finally figuring out that Reid hadn't searched the world just to find her and bring their friendship to the next level. From Reid's reaction, now that I was paying better attention and not focusing on the burning jealousy in my gut, I could see he was happy to see her, but there was no romantic passion, no lust when he looked at her. I let out a relieved sigh internally and tried to relax.

His smile fell, and he looked a little embarrassed at her assumption and genuinely sorry. "Yeah, that's why I'm here. He requested the transfer so I could go to this high school. We knew I would have better prospects here than I would have if I'd stayed in California." He looked over at me and put his arm around my shoulders as he had earlier. "This is Paige, my girlfriend. But I bet you probably already know each other, right?" He grinned, looking back and forth between the two of us while I tried not to fidget. Jenna had never done anything outright mean to me before, but she had never strayed too far from Jessica's group of minions. She'd done her fair share of taunting me, just like the others.

I lifted my hand slightly and gave a small wave. "Hey, Jenna."

Jenna just stood there in her tight cut off shorts and strategically ripped t-shirt and blinked at me a couple of times before she burst out laughing. I immediately dropped my hand and tried to back out from under Reid's arm. He looked confused but didn't let me go.

"Oh, this is fabulous!" Jenna was laughing so hard she held onto her side. I noticed the class schedule in her hand. That explained why we hadn't seen her yesterday. She must have missed the first day of school yesterday. I couldn't help but wonder if things might have ended up differently if Reid had seen his old friend before he'd seen me for the first time. "You want DSL as your girlfriend? Reid, come on. I'll take care of you if you want a girlfriend. Trust me. You do *not* want this one." She was still giggling and trying to wipe under her eyes to clear any smudged mascara. She didn't notice Reid's posture change or the anger that was building behind his eyes. But she must have finally felt the tension coating the air because she stopped giggling and really looked at him.

"You've changed." He said it quietly. Disappointment and sadness warred with the anger that he was holding back. "Someone who used to be bullied in middle school should know what it's like and not repeat it on someone else." He took a step back and turned to me, missing the crestfallen look on her face and the pain that flashed behind her eyes. She lifted her hand back to him but let it drop again. She stood there with her shoulders slumped and looked at him as he looked at me.

"I'm sorry." He whispered. He looked truly devastated. I imagined a lot of the devastation was for the friend that had disappointed him so much. It would be hard to find out that someone you had once cared so much for had turned into a different person.

"It's okay, Reid. I told you before; I'm used to it." I shrugged one shoulder in defeat.

His lips thinned as his face got hard. "No, that's not okay. No one will ever bully you again." He sounded determined to single-handedly stop any bullies from getting within a hundred feet of me. It wasn't possible, but it was sweet. I also didn't have the heart to tell him that he had painted an ever bigger bullseye on my forehead just by claiming me.

He turned back to Jenna, who looked like she was ready to cry for real. She put her hand out again and whimpered. "I'm sorry, Reid, I didn't mean it."

"Yes, you did. You may not have started out wanting to be a bully, but the moment you laughed at her, called her names, you became one." The anger bled out of his expression, and he just looked disappointed. "It was good to see you again, Jenna."

He turned me towards the door to the office and opened it for me just as the final bell rang, indicating that everyone needed to be in their seats for the first class of the day.

He sighed, and I squeezed his hand. "Let me write you a note so you don't get a tardy."

"It's a secret, but nobody is handing out tardies for the first week of school." The secretary winked at Reid. "I saw what happened out there. I'm proud of you, young man. There are too many bullies in this world and not enough white knights. Always keep your honor and never let the weaker ones suffer because of you."

Reid straightened his shoulders and nodded. His voice was dead serious when he replied, "Yes, ma'am, always."

He turned back to me, smiled a crooked smile, and walked back out the door to his first-period art class.

Both Mrs. Walker and I stared after him, and both sighed at the same time. She turned to me with a wink. "That's a good one right there. Don't ever let him get away from you. If I were 30 years younger, I might have tried to fight you for him." She laughed a sweet laugh, and I smiled at her. She may have been older, but Mrs. Walker was still beautiful with her flawless dark skin and braided hair.

"I bet you would have won, too." I teased her back.

"No way, I bet you'd fight me dirty to keep him to yourself. Besides, my Reggie would never have let another man turn my eye even back in high school. He was one of those, like your young man out there." She nodded her head towards the way Reid went while she sat down in her rolling chair and pulled out a binder. "Reggie took one look at me, and within minutes, he told me how it was going to be. As long as I let him, he led me through every up and down we had throughout our lives. Thirty-five years now, we have been together. I can see your man out there is the same. Determined, bossy, loyal, cocky," she smirked at me, "and worth it all."

"Yeah, that sounds like Reid." I cleared my throat as I sat down and opened my bag to pull out the pirate romance I had been reading yesterday. Usually, I would read in the bath and would have finished it last night, but I was too depressed. Now, I just wanted to get back to the Mallorys. "How did you know?"

"How did I know what, dear?"

"How did you know that he was the right one. That his bossiness and...dominance was worth it?"

She hummed and tapped her fingers on the arm of her chair and cocked her head to the side as she studied me. "Well, I had good advice from the best woman in the world."

"What was that?" I asked quietly.

"My granny was the wisest, meanest old woman anyone had ever met. She always had pearls of wisdom to hand out. But the best advice and the one I still live by to this day?" She paused, and I leaned forward eagerly, needing to know what I should do about Reid, about Jessica, about everything. "Follow your heart." She laughed softly. "That's it, Miss Paige. Follow your heart."

I sat back, almost disappointed. "That sounds so easy and so hard all at the same time."

"Of course it is! Nothing worth having ever came easy. But if you follow your heart and trust your instincts, it will be worth it in the end. You feel something gnawing at you in here," she tapped her chest, "you run far away; that man won't be any good. But if your heart feels warm and he treats you like gold, you owe it to your future happiness to give it a chance." She smiled and looked down at my book. "Ah, I see we have more in common than our taste in men. Aren't the Mallorys delicious?"

I laughed and nodded then we both settled in for the rest of the first period.

CHAPTER 12

Paige

The rest of the week went by surprisingly drama-free. Well, for the most part.

Reid and I shared our classes together, sitting side by side, while we went our separate ways for the other periods we didn't share, though he walked me to those and met me at the door after. After school, I went home right away while the twins were busy with their after school practices and grabbed food for my dinner, then barricaded myself in my room for the rest of the night

In the cafeteria, we sat with Lisa and Chad at one of the circular tables. I wasn't surprised that nobody joined us. Chad had never been bullied in any way. He was actually fairly popular as a baseball player, but because he was associated with Lisa and me, everyone pretty much ignored him until he was alone. It was actually kind of funny how they would suddenly swarm in around him the moment we walked away.

I was a little surprised that no one spoke to Reid, though. I knew it was because of me that they stayed away, and I mentioned to him on our second day of school that I didn't mind if he wanted to hang out with his football team but he just looked at me for a solid 30 seconds before turning back to his lunch tray to finish eating his meal. I never mentioned it again.

One thing that was becoming real annoying real fast was the sad doe eyes that kept being sent his way. Jenna was always nearby. Whether it was at lunch or in the hallways between classes, she could be found staring in his direction. I got it, he was her best friend for a long time, and when she saw him, she had immediately hoped for more than friendship.

I could tell Reid was sad when he would see her in the halls, but he told me when I had asked him about it that he had no patience whatsoever for bullies, and forgiveness would be hard to find for someone that had hurt me. I tried to explain that she was only following the rest of Jessica's followers but that only made him more determined. Apparently, she had gone through something similar in their old middle school. He hated that she knew what it felt like but decided that popularity was more important than doing the right thing.

Of course, I had also pointed out that the football jocks had been some of the worst offenders. He just gave me a chilling smile and said that he was making them pay for it. I'd also noticed that most of the players were very respectful towards him. They showed him more respect than their football captain that they had played with most of their lives. Having a strong moral character earned more respect than someone that preyed on the weak. Who knew, right?

It was the last day of the first week at school, and the first football game of the year would be that night. The entire school had been decked out in red and white. Streamers covered the hallways, and signs with glitter were everywhere. As soon as Reid walked me in through the school's front door, it was like being sucked into a vortex of school spirit. Reid had to wear his football jersey over a button-down shirt with a red tie like all the rest of the football players, while the cheerleaders wore their uniform all day. I never quite understood the reasoning behind them dressing up on game days, but it was definitely nice to see him in it. Nice really wasn't the right word. Sexy, hot, drool-worthy, those were far better words. His biceps strained the fabric, and the buttons pulled tight across his chest whenever he flexed. I mentally waved my hand in front of my face to cool myself off.

He dropped me off at the office door with the now-familiar kiss to my temple with a smile when he waved goodbye and threw out a "see you, buddy". I got myself settled into my usual seat behind the counter. I was just about to crack open the latest book on my TBR list about a princess from a foreign land that had been hidden away in America as a child when Mrs. Walker handed me a slip of paper to take down to one of the teachers.

It always felt strange to walk the empty halls while the classes were in session all around me. I tended to walk as quietly as possible. It felt like I was doing something against the rules instead of sitting at a desk with the rest of the students. I rarely saw another person in the halls so I was surprised when I came up to the teacher's door I needed to drop the paper off to and saw a couple of students standing nearly hidden at the end of the corridor where the row of lockers ended.

I paused with my hand on the classroom door handle. I couldn't help but be curious about who was out of class. Mostly since they were whispering as if they were trying to hide that they were there at all. I debated walking past them since my curiosity was running on overdrive, but before I could let go of the handle and take a step in their direction, the two people stepped out and went in opposite directions.

I was momentarily stunned to see Jenna coming my way. She was wiping her eyes and looking at the floor as she quickly walked past me. I didn't think she even realized anyone was standing there at all.

"Hey," I said softly, lifting my hand to touch her arm. "Are you okay?"

She jumped, startled, and looked up at me. Her mascara was

running down her cheeks, and it would take more than a tissue to fix her makeup. Her eyes were red and puffy. She was clearly upset, and I wanted to see if there was anything that I could do to help her. The guy she had been with left the hallway pretty quick, but I was almost completely certain that it had been Jason. I didn't know that Jason and Jenna had been dating or had hooked up, or whatever they were doing that would cause her to look so distraught after talking together.

Jenna gaped at me for a few seconds, and distress passed through her blue eyes so quickly I almost thought I had imagined it before her face shut down and her pretty features twisted in disgust. She pulled her arm away from me as if I had burned her and snarled, "Eww, don't touch me, gutter trash. Why don't you mind your own business." Then she took a step closer to me and looked into my eyes. "Why don't you do everyone a favor and just leave? No one wants you here."

I felt a sharp stab of pain in my chest. It never got any easier no matter how I got used to hearing those types of words from my fellow students. I usually put my head down and walked off as quietly as I could to get away from the person before they could get worked up and really sling insults my way. It usually drew a crowd and incited others to do the same, but being with Reid for the short time that I had known him had given me the courage to hold my head up.

"First of all, I could hardly be considered gutter trash. I may be living under my uncle's roof, but my parents owned more than he does, and all of that will pass to me soon. You might want to find a new insult." It was petty, but I was tired of the insults, of being put down for being a charity case. "And secondly? Reid is more than happy to have me here." I smiled sweetly at her.

She scoffed and threw her curly blond ponytail over her shoulder. "Count your days with him, whore. We have a history. He won't be able to stay away from me for long." She winked and spun on her heel away towards the bathrooms. Her words didn't hurt me, I knew what she was insinuating, but I also knew they just weren't true. Yes, they had a history together...as friends only. They'd never dated, or kissed, or even held hands. Reid had told me that he never once felt that way about her. She had been more like a sister to him than anything. And that was the only thing that actually managed to dig a barb into me.

He couldn't possibly stay mad at her for long if she had been so important to him. Reid was a good man. I couldn't see him holding a grudge for long. Once they actually sat down and talked, I was sure he would get over his anger towards her. I had no problem with that. It was just that I didn't want to share Reid with anyone else. I was being selfish, I knew. But we had only started out in our relationship. I didn't want her to take his time away from me.

I finally turned the door handle, walked the paper over to the teacher's desk, and nodded when he said thank you. The whole walk back to the office, I thought about what I had seen and what it might mean. Really, there was no telling. Maybe they had hooked up at a party and had just broken up. Perhaps he was bullying her too. I wished that she had spoken to me instead of pushing me away. I sighed deeply and hung my head when I sat back down in my chair in the office. I was going to have to talk to Reid and tell him about it so that he could speak to her.

It wasn't long before the bell rang, ending the first period. I gathered my belongings and slung my bag strap over my shoulder, and stood up, waiting for Reid to appear outside the glass door. I was a coward. I didn't like waiting in the hallway, letting other students snicker at me as they passed by. I couldn't hear their whispers if I stayed in the office.

Finally, Reid walked up to the door and smiled. As soon as I saw that beautiful grin, I immediately felt my tension start to melt. I definitely didn't like that I was finding myself relying on him to protect me. I didn't want to go back to being alone, though, either.

We walked down the halls heading towards our shared locker without saying a word. The halls were noisier than usual due to the hype of the coming football game. The energy from all the students surrounding me was practically electric. I could almost reach out and touch the sparks flying. As a school, they would get excited over football each week, but few of the games would elicit as much excitement as the first game of the season. Homecoming was a big one, and any playoff games, of course. But coming straight off of summer vacation and suffering through the first week of school, not much could beat the first game of the season.

I could feel that Reid was starting to be affected by the other student's excitement. It was the main reason for getting the students hyped up, I supposed. The actual football players would eat up the energy and excitement and let it fuel them for the upcoming game. I couldn't deny it was a great idea. Now that I had a... friend-boy, a friend that was a boy, boy...friend? We certainly hadn't discussed titles, but whatever he was to me, I wanted him to do well. Go team! And all that stuff.

The senior hallway was crowded as usual, so I didn't catch sight of the monstrosity that was his locker until we were right on it. Due to the school colors being red and white, the glitter and ribbons that decorated the entire 5 ½ foot locker door looked more like a valentine greeting from an overzealous lover.

Small bits of glitter slowly floated to the ground in shiny displays of tiny disco balls each time the breeze from a passing student stirred up the air around the...artwork? There was a decent-sized little pile of discarded glitter with more spread several feet away through the hall. The poor janitor would be sweeping, mopping, and burning those teeny tiny pieces out of every nook and cranny for the next year.

Reid stopped us in front of his locker, and we both stood there, staring. There were multiple sayings written on the poster board that looked like it had been cut and re-pieced together to make a full-length example of what a teenage girl with too much time, money, and glitter on her hands should never do. There was Go Team Go! along with his number 81 in red and silver glitter in at least five sizes and as many places. Of course, his name was plastered on there, too. If anyone in the school hadn't already known who he was, they would have to be completely oblivious to miss this display.

He reached for the combination dial with a slight bit of dread on his face. I thought he was doing a pretty good job of trying to hide it from the rest of the students, though—what a trooper.

He leaned over to me and whispered out of the corner of his mouth, "Do you have a tissue or a napkin?"

I snickered and quickly clamped my mouth shut when his head spun to meet mine. I shook my head with wide eyes while he narrowed his dangerously on me.

"You know, I think it's time for you to learn how to open the locker since we share it and all."

I blinked my eyes a couple of times and stared up at him, widening my eyes as big as I could. "You don't want to open it for me anymore?" He'd been such a gentleman, demanding to open all my doors, including the locker door, that I couldn't help the tease now.

He sighed deep and loud, causing more glitter to rain down to join their lost little brethren. We both snickered at the sight. He turned to me, a pleading look on his face. The gleeful look in my eyes must have clued him in that I wasn't going to save him from his fate.

"You're really going to make me do it, aren't you?"

The pop in my 'p' was as drawn out as I could make it when I responded with a resounding "Yep!"

His hand paused only once, and then he managed to get up his courage to touch the combination dial that was covered entirely in red and silver glitter.

I took pity on him and exchanged both of our sets of books, and yelled at him to stop once when I saw out of the corner of my eye that he was going to attempt to wipe his fingers on his jeans.

The warning bell rang, letting us know we had one minute to get to class. That surprised me since I was sure we had spent at least two weeks in front of his locker while he tried to wish the glitter away.

"Run into the bathroom and wash your hands. I'll go to our class and distract the teacher." I giggled, watching him try to pick individual pieces from his fingers.

He looked relieved and leaned over to kiss my hair as he had gotten into the habit of doing, but I backed away quickly. "Not uh. Nope! You go wash first before you touch me again."

He looked down at his hands and grimaced. "You're probably right. These things migrate. Or multiply. I don't remember seeing that one on my wrist a minute ago." He dropped his backpack on the ground and took off to the bathroom without looking back.

"Good luck!" I wished him solemnly and backed away to head to class. I wanted to laugh, but I was too scared that he'd manage to get it on me, too. And we still had the rest of the day and at least four more locker trips to make today.

CHAPTER 13

Reid

I walked into second period Government just after the final bell rang. I still didn't feel like I got all the glitter off of me and had a feeling I was going to be seeing glitter in my nightmares.

The teacher gestured for me to move on back to my seat in the last row, conveniently next to the prettiest girl I had ever seen. I grinned and winked at her just as I was passing the girl's desk, Roxanne, and nodded to her as I passed. I can't help but feel a little...uneasy around her. It was obvious she had a crush on me, and I didn't want to encourage her, but I also wasn't raised to be rude either. I could only try to be polite but show that the only girl for me was and always would be Paige. I just had to convince my buddy of that.

I sat down and held out both my hands and turned them over to study them from every angle.

"Do you see any pieces I missed?" I hissed at Paige, who should have already been helping me out of the crisis I was thrown in.

Honestly, as a good girlfriend, she should have volunteered to open the locker for me. I side-eyed her. I may have to rethink our future.

"Actually, I do see a piece." I was horrified that there could be more and practically twisted my wrists into pretzels trying to find the glitter I missed. When I couldn't see it, I looked at Paige for guidance, but she wasn't looking at my hands.

"Oh hell no!"

"Yep." She looked way too chipper for the situation.

"Get it off!" I knew I was almost whimpering, but the situation was dire and had to be excusable.

"You big baby." She scratched the tip of her fingernail against the side of my nose and pulled her hand back only to hold it up so I could see the offender. And there it was, right at the end of her fingernail, a red glitter herpy. She flicked it, and I watched it fall slowly to the floor. Somehow it would make its way into my hair. I was sure of it.

"I'm doomed." I groaned, about to drop my face into my hands but thought better of it. I could get more on my face. Or on my hands.

"If you are done, Mr. Johnson?" The teacher looked highly amused at my expense.

"I certainly hope so, Mr. Ortiz." I sighed and leaned back in my seat, and tried to resign myself to a lifetime of finding red glitter in random places.

As we were told about our assignment, I suddenly remembered about the surprise I had for Paige today. As soon as he told us that we would be watching a documentary about the Constitution, I tugged my backpack over to me.

When he turned the lights off, I unzipped my backpack and pulled out the folded jersey that I had placed in there last night. I had asked my mom to have this jersey made with my name on the back with my number. It was a fan jersey but closely resembled our official jerseys in the school colors. While he was getting the movie started, I leaned over to Paige.

"I have something for you."

She turned to me, looking up from her notebook and pen where she had already written the date and what the class was doing today. At that moment, I couldn't be any happier that we were study buddies.

"What is it?" She looked apprehensive, but I could also see the excitement at having a random present being given to her. I hated that she likely had very few gifts recently.

I put the folded jersey on her desk and slid it closer to her. I hadn't felt nervous about her accepting it until just then. I suddenly realized that she may very well be offended or just not want gifts from strange guys...

She picked it up and let it unfold to show the front. "Turn it over," I whispered.

By now, the documentary had started, and the teacher had planted himself back at his desk. The last thing I wanted to do was get on the bad side of one of my teachers, so I kept my head facing the television screen but watched my girl as well as I could in my periphery as she turned over the shirt and looked at the back. After a long beat of silence, I gave in and looked at her.

"Do you like it?"

"You had this made for me?" Her voice was quiet so that the teacher couldn't hear, but there was a softer quality to it even through her whisper.

"Well, I asked my mom to have it made, but, yeah." I cleared my throat and looked back at the tv. "I was hoping you would wear it to the game tonight."

She didn't say another word, just held the jersey in her left hand and picked up her pen with her right, and started taking notes on the amendments to the Constitution.

A full 45 minutes later, the lights were finally flipped back on, and the class started putting away all their writing implements and note-books. As soon as the bell rang and the class stood up to leave, I saw Paige stand up too, still holding the jersey. I expected her to walk out of the class and put my hand on the top carry strap of my backpack so I could follow her out because, let's face it, I would follow her anywhere. She may not have liked the jersey, but I would just keep working on her until I found something she would like.

Before I could stand up, though, Paige took her cardigan off and stuffed it into her bag. I then watched as she pulled the jersey with my name and number over her head and tugged it down her body. It was loose and long like most jerseys were, but it looked cute as hell on her with the bottom hem stopping just a couple of inches from the hem of her denim shorts. It made her already gorgeous legs look even longer. When she turned around to show me her back, a shot of lust like I had never felt before in my life hit me.

My girl was wearing my name on her. I had marked her as mine, and anyone looking would be able to see it. I wanted to pound my chest like a gorilla, and I wanted to bend her backward over my arm and kiss the hell out of her.

I finally realized that she was waiting for me to say something. I cleared my throat. "It looks great."

"Does it really? It doesn't look like it's swallowing me?" She looked down her body and smoothed the shirt over her butt and thighs, making me groan on the inside. On the outside, I tried to show her I was still a gentleman.

"It looks like it's a football jersey. All jerseys are big. But it looks perfect on you."

She beamed at me, the biggest smile I had ever seen her give me so far, and I vowed I would try to make her smile like that at least once a day from now on. "Thank you so much! I love it! Can you tell your mom that I love it?"

I sighed in relief and picked up her bag along with mine. We were going to be super late if we didn't get moving. "You can tell her yourself tonight, buddy."

"Your parents are going to be at the game?" She sounded worried, but I could have told her that she never had anything to be worried about when it came to my parents. They loved her already, just from what I had already told them.

"Of course they are. They love going to my games. I asked them to keep an eye on you for me so I know you're safe while I can't be there for you. You don't have to sit with them, but I would feel better knowing they can see you."

"I'd say you were overreacting and that having them watch me would be overkill, but you never know how some of these kids are going to act sometimes. It's been a while since anyone has thrown anything at me, but I can't ever let my guard down. If your parents are as amazing as you make them sound, maybe I will sit with them?"

"I'm sure they would love that, and I know I would." I swung my arm around her shoulders and led us to our next class.

WHEN WE WALKED into the cafeteria, I was immediately accosted by my football coach.

"Over here, Johnson! Team bonding time!" He clamped his hand on my shoulder and started to lead me over to one of the long tables that were crowded with my teammates. Our cafeteria had several round tables, but there were also a couple of long tables along one wall.

I grabbed Paige's hand and started dragging her with me, but Coach was quick to separate us.

"Nope, sorry, bud. Team bonding means no girlfriends." He looked over at Paige. "Sorry, Ms. Anderson, you know it's a tradition."

Paige nodded her head and smiled sweetly. "That's okay, Coach." She turned to me and squeezed my hand before slipping her hand out of mine. I felt the loss immediately. "I'm going to go eat with Lisa and Chad. I'll see you after lunch, okay?"

Well, I had absolutely no argument I could make to keep her by my side, so I nodded and kissed her head, lingering just a second so I could breathe in her strawberries and cream scent. I would never be able to smell strawberries again without thinking of her.

Coach pointed to the table filling up with rowdy football players, and I reluctantly walked over to the table. It wasn't that I disliked the guys; most of them were actually pretty cool. I was still kind of irritated with a few of them after finding out that they had helped terrorize Paige over the years, though. It wasn't something that I could easily let go of and forget about. There wasn't much I could do on the practice field, but I had given enough extra hard knocks during tackles that they knew I meant business. It was the only way to get through some people, and I didn't want to do anything violent off the field that would get me in trouble.

I knocked knuckles against a couple of the guys and found me a spot facing the rest of the cafeteria and Paige's table. I watched as she threw her head back and laughed. She was breathtaking, and her joy was enough to light up the entire room. It certainly lit something up in me.

"She smiles now."

I turned to John, "What was that?"

He tilted his chin in the direction I had just been looking in and took a massive bite of his pizza. He had at least three giant slices on a paper plate in front of him. I looked down the table and saw the small tower of pizza boxes. Apparently, game days and team bonding was also pizza day. Nice.

"Your girl. She used to walk around here like she was nothing more than a shadow. She rarely looked up and never, ever laughed." He took another bite and was polite enough to actually wipe his mouth on a napkin. His mother must be proud that she didn't raise a heathen like most of these guys on the team. "Everyone is noticing it." He lowered his voice and leaned in closer to me. "A lot of the guys are kicking themselves that they didn't notice, really see her for what she is instead of getting caught up in Jessica's bullshit."

I got up and grabbed a couple of slices of pepperoni pizza before it was all gone and sat back down next to John. I looked over to Paige and caught her looking at me with a small smile on her face before turning back to her friends. I was glad to see her happy today. Until today she still seemed mostly cautious around me. Around everyone, really. She had been conditioned to stay in the shadows, hidden away from others, so she didn't catch her cousin's wrath. It seemed that Jessica really was so jealous of her prettier, more intelligent cousin that she made sure she would never be able to outshine her.

"Oh, shit." was mumbled next to me. I looked over to John just to see him looking back in Paige's direction again. For a brief moment, a flash of jealousy ran through me that he was staring at my girl so much. That was, until the look of horror on his face registered, and I swung my head in the direction he was looking and saw what caused it.

The back of my jersey-Paige's jersey-was covered in chocolate pudding. It looked like someone wasn't happy about Paige wearing my name and number. I looked around to see where the pudding might have come from, but every person in the cafeteria was frozen in shock. And then, as if on cue, at least half the students started laughing. The other half turned to look at me with grimaces on their faces. All the football players looked at me, waiting to see what I would do. Not one of them laughed. Not one except for her own fucking cousin, that is.

"Did anyone see what happened?" I growled to John as I stood up and walked around the table, swiping a stack of paper napkins as I passed the now mostly empty pizza boxes.

"Nah, man. I'm sorry I didn't see anything. I will double-check with the guys, but they were mostly all eating and fuckin' around. I'll get them to help me ask around at the rest of the tables to see if anyone knows what happened." He clapped his hand on my back and turned back towards the table we came from as I continued towards my girl, who was sitting frozen in her seat. I wanted to yell at the students that were laughing at her. I wanted to bash their heads together. I hated that I had to accept that glaring them to death was the most revenge I'd be able to get away with at this time.

I leaned over Paige's shoulder and put my hand on the table next to her elbow. Her hands were frozen with her chicken nugget halfway to her mouth. She was staring wide-eyed at Lisa who's facial expression was morphing from one of confusion to one of rage. She was realizing what had happened to her friend. Chad quickly stood up and looked around the room, trying to see if he could find the culprit.

"Hey, buddy," I whispered softly into her ear. "You doing okay?"

She nodded her head slowly. And then took in a deep, ragged breath before asking me in an equally quiet but raspy voice, "Is it bad?"

I shook my head and kissed her head. "Nah, it's fine. No big deal." I started wiping the pudding off her back with my stolen stack of napkins. "A little rinse in the sink and a couple of minutes under the hand dryer will have it good as new. These jerseys are great. They don't hold stains, and even mud rinses right off. A little chocolate pudding shouldn't be a problem at all."

She took another deep breath and turned her head, and smiled up at me, but I didn't miss the extra sheen to her eyes. Seeing my girl holding back tears made me want to jump on the table and issue a challenge to the death to whoever was responsible. I couldn't help but be proud of her, though. These pricks would get off on seeing her tears, and she was denying them the pleasure.

Lisa stood up. "Come on, girl. I'll help you get cleaned up in the bathroom. We'll have you good as new before the next period starts."

"I'll meet you at our locker, alright?"

She nodded at me and murmured her thanks for wiping the pudding off her back before walking away with her friend. I stood there feeling helpless as she walked off, clenching my fists and grinding my teeth until my jaw ached.

"I hate to say it, man," I heard Chad say quietly, "but she's actually used to this. She was probably hoping that things may have changed for her since you came along, but that doesn't mean she didn't expect something like this would happen soon. She'll be okay."

I turned to look at him, incredulous. "She's okay? She's expecting to have food thrown at her? None of this is okay. These assholes think it's funny to see one of their classmates assaulted and not one single person saw anyone throw a container of pudding?" I kicked the plastic pudding cup that obviously been what hit Paige.

Chad held his hands up in surrender. "I'm sorry, man. I'm only trying to make you feel better. As shitty as it seems, this is not the first time or even the 20th time that Paige has been the victim of some type of food assault. She's probably embarrassed, yeah, but she has experience with this kind of thing."

I shook my head in disgust. If it weren't for the fact that I would never have met Paige, I would have wished I had never stepped a foot over the threshold of this shitty school.

CHAPTER 14

Paige

I followed Lisa into the bathroom closest to the cafeteria. She flung the door so hard that she nearly hit a girl coming out of the bathroom. I recognized Suzanne and gave her an apologetic smile and cringed when she glared back at us as she left the room. Oops. Lisa was so pissed off that she almost took out another student with the door. I thought maybe she was angrier than I was.

I was definitely angry, though I was more resigned than anything. I didn't know why I thought that all the bullying would stop just because Reid had taken a liking to me. He'd been a buffer for this last week. The football team respected him, and the rest of the student body seemed to like him because of his football star status. But apparently, that status wasn't going to protect me.

"What the ever-loving hell?" Lisa's shout had me jerking my head up to look at her. I was trying to remove the jersey without getting anything in my hair or on my shirt, though that might be a lost cause with the tiny holes the jersey had. Pudding was probably already dotting my back.

"What's wrong?" I asked once I finally, carefully, had the jersey off.

"This is what's wrong!" She threw her hand to the side.

I looked over at what she indicated and jolted when I saw the words written on the mirror in what looked to be black permanent marker.

Stay away from Reid Johnson

"Seriously?" I stood there dumbfounded. It had to be Jessica. She probably had someone throw that shit at me and left me this little note, knowing that I would come in here afterward.

"God, those bitches are just flat-out crazy!"

I could only nod. It seemed so ridiculous to go through all this trouble just to be a mean girl warning off her competition. I wasn't falling for it, though. Reid was the best thing that had happened to me since my parents died. For the first time in over three years, I was finally happy. Like, really happy.

I watched Lisa rub at the words on the mirror and huff when the letters didn't come off. "Whatever. Let's get you cleaned up. When you show up to the game in a clean jersey and end up standing with Reid at the end of the game, I want to watch them turn green with envy."

I held out the jersey and was surprised to see that most of the pudding was already gone, and it hardly left a spot at all.

"Wow, these things really do clean up well," I said as we finished rinsing the hand soap off.

"Jersey material." Lisa replied with a laugh, "It's meant to take mud and grass stains."

I nodded and held it to the hand dryer for a few minutes, and sighed when the next period bell rang. "Go ahead to class. Thanks for helping me, Lisa."

Lisa huffed again; her anger had barely started to subside after all the ranting and cussing she did while cleaning off the few splatters that had landed on my neck and hair. She hugged me and swayed me side to side. "Don't let them get you down, girl. Promise me?"

I smiled at her weakly. I was definitely sad that I was still being targeted, but I also knew it wouldn't be long before this entire nightmare of high school would be over soon. "Nine months until freedom. I know, Lisa, it's fine. I won't let them keep me down."

"Good. Alright, I'm out. Call me when you get to the game if I don't see you again between now and then."

"I will. Thanks again."

I tugged my new jersey back on after she left. It was still slightly damp, but the hand dryer actually did a pretty decent job. Between the jersey being so easy to clean and the dryer, I looked like nothing had happened.

I walked out of the bathroom and ran into a hard chest. Arms came around me and held me tight. I sighed and relaxed into Reid's embrace.

"I'm okay, Reid." I looked up at him and saw that he was practically vibrating with fury.

"Can you believe that nobody saw what happened?" He growled.

I sighed again. "Yeah, actually, I can."

"It's bullshit."

I nodded at his assessment. "Yes, it is. But there's nothing that I can do about it. Reid, I'm okay. It's childish and petty, but I wasn't hurt. A little bit of food thrown on me isn't going to kill me." I was never going to mention to him that the center of my back smarted a little bit from the plastic cup's impact. It was a minor pain that would fade by the end of the next period. It would only get him even more riled up, and I didn't want him to do something that would get him into trouble. I tugged on his hand and started walking. "Come on. We're going to be late as it is."

AFTER THE LAST BELL RANG, signaling the end of our day, Reid stood up and helped me pack up my study notes for the statistics test we were supposed to have the following Monday. He was turning out to be a pretty good study buddy. I wasn't surprised. He had said that school and getting good grades was a priority for him, and it showed.

"What are you going to do before the game?" He asked me as I stood up with my backpack.

"I don't know." I shrugged and hefted the bag over my shoulder. He eyed it, and I could see that he wanted to carry it for me. His fingers twitched, and I smiled. "I guess the best thing to do would be to head home and get something to eat and wait until it's time to head back over here for the game." I took the backpack off my shoulder and handed it to him. He grinned like he won something as he slung it over his own shoulder.

"Your cousins won't be home?"

"They have never gone home before a game in the past."

His worried frown didn't lessen.

"Text me when you get safely to your room. And text me again when you are leaving."

"Yes, sir!" I gave a mock salute as we walked out the school's front doors and headed towards my Jeep.

"I mean it, Paige. I have a meeting with the coach and a quick meal with my parents, but I will be worried the whole time if I don't know you're safe." He set my bag down on the back floorboard and turned to face me. "I want to introduce you to my parents, so I need you to be there at 6:30 next to the gym, okay?"

My heart sped up with nerves at the thought of meeting his parents. They sounded like wonderful people, but I'd never had a boyfriend before and definitely never a guy's parents. Not that he was my boyfriend. Or was he? I had no idea and was a bit confused. We hadn't talked about it, but he seemed determined to take us in that direction. Other than holding hands or him putting his arm around me, we hadn't really acted like a couple that were dating. Though he *had* introduced me as his girlfriend to Jenna. I mentally stepped back from that thought.

I had a feeling that he was trying to take things extra slowly for me.

"I'll be there, I promise."

"Good." He looked at my eyes, seeing the nerves. "They'll love you, and you will love them."

"If you say so."

"I know so." He leaned down and kissed the top of my head and waited until I was in my seat and buckled up before stepping back to watch me leave. I looked into my rearview mirror one last time before I turned out of the parking lot and headed towards my uncle's house.

That boy was everything I could ever ask for. I wasn't sure where the future would end up taking us, but I knew I would probably never do better than having him by my side for the rest of my life.

I sent the promised text once I entered the quiet house and made it to my bedroom with a sandwich and a bottle of water. I spent the next three hours reading one of the books on the AP English teacher's reading list and listening to 80's pop music.

The closer the time ticked to 6:30, the more nervous I got and the less I was able to concentrate until I found myself repeating the same paragraph five times without comprehending a single word. I groaned and tossed the book onto my nightstand, and picked up my phone. I opened my social media app and started scrolling through the feed.

I wasn't surprised to see a picture of my back covered in the chocolate pudding on Jessica's page and rolled my eyes. She didn't write anything on it, just posted an upside-down smiling emoji. She was too smart to incriminate herself or write anything publicly that would get her in trouble for bullying, but she also wouldn't be able to resist rubbing it in my face either.

I kept scrolling, ignoring the likes and laughing faces. She had the comments turned off, so at least I didn't have to read what the other students thought. The reactions were enough for me. I scrolled past the excited posts about the first game of the season and the multiple photos of the banners and posters that had been posted all over the school. School spirit was a real thing when it came to sports. But football? Football was its own beast. The stands would be packed tonight, filled with students, teachers, and parents alike. Even the people of the town that hadn't gone to the school in the last decade or more would be at the game. Afterward, every pizza parlor and diner would open their doors wide for all the students that would be still high on the game. If there was a win? They wouldn't shut down until well after midnight.

There would be at least a couple of parties, too. I had never been to a party, and I had absolutely no desire to ever go. I wondered if Reid would want to. There was no way he wouldn't be invited; he'd probably already been told exactly where to go and how to get there. If he wanted to go, I would just have to wish him well and head home. Walking into the lair of one of the students that might have been responsible for the pudding incident today? With zero parental supervision? Yeah...no.

I stopped scrolling when I saw a picture of the bathroom mirror from lunchtime. The message was very clear, but the photo had been taken at an angle, so it was impossible to see who was taking the picture. The message written on the post was almost eerie. It questioned if I would listen to the advice without actually stating my name.

It could have come from Jessica, but there was no telling. It could even have been from a guy if he decided to enter the girl's restroom or was sent the picture from a girl. But whoever posted it had a fake profile. It had the name Rocky Hills as the first and last name. I rolled my eyes. Real original. It wasn't the first time someone created an anonymous profile to post on social media, but they were usually taken down within a couple of weeks after being reported a few times.

I clicked on the profile and wasn't surprised to see that was the only post so far. The profile picture was black with the number 81. Reid's football jersey number. My skin prickled. The person had to be a fan, but it was really creepy. As I sat there looking at the profile picture, I saw another post pop up on their page.

A picture that had to have been taken this morning without us realizing. Reid and I were standing at his locker while he was trying to get the courage up to open the locker door. I would have smiled at the picture, but my face was crossed out. The caption read:

Reid Johnson is MINE

CHAPTER 15

Paige

W hile driving back to the school, my hands were gripping the wheel tightly, mostly to stop them from trembling. I tried to keep my breath steady and counted each one in hopes that my whole damn body would start to settle.

Earlier, I had rolled my eyes so hard I almost saw the inside of my brain due to someone's utter stupidity, thinking that it was possible and appropriate to try to claim another human being. Reid obviously wasn't interested in Jessica. The only girl he even seemed remotely interested in was me. And, after spending this week with him, getting to know him, I was finally becoming convinced that he was serious about me. He had wormed his way into my life in a way I didn't want to pull him out.

I was starting to look forward to seeing him every day, and I was actually feeling dread for the upcoming weekend where I wouldn't see him for two days in a row. The feeling worried me. If I grew too attached and then it was ruined somehow...that might just be my breaking point.

Jessica had been mostly quiet this whole week after the tennis racket incident. Other than a few death glares and the words on the mirror after the pudding attack, she was being surprisingly calm. Reid wasn't giving me any space, always by my side and walking me to our classes. I would have thought Jessica would have detonated by now. Even at home, she was leaving me alone. Not that I gave her a chance to threaten me since I kept to myself inside my locked room. The whole thing was wearing on my nerves. I was purposely ignoring her warning. It was a dangerous move on my part and I knew it.

After I closed the app, choosing to ignore the ridiculous picture, I took a quick shower for something to do to keep my mind off meeting Reid's parents. Of course, it didn't help ease my worries, but at least I was clean and freshened up. I thought about wearing my hair down for once but immediately discarded the idea. I was already ignoring Jessica's threats, and I didn't need to piss her off even more.

I put Reid's jersey back on and put on a clean pair of denim shorts. The game wouldn't be over until around 10 pm, but it would still be hot even that late. I thought about putting some makeup on but nixed the idea almost as soon as it entered my brain. I would just sweat off anything I put on. I didn't have much skill with it anyway. I could put on a mean lipgloss, though.

While driving back towards the school, my mind wandered back to Reid. He was unlike any guy I had ever known. He was so sweet to me, and his protectiveness made me feel safe in a way I hadn't for over three years. I was definitely caving. I was beginning to daydream about him kissing me in a way that was definitely more than the sweet pecks he landed on my hair or cheek. I'd been daydreaming about what it would be like to be kissed by him. Just the thought of him changing those cute little kisses to ones that were decidedly less PG and would likely get us sent to the principal for a lecture on appropriate behavior at school had my face warming and my heart beating faster.

Before I knew it, I was back at the school and looking for a spot to park in. The football field's parking lot was fairly large and still had a lot of spots, most of the closer ones taken by the parents of the JV team. But the lot was starting to fill up fast. The varsity game would be starting within the next 30 minutes. I found the closest spot to the field that I could and turned off the engine, and took another minute just to take a few deep breaths. I tried to remind myself that it wasn't a big deal to meet his parents. He had promised that they would love me.

Honestly, I thought my anxiety had a lot to do with my own parents being gone. I would never be able to invite Reid over for dinner. My dad would never be able to ask him what his intentions were towards his little girl. I swiped a tear away from my cheek and blew out a shaky breath. Everything would be fine. And my parents would have loved him exactly the way he was. My dad would have given him a hard time, but he would have seen how protective Reid was towards me and would have easily given his blessing.

I slid down out of my Jeep, stuffed my keys into my pocket, and felt my back pocket for my student ID and the cash I had put there before leaving the house. Then, I made my way over to the entry booth and stood in the line that, thankfully, moved rather quickly. After paying, I accepted a stamp to the back of my hand and looked around.

Even though I had never been to a game before, it was pretty obvious what was going on. The stands were filling up, most of the center already packed with the JV fans and parents. I looked to the left towards the gym and started walking in that direction. Reid had told me to meet him there as soon as I made it to the field. He wanted to introduce me to his parents right away so I would know who they were and so I would feel more comfortable sitting with them.

I turned the corner past a small building that was probably a maintenance shed and caught sight of Reid. My breath caught in my chest at the beauty of him. He was wearing all of his football gear except his helmet and was pacing back and forth in front of the gym entrance.

I walked towards him and watched as he stopped pacing, his eyes on me—his look of relief at seeing me quickly faded into a grin. Once

I stepped closer to him, he held open his arms in invitation, and I didn't hesitate to step into his embrace.

"Hi," he whispered into my hair. I suppressed a shudder and whispered, hi, back.

We just stood there like that, simply holding each other loosely, enjoying being in each other's arms. It felt peaceful, safe, and just right.

When we heard footsteps coming our way, I reluctantly pulled my arms from around his waist and stepped back and to his side, and tried not to fidget. He took my hand in his and gave me a reassuring squeeze.

His mother was beautiful, shoulder-length brown hair with attractive golden highlights. She had the same blue eyes that Reid had. It was easy to see why Reid was so gorgeous. While both of his parents were good-looking, his dad was like a replica of Reid, just a couple of decades or so older. If Reid grew older the way his dad did, then he would only continue to get even more good-looking than he already was.

It took me a minute to realize they weren't alone. His mother was arm in arm with none other than Jenna, Reid's ex-neighbor and childhood best friend.

Swear words started going off in my head, and I was struggling to maintain the pleasant smile I had plastered on my face when what I really wanted to do was shove Jenna away from here. I could admit that I felt jealous that she was friendly with Reid's parents, and they obviously liked her. I was still nervous that they wouldn't like me, so it was a bitter pill to swallow that another girl wanted Reid, and she already had an in with his parents.

I swear I heard Reid growl as his grip tightened on my hand, and I almost wanted to laugh. Jenna didn't realize what she was doing by trying to ingratiate herself back into Reid's life through his parents.

Reid looked right at Jenna and demanded, "What are you doing, Jenna?" His tone couldn't be mistaken for anything other than irritation.

Jenna stopped short and glanced around quickly, realizing that she had made a mistake that was about to bite her on the ass.

"Reid!" his mother admonished him and put her arm around Jenna's shoulders as if to shield her from Reid's wrath. "Don't be rude!" She looked over at Jenna, who looked like she wanted to just slip away unnoticed, and smiled at her. "We ran into Jenna on our way in the gate. Isn't it amazing that you two are back together again!"

Reid frowned. "What?"

His mom was starting to look a bit unsure, looking back and forth between Reid and Jenna. A small line developed between her eyebrows as Jenna managed to back up enough to escape his mother's hold and started walking backward. "Umm, I need to get back to the cheer team before I get into trouble. It was, umm, great seeing you again, Mr. and Mrs. Johnson. Bye Reid, and good luck on the game!" She spun around on her heel and took off, jogging towards the stands where the rest of her team were likely waiting to go on the field as soon as the JV game finished.

Mrs. Johnson followed her departure and finally turned her eyes back to us. She seemed to finally take us in, the fact that we were standing close together and that we were holding hands. She cocked her head to the side for a minute as if coming to terms with the situation. Then, she pointed her thumb over her shoulder and said, "She played me, didn't she?"

"Yeah, mom, she did." Reid sighed and shook his head. Then, he turned to me and asked quietly, "Are you okay?" I nodded and gave him a small smile. Yes, I was okay. But, it wasn't like she would have been able to keep up the charade that she had attempted to pull off. It was kind of sad, really. "Mom, Dad, this is Paige...the girl I wanted you to meet."

I lifted my hand and gave a little nervous wave. "Hi."

Reid's dad chuckled. "I knew Jenna had to have been full of shit. Your mom is just nicer than I am." He stuck his hand out to me, "Nice to meet you, Paige."

"Thanks, you too." I felt awkward as hell, but I was so glad his parents seemed to be as lovely as he had made them out to be. I turned to his mom, ready to be introduced to her too, but I found myself swallowed up in what could only be considered a mom hug. I was stiff for all of 3 seconds before I allowed myself to relax fully and let the warmth of being held by a mom seep into me. I hadn't been hugged like that in way too long, and it took everything I had within me not to burst into tears at the sudden and genuine feeling of loss. I thought of my parents every single day, but it was moments like this, ones out of left field, that brought home to me exactly what I had lost when my parents died.

She finally let me go and held me back from her by my shoulders so she could get a good look at me. I felt her eyes roam over my face and down my body, and back up again. It didn't feel invasive or judgy, but I did feel like she was sizing me up. Then, finally, she looked over my shoulder to Reid and smiled at him. I was finally able to relax once I saw that smile.

"You are so beautiful, Paige. I can't wait to get to know you better. Do you like to get your nails done?"

I smiled back at her and shrugged, "Actually, I've never been."

"Well, we will just have to change that, won't we? Are you free tomorrow? We can make it a girl's day."

Reid laughed and pulled me back to him before I could answer and put his arm over my shoulder. "Mom, give my girl some time before you overwhelm her, alright?" He was right, she was so sweet to invite me when we had literally just met, but I wasn't used to so much attention anymore.

She pouted a little and said, "fine." a little grudgingly but smiled again quickly. His dad chuckled at all of us.

Reid and his dad did manly back pats, and his mom gave him a squeezing hug and kissed his cheek when he announced that he had to get back into the locker room before he got into trouble. Then, before he left us to head back to his team, he pulled me in for another hug and kissed the corner of my mouth. "For luck," he whispered, gave me a wink, and backed up to the door and knocked on it so someone could let him back in. "Make sure you cheer for me, buddy." And then he disappeared, the door shutting heavily behind him.

I stood there, the spot on the very edge of my lips tingling. My thoughts were running crazy. Did he mean to kiss me there? Maybe he was aiming for my cheek and got too close to my mouth? Why was I so light-headed all of a sudden?

A touch on my arm jerked me out of my musings.

His mom gave me a knowing look. I wasn't sure what she knew, but she seemed to know something that I didn't and wasn't sure I was ready to.

"Are you ready to go find some seats?"

I nodded my head and forced a smile on my face. Damn Reid for getting me all discombobulated like this.

We walked back towards the stands, and it was so obvious that we would have a hard time trying to find a decent spot to sit. The stands were already stuffed nearly to capacity. Some were on their feet staring intensely at the game that was still going out on the field, while others, mostly students, were talking animatedly to their friends.

A couple of police officers roamed the stands both on the Home and the Away sides, looking for, or hoping to prevent, any trouble. In addition, several teachers wore t-shirts in the school colors that had a large white STAFF printed on the back ushering students to their seats and preventing anyone from standing up against the fence that separated the spectator stands from the football field.

It was loud. It was chaos. It was amazing.

I followed his parents through the crowd that was still trying to find their own seats or just milling around trying to see and be seen. Finally, we turned and started climbing the steps until we got about halfway up the stands and then started making our way to seats I couldn't see but apparently, his father could. I gingerly stepped over feet and around bags or drinks and had to say excuse me several times. By the time we made it to the middle of the stands, I was so relieved. I planned to stay right where I was for the rest of the night until the game was over and all the rest of the people left.

CHAPTER 16

Paige

It was much too loud to try to hold a conversation with a near-stranger, and I wasn't sure if I was glad of that or disappointed. Reid's parents were turning out to be pretty fantastic so far, and I was looking forward to getting to know them better. Unfortunately, my awkwardness and the noisy crowd weren't really helping.

I sipped at the soda that Reid's dad had bribed a kid on the other side of him to run and buy from the snack bar at the end of the field near the entrance. I hoped he paid the kid well because that line was long, and the walk through the crowd looked like a bitch.

The JV game had ended a while ago, and the entire crowd seemed to be holding their collective breaths waiting for the varsity team to be released onto the field. Music started playing from the speakers and announced the name of the away team, a team from a few towns over that was pretty serious about football, too. But from what I heard, their quarterback had recently gotten arrested for car theft and was currently serving some time in jail. Apparently, the car was a junker and barely made it a mile before breaking down on him right in front of a police car. The story sounded too ridiculous to be real, but it was in the paper, so unless the newspaper lacked integrity, it was completely legit.

After a few minutes of announcing the team and its team members, a hush fell over the crowd. The cheerleaders stood at one end of the field holding a giant banner with the team name on it covered, once again, in glitter. I couldn't help but wonder where the hell they got all their glitter from. They had to order it in bulk.

The music started back up again, pounding music that I felt rattling my bones. Suddenly every person in the stands shot to their feet as the first varsity football team member tore through the banner and ran onto the field. I didn't have to hear the announcer to know that it was Jason. As the quarterback and team captain, it was his right to be first.

Each player was announced with their name and number until, finally, the announcer called Reid's name and number. If the crowd was loud before, that was nothing compared to the crazed excitement that started as soon as he ran out onto the field. I couldn't stop the thrill I felt seeing him out there, and my cheers and clapping joined in with the rest of the spectators. I felt a nudge against my shoulder and glanced over to see Reid's mom smiling at me. I gave her a huge smile back, my excitement overriding any hesitant shyness I had been holding on to before Reid ran out onto the field and allowed the two of us to bond over our pride for this one man.

Once all the guys were on the field, the two teams separated to opposite ends and began warming up. Some were tossing balls. Others were running in place or stretching.

"So, this is the first football game you've been to?" Mrs. Johnson spoke close to my ear so I could hear over the raucous yelling of the teens that surrounded us.

"How could you tell?" I asked, even though I knew it had to be obvious.

"No reason," she laughed, "only because you keep looking around and look uncomfortable as if you wish you could disappear."

I shrugged, "I'm not popular. Most of these guys don't really like me, so I am having a hard time feeling comfortable sitting with them." I wasn't trying to whine or get sympathy. It was what it was.

Mrs. Johnson took my hand in hers and squeezed it gently before placing it back on my leg. "Reid told us a little about you. I'm sorry that your cousin has made it rough on you."

I couldn't respond with words. Hearing from someone that seemed to genuinely care made my eyes burn and my nose tingle. I smiled my thanks and looked back towards the field, and blinked a few times quickly. Mrs. Reid just smiled softly and let me be.

I couldn't see Reid right away; he was probably in the large huddle that held most of the players. They were all kneeling and looking up at the coach. A few were walking towards the sidelines, obviously not going to play in the game that evening.

My eyes roamed over the rest of the field and drifted towards the cheerleaders. I saw them all bouncing around, laughing, and obviously energized for the game that was about to start within the next few minutes if the clock counting down on the giant scoreboard were any indication. I stopped on Jessica, seeing that her gaze was trained on Reid, a look of longing on her face. I suddenly felt like rushing down the steep steps of the bleachers and challenging Jessica once and for all. I was willing to fight for Reid. I'd be damned if I let her dictate who I could date.

I followed where her eyes were trained, expecting to see Reid, but I didn't see him. I looked back towards her and tried to follow her line of sight again but still didn't see Reid. There was only the assistant coach standing to the side of the huddle. Another quick glance around the huddled group of football players finally revealed the 81 on the back of one of the red game jerseys. He was definitely not where she was looking. What the hell?

I looked back at Jessica. She was no longer looking at the huddle but, instead, was eyeing the crowd, smiling or waving at people that called out her name. When her eyes rolled over mine, she stopped. Her eyes narrowed, and the usual malice I was used to seeing from her was coming off of her in waves. If her eyes were lasers, I would have a hole in the center of my forehead.

When she finally looked away, it felt like I was released from her hold. It may not have been Reid she'd been watching intently, but I was still on her shit list. I couldn't help but wonder, though, about who had held so much of her attention.

Once the time had counted down to zero, all the members of the football teams, their coaches, and the cheerleaders lined up and faced the large flag that was planted just behind the scoreboard. Every person in the stands began to stand up, and it didn't take but a second to realize that they were ready to sing the national anthem. As soon as it was over and the senior girl that I hardly knew was done singing, everyone sat back down again. As I sat there wondering what was going to happen next, there was a whistle blown, and I watched as three members of each team walked out to the center of the field where a referee was waiting. All the rest of the team members quickly lined up on the sidelines, ready to enter when it was their turn.

I had no idea what was happening on the field, but it must have been something important. Everyone cheered and clapped when the ref made a hand gesture, and the players who had entered the center made their way back to their prospective sides. I wasn't exactly thrilled to be sitting in the Texas heat waiting for a game that I didn't know much about, but I could feel the buzz of energy sweep over the crowd as players took their places and waited for the signal to begin.

By the time the scoreboard had counted down the first 15 minutes of the game that seemed to take a hell of a lot longer than just 15 minutes, I was starting to feel the buzz myself. Watching Reid out on the field and listening to his parents explain the finer points of the game, hearing the fans call out his name, and cheering wildly when he carried the ball into the endzone was starting to make my heart race.

Obviously, I knew that he was a good player, one of the best according to his parents, but seeing him in action really brought home for me the reality of the situation. He was good. Really good. And if it could be believed, he was being scouted and would continue to be scouted by more and more colleges until he had his pick of the one he really wanted. I wondered if it was one that I would want to go to as well. The more time I spent with him, the more attached I was becoming. Just the thought of not seeing him every day sent a pang to my heart. Such a short time had passed, but he had, without a doubt, wormed his way into my heart.

I'd had an immediate crush on him with his baby blue eyes and fantastic physique. But his personality made him someone that I wanted to be with. He had been clear from the beginning that he was looking to be more than friends, and he had been very patient with me, not pushing for a single inch more than I had been willing to give, but I was starting to itch for more.

Midway through the next fifteen-minute countdown, I decided I needed to use the restroom after the large soda Mr. Johnson had bought me. I looked over to see the row of people I had to squeeze past and figured there was nothing for it. I had to go. I leaned over and told his mom where I was going, and she offered to go with me, but I waved her off. I was in a rather large crowd of people, and most everyone was engrossed in the game. I assured her that I would be fine.

I stood up and squeezed through, mumbling apologies as I went and was relieved once I made it to the end and vowed that in the future, I would be careful not to drink so much that I would have to leave my spot once my ass was parked on it.

I looked down the steep stairs that still had several people heading up and down, either looking for snacks to buy or heading to the restrooms like I was. It wasn't too bad. The stairs had a rail going down the center every few feet to hold onto, which made me feel better, knowing that I had to make my way down the crowded steps. It was steep enough to cause me a slight bit of vertigo, so I was sure to hang onto the rail as I slowly made my way down.

I was nearly to the bottom when I felt my foot knocked out from under me. My body began to pitch forward. Then, in slow motion, I felt gravity start to pull me head first towards the metal stairs. I reached out blindly for the beginning of the next railing in front of me but only managed to skim it enough to bend the fingernail back on my left pointer finger.

I didn't even have time for a startled gasp. The air in my lungs froze as my heart picked up a mad tempo and the sound of the crowd and game disappeared as a rush of static filled my eardrums.

I was about to hit the stairs, so I shut my eyes tightly, just knowing that it was going to hurt and I was going to roll head first to the bottom. I had a quick thought to be grateful that I was already near the bottom. The journey down would be swift but short.

Suddenly I was jerked upright and held still. It took a few seconds for the world to come back into focus and hear the man calling to me. I felt hands gripping my arm tightly and turned to blink at the man who had saved me from the bruises I was sure to get and the other possible injuries I might have been in danger of.

"Hey! Are you alright?" He was older, probably someone's dad, and all I could do was blink stupidly at him a few times before I was finally able to snap out of it enough to nod my head. He slowly let go of my arm. "Are you good to walk now?" I nodded again and placed my hand over my heart in an attempt to get the organ to slow the fuck down.

I took a deep breath and then once more before opening my mouth and thanking him. "Th-thank you for stopping me. I don't know what I tripped over." I could hear the shakiness of my voice, but it couldn't be helped. That was scary.

"I don't know either. I didn't see what happened; I just grabbed you when I realized you were going to tumble down. Be more careful, okay?" His voice was gruff, but I didn't think it was because he was annoyed. On the contrary, I had a feeling that my tumble, as he put it, had shaken him up, too.

"I will," I promised, sure that it was a promise I would have no trouble keeping in the future because there was no way I wanted to go through that again. "Thanks again."

He nodded and sat back down in the end seat, a row above where he had caught me. I turned to look up the stands to where Reid's parents were sitting, and I saw the concern on both their faces. They both looked frightened for me. I felt terrible that I had scared them. I waved at them to indicate that I was alright and then glanced at the stairs above me, looking for whatever I had tripped on, hoping that I could move it to prevent anyone else from taking the same fall I had, but there was nothing on the stairs.

I avoided the looks on the spectator's faces, not wanting to see what they thought of my clumsy fall, and instead made my way the rest of the way down as carefully and quickly as I could. Once I reached the bottom, I hurried to the opposite end of the stands from where the entry was. I was relieved to see there wasn't a line for the girl's restroom.

The building was a small brick structure big enough for three stalls for the girls and two sinks. I imagined the boy's wasn't much bigger. As soon as I walked in, someone was coming out of a stall. It was a student that I often saw hanging out with Jessica, so her sneer wasn't a surprise, and I just hurried past her, ignoring the silent taunt she was giving with her eyes. There was probably an adult, maybe a teacher, in one of the stalls, or else she wouldn't have held back.

Once I was in the stall, I locked it behind me and leaned my back against the door, and breathed out heavily. That had been one of the scariest moments of my life. I was sure that I had tripped on something. I had felt my foot hit before I tipped forward. But there had been nothing on the stairs. If I hadn't actually stumbled over anything, did that mean that someone had purposely tried to trip me? Was it only an accident? I could have been seriously hurt. No one had tried to hurt me that bad before. They had always done things to humiliate or embarrass me. Having someone try to cause me serious harm was new, and I wasn't sure how to handle it.

I hoped it was the one and only time I would be in danger of being injured.

CHAPTER 17

Paige

I made it back up the stairs and to my seat without further incident and spent the rest of the game chatting with Mrs. Johnson and watching the activity on the field. When my eyes weren't on Reid, I watched the cheerleaders.

Jessica rarely looked in Reid's direction, which I found extremely odd considering all her threats. It just pissed me off even more that she didn't even really want him but would deny me the chance to be with him. I did my very best every day never to be alone with her. I stuck to Reid's side most of the day at school and always locked myself in my room at home. I didn't want her pushing me around, but I also couldn't deny that she held the upper hand when it came to strength and viciousness.

I also watched Jenna. Jenna definitely watched Reid a lot. She also looked sad. When she wasn't actively cheering with the rest of the squad, she spent her time either sitting quietly on the bench or standing with her arms wrapped around herself. I wanted to feel sorry for her since she looked so miserable, but I couldn't forget the way she had acted since she saw Reid had moved here.

The entire stadium jumped to their feet, and their cheers were so loud I put my hands over my ears in self-preservation. Reid's mom turned to me and tugged on my elbow, and laughed at my expression as she hauled me to my feet. I reluctantly lowered my hands and looked to where she was pointing. Reid was running with the ball, and from the looks of the field and where most of the players were, it appeared that he had run it all the way from one end of the field to the other.

I didn't think it was possible, but the noise from the crowd went up another notch when he crossed into what I now understood, thanks to his mom, was the end zone. One of the referees standing at the end threw his hands up in the air along with half the crowd. I turned to his mom and leaned in so she could hear me. "I'm guessing that's a good thing?" I asked wryly.

She laughed out loud and hugged me to her, bouncing the two of us around in her excitement. "You're adorable, Paige. Yes, that was a very good thing." She was so cute with how proud she was of her son. A wave of melancholy hit me for a moment as I thought of my own mom. I just smiled at Mrs. Johnson and hugged her back a little tighter.

I may not have known the technicalities of the game, but that didn't mean I didn't understand the importance of a good gameplay. Mrs. Johnson tried to teach me the basics, and I was pretty certain I picked up most of the important parts, though there was no way I'd be able to explain the game to anyone else at this point.

"You don't have to learn everything all at once." Mrs. Johnson laughed and bumped her shoulder against mine. "I bet by the third game you'll be a pro at it. Reid tells me you're pretty smart."

I blushed and looked at my lap. I gingerly touched the tip of my finger where the nail had bent back from my near fall down the stairs. It still throbbed, and there was a little bit of blood under my nail. "I don't know. I just try really hard to do the best that I can so I can get into a good college so I can move away from here." I swallowed hard and shrugged one shoulder. I hadn't meant to confess that; she didn't have to know about my crappy home life.

She leaned over so she could talk closer to my ear without yelling and having someone overhear her. "Reid's told us some of that, too. I hope you don't mind that we know." It sounded like Reid had told them quite a bit. I wasn't sure, yet, if that bothered me or not. She squeezed my arm, "We are here if you need someone, okay? You aren't alone."

I looked over at her and studied her face. Her kindness showed in the tiny lines around her eyes and mouth and radiated from the warmth in her eyes. I felt my nose burning and blinked my eyes, hoping I wouldn't embarrass myself in front of the entire crowd.

"Thank you," I whispered. There was no way she could have heard me, but she must have known anyway. She just smiled again and gave me another small squeeze.

"So, I wanted to invite you to dinner. Will tomorrow night be a good night? I can make meatloaf."

"Meatloaf sounds delicious; I'd love to come over for dinner." I smiled at her, and we both turned back to watch the rest of the game, with her snuggled up to Mr. Johnson and me feeling warmer inside than I had in a long time.

AS SOON AS the final seconds ticked off the clock and the Rocky Hills Hawks were pronounced the winners, it seemed as if the entire stadium, students and adults alike, emptied out right onto the field in seconds. Reid's parents sat with me for a few minutes as the stands quickly emptied. Then, once it was cleared enough to avoid being trampled by an over-enthusiastic fan, we finally descended the steps to the concrete walkway, went through the now open gate, and followed the rest of the crowd onto the thick grass.

I looked around but couldn't see Reid through the mass of bodies. I wasn't short, but I wasn't exactly tall, either, and standing on my tiptoes wasn't helping. I turned to his parents, that seemed to be having as little luck as I was, and shrugged my shoulders at them.

"Paige!"

I turned sharply to follow the sound of my name and saw Reid pushing his way through the horde that was trying to pat his back, shake his hand, or, in a couple of instances, hug him. The latter had me narrowing my eyes at the two girls, one of which was Jenna. The girl was never going to learn. He held her off with a hand to her shoulder and a shake of his head. When he looked back towards me, I was already running.

He caught me with a laugh as I launched myself into his sweaty, dirty arms. "You were great out there!"

"Yeah? Did my parents help you understand what was going on?" He laughed as he squeezed me tight before letting me slide back down the front of his body. Being held against a full suit of football pads wasn't exactly comfortable, but I was more than happy to show my appreciation for his great playing-and to put my claim on him once and for all. We had been dancing around our instant attraction to each other with talks of being friends or study buddies. He and I both knew from the beginning what we really wanted. I was done with pretending that we weren't going to be something amazing together. I was sure he'd agree with me that we needed to have a serious discussion.

He let me go for a hug and a pat on the back from his dad that would have pulverized my bones, then he hugged his mom, lifting her feet off the ground making her squeal, "Let me down!". She smacked his arm as we laughed. "Brute!" But her smile was big, and her love was plain to see.

He tugged me back to his side and threw his arm over my shoulder while his parents recounted the game with him and told him what a great job he'd done. I was startled when a heavy hand clamped down on my arm and squeezed.

"Hey, there's my best wide receiver." Jason reached his hand out to Mr. Johnson. "Hi there, I'm Jason, the quarterback. I can't tell you how glad I am that you moved him out here. He's really been an asset to the team. I can tell we are going to do great this year with his help."

That was probably the nicest thing that Jason had ever said about anybody in his entire life. I narrowed my eyes at the side of his face and wondered what he was playing at.

"Great game out there, Jason. We're glad that your team accepted our boy so easily." His dad shook Jason's hand.

"Congratulations, Reid! You were so great out there!" Jessica's voice came from the other side of Reid and took a step into his personal space going for a hug.

"Thanks, Jessica. I couldn't have done it without my own personal cheering squad, though." Reid turned away from her before she could latch on, picked me up again, and spun me around, making me laugh. The movement caused Jessica to have to back up a few steps to avoid being hit by our bodies. Reid set me back down and placed a kiss on my head in his usual spot. I returned his grin, his adrenaline was still high from the game, and it was cute how energetic he was.

"Hi, Reid, good game." Jenna's small voice could barely be heard over the sounds of all the voices around us. His curt nod had her smile fading, and I watched as she jerked her head over towards Jason and then put a hand to her stomach before turning around quickly and disappearing into the crowd. I noticed Reid's mom watching with a slight frown on her face. I wondered if she had noticed the gesture, too. I didn't know if Jason was the guy she had been talking to earlier in the week, but the way she acted around him almost made it seem she was scared of him. He was not a good guy and could definitely be called a player with the way he went through girls.

"So the team is having a party tonight to celebrate the game, and you have to come." Jason interrupted my thoughts. He turned to Reid's parents. "Not to worry, there will be adult supervision. It's important for the team to get together and celebrate. The coaches throw a party for us after every win, and all the players are expected to attend."

I frowned at the news. It was the first time I had ever heard that information. In all the years at the high school, no one had ever mentioned it. I knew that the players partied, of course, but I was under the understanding that the popular kids went to someone's house and drank and had sex. I had a hard time believing that the coaches condoned that kind of celebration.

"Nah, man. I don't go to parties. You know that. I'm just going to hang out with my girl here. I'll see you on Monday. But you guys enjoy." Reid turned to his parents, cutting off whatever else Jason was going to say, and said, "Thanks for sitting with my girl."

"Of course, son." His dad took his cue and dropped his arm from around his mom's shoulders. "It was good meeting you, Jason. I look forward to the rest of the season." Then he took his wife's hand and led her away from the crowd and off the field while Reid followed after them. I peeked over my shoulder as inconspicuously as possible and saw Jason watch with his jaw clenched. Jessica was still standing there with a couple of her cheerleader friends, but she wasn't watching our departure. Instead, her eyes were focused further down the field near a different group.

When we got to the exit, we all stopped, and Reid let me go.

"Do you mind keeping an eye on my girl while I run and change?"

I wanted to protest that I needed to be supervised like a toddler, but I couldn't. I was in the lion's den. Any one of these students could decide I was fair game and do something to ruin my night. It was sweet that he wanted to protect me and that his parents were willing to wait around with me, but the fact that I needed protection chaffed.

He looked down at me. "I'll be as quick as possible, okay, buddy?"

I nodded my head and gave him a small smile. His responding grin and wink had butterflies erupting in my belly. He didn't have dimples as I had initially imagined in the picture I had seen of him before we met, but he did have a bit of a crease that was enhanced when he grinned the way he was. His bit of stubble was just thick enough to shade his face, and I realized I had never seen it so dark. Tonight was the first time I had seen him after school hours.

I watched him jog off and sighed. I turned back to his parents and felt my cheeks warm that they had caught me mooning over their son.

"Come on, let's walk to the car." His dad smiled and gestured towards the parking lot.

Once we got to the lot, we stopped by a shiny new Mercedes. I could see my Jeep a couple of rows over, and Reid's motorcycle was visible from the student lot where the rest of the players parked before the games had begun.

I suddenly felt awkward and didn't know what to say, so I just took my keys out of my pocket and fiddled with them while I continued to glance around as if I had never seen a parking lot before.

Mrs. Johnson spoke up, making my head jerk up to see her face. She looked contrite and a little sad. "I'm sorry about the scene with Jenna earlier before the game. I didn't mean to make things weird or uncomfortable. I didn't know there were any issues with the two of you." She sighed and looked over at Mr. Johnson. "She used to be such a sweet little girl. We were all very close with her family. It makes me sad that she's changed, though I don't really know the story yet. I know Reid wouldn't be upset with her the way he is if she hadn't done something to warrant it."

Her apology was something I didn't even realize that I needed to hear. When she had walked up with Jenna earlier, it had hit me harder than I would have expected in such a short amount of time that she might want Reid with someone other than me.

I shrugged my shoulders and looked down at my feet. "She fits in here at the school, and I don't." Then, I shrugged again, "Most of the students actively dislike me."

Mrs. Johnson startled me as she yanked me into her embrace and squeezed me within an inch of my life. "That's your kind way of saying that she bullied you." She took a deep breath while still holding me. "Oh, sweet girl. I'm so glad Reid found you."

All I could think to say while being held by his mother was, "me too."

CHAPTER 18

Reid

Seeing my parents and my girl getting along so well already was a great feeling. Knowing that this was the girl I planned to spend the rest of my life with, I would have done what I could to make my parents like her, but seeing that she won them over without any help on my part was an incredible sight to see.

I walked up to their little group, ignoring the rest of the students and families that were making their way to their own cars to either head home or find a party where they could get wasted. I had plans tonight that I hoped my little buddy would agree to. I took the bracelets and leather cuff that my mom had kept safe for me while I played and thanked her with a kiss on the cheek.

I wrapped my arm around Paige's shoulder and kissed her head, something that had become one of my favorite things to do, and said, "Hey, are you ready to get out of here?"

She turned her head to look up at me with a beautiful smile on her face. "Yep! What did you have in mind?"

"Do you have a curfew?"

She scrunched her nose up and tilted her head to the side while thinking. She was adorable. "Honestly? I don't know." She shrugged her shoulders. "I never go anywhere. But Jason and Jessica go out all the time on the weekends and usually come home around two or three in the morning, I guess. Sometimes they don't come home until the next day."

"I won't have you out that late anyway, so no worries then." I turned to my mom. "Hey, mom? Do you think you could drive Paige's Jeep to our house? I don't trust it out here while we are gone." I plucked the keys from Paige's hand before she could protest and dropped them in my mom's already waiting hand.

"Of course, son." She pocketed the keys and kissed my cheek. "Have fun and drive safe." She turned to my girl and pulled her in for a hug. "I'll see you tomorrow for dinner, right?" She held her out by her shoulders, staring her in the eye. I'd been victim to those mom eyes before; they could get you to agree to anything.

Paige nodded her head, then turned to me, eyes wide. I grinned.

"Ready to go?"

"Ummm, where are we going?"

My dad reached into the trunk of his car and pulled out the brand new shiny black helmet with purple flowers on each side. He handed it to me and slammed the trunk. "Be safe, son," he said, then took my mom's hand to walk her to the Jeep and helped her climb in. Taking my queue, I took Paige's hand and walked her across the street to the student parking lot.

"Reid?" Paige was eyeing my bike and when we stopped next to it.

I reached up to her hair and carefully tried to pull her bun down from the back of her head.

"What are you doing?" She laughed and swatted at my hands.

"You can't wear a helmet with your hair up like that."

She sighed and started grumbling under her breath, but she pulled her hair down. I stood, dumbfounded, as I watched her shake her hair out and then started braiding it after finger combing the waves. Her hair was as beautiful as she was.

"Fuck. You're so fucking beautiful."

Her cheeks turned pink, but she didn't seem bothered by my outburst.

She had her hair braided and tied off with the hairband that she had used to keep her hair in her ever-present bun within seconds. She stood there with her arms out and said, "Alright, I'm ready. Plop the helmet on me, and let's get going before I change my mind."

I chuckled but did what she said. I carefully placed her new helmet on her and took the time to make sure the chin straps were just right. It was hers, and she would be wearing it a lot, so I had to make it perfect.

Once I was satisfied, I threw on my own helmet and tossed my leg over the seat before I turned back to my girl and held out my hand. "Alright, slide your leg over the seat and scoot in close to me."

"I just want you to know," she started as she did what I said and scooted forward until her front was like a second skin against me. It felt like heaven. "The only reason I am doing this is because I trust you."

I felt something dip and swirl inside. I never knew I would need to hear those words from her, but now that I had, I vowed to myself that I would never make her regret them.

I showed her where the footpegs were and explained good passenger etiquette before starting the bike and taking off. The night was hot, but the wind felt great against my skin after the heat of the game. The ride was relaxing, it always was, but having the girl I had been steadily falling for since the moment I saw her made the ride the best one I had ever taken.

I drove us out of town, not too far out but far enough. I slowed down once we reached the lake and slowly cruised down the packed dirt road until we reached the spot I was looking for. My family had been told about this area earlier in the summer and had a nice day fishing and bar-b-queuing burgers. I was hoping that there wouldn't be any parties out there tonight and was glad to see the night was dark and quiet except for the sound of my engine. I was sure the night would come alive with the singing of insects and frogs once I shut down my bike.

I stopped in the secluded space I had found while looking for a good fishing spot. It was perfect for sitting near the water since it had a private, grassy shoreline and a large tree that stretched over the water.

I helped her off the bike and grinned at her, finding how shaky her legs were after her first motorcycle ride. "You'll get used to it," I told her and winked when she glared, but she didn't look angry at all as she took in her surroundings. She didn't even take her eyes off the water as she absently handed me her helmet. I couldn't hold back the chuckle as she walked straight to the shore and started taking off her shoes.

While she was busy dipping her toes in the water, I pulled the small blanket I had stowed in the storage under my seat. I had no plans tonight other than to enjoy some quiet time with my girl. Every time we were together, I felt our hearts connect little by little. I was patient. I would wait an eternity for her. I couldn't begin to tell someone that held a gun to my head why, exactly, I knew she was mine. It was just a feeling and a knowing that couldn't be denied. No one else would ever do.

I spread the blanket at the base of the tree and sat with my back against the trunk to watch her. She was so beautiful she took my breath away. She turned to face me, and with the moonlight shining behind her, causing a glow to surround her, I could believe she was an ethereal goddess standing there at the water's edge.

She slowly walked to me and my breath caught in my throat. She had me spellbound, and I never wanted to be released.

She knelt on the blanket and turned back to face the water before leaning her back against me.

"This place is beautiful," she whispered.

I wrapped my arms around her and rested my chin on the top of her head. Not as beautiful as you.

I could feel her fingers brush along the leather band I always wore and lightly played with the beads on the bracelets.

"We should talk about college."

"Hmm."

"Did you have a specific school in mind?"

"I had planned to go as far away from here as it was possible to go. I planned on the northeast coast, but I'm not opposed to the northwest." She tilted her head back to look at me. "What about you?"

"Honestly, I didn't really have a preference. I was going to wait until I got offers and pick from there. I seriously don't have a school that I just had to go to. I could try for my dad's alma mater, but that hasn't been a dream of mine."

"What do you want to study? Other than football, that is."

I chuckled. "I was thinking that I could get a degree in sports education and become a high school football coach after I retire. Of course, I could also be a P.E. teacher at the same time."

"I could see that. You would probably be good at it."

I squeezed her waist a little. "What about you? What do you want to be when you grow up?"

She was quiet for a long minute, and I was beginning to think she either didn't know or didn't want to answer. Then, when she did, her voice was soft and layered in sadness.

"My mom was a pediatric nurse at a children's hospital. When I was little, sometimes she would let me spend the day in her ward and, if the kid's parents agreed, I would play with the long-term patients there. Sometimes I would just read to them. Other times I would play with them. They all loved my mom, and I know she loved them. Sometimes she would come home, and I could feel the sadness radiating off her and just knew that one of her patients had died." She sighed and shifted a bit against me. "I want to do what she did. I know it was hard on her sometimes, but she really made a difference in their lives, you know?"

I grunted, knowing exactly what she was talking about.

We sat in silence for a few minutes, just listening to the sounds of the night.

She whispered suddenly. "You win."

I stilled, every part of me going on alert. "What?"

"You win, Reid. I can't fight it, and I don't want to anymore. I want to be yours. I want you to be mine."

I turned her body around to face me, her legs straddling my hips so that I could see her eyes. I cupped her cheeks and made sure she was looking at me before I spoke to her.

"It was never a contest, Paige. I never wanted you to feel that way. I could see that you were struggling with your feelings, but I would have waited forever for you."

She squeezed her eyes shut.

"It will be hard to do this, for others to accept that we are more than friends. Jessica threatened me more than once." She looked at my face, her eyes taking in everything before settling back on my own. "It is a battle, maybe not between us, but between us and everyone else."

"Then I will fight for you, for us, but we need to stand together."

I watched as a tear gathered and fell from her bottom lashes. It broke my heart to see her this way. I swept my thumb over the wetness, wiping away the tear the way I wish I could wipe away her fears.

Slowly I lowered my head, my lips a hair's breadth away from hers, and waited. I watched as another tear slowly made its way down her cheek. She sighed, her breath fanning over my lips before she finally took away the small space between us and pressed her lips to mine.

The kiss was soft, gentle, just a press of our lips before she let out a shuddering sob, and we both let go. After that, the kiss turned harder, and I didn't know who made the first sweep of the tongue, but soon we deepened that first kiss into something more.

My heart ached with pain for her but also beat harder as we finally gave in to the passion that was always under the surface. I felt like I was walking a tightrope every minute I was with her, always trying to keep my balance, to keep from giving in to what I wanted from her before she was ready. Now that she had finally opened herself up to me, I felt myself fall off that precipice and into her waiting arms.

I tilted her head with the hands that were still cradling her cheeks and deepened the kiss further, showing her everything I felt with my kiss. I soon realized I was tasting her tears and pulled back, looking into her aqua-colored eyes.

"Please don't cry, baby. I don't want you to be scared. If you need more time…"

"No," she shook her head, "I'm not scared right now, Reid. I'm happy. For the first time since my parents died, I actually feel happy."

I swiped my thumbs over her cheeks again. "Is that why you are crying because you're happy?"

"Sometimes tears are made because the rush of emotion is just too much to handle. Tears aren't always because of sadness or pain. Sometimes it's because you feel too much good, and it needs to escape."

I rested my forehead against hers and nodded in understanding.

"I love you, Reid," she whispered so low I almost missed it.

"I love you, too, Paige. More than I ever thought possible."

She nodded and laid her head on my chest.

"It's fast, isn't it?" She said after a few minutes.

"I don't know," I said honestly. "In a way, it feels like it's been forever since I saw you for the first time. But in another, yeah, we are young, and we haven't known each other long. People will look at us and say that we don't know what we are doing. But do you care what other people say?"

She was quiet for a long minute before whispering again. "No, Reid, I don't care what they say. All that matters is us."

I couldn't agree more.

CHAPTER 19

Paige

I t was quiet when I walked into the house last night. The twins were either sleeping or still out with friends. My bet was on the latter.

I spent the night staring at the ceiling and thinking about everything. The past. The future. I had been doing my best to dodge Jessica since the day she threatened me at the stairs. I should have done what she said and stayed away from Reid because I knew that it would be worse than the last time when she finally pinned me down again. She hadn't hurt me physically, but she wouldn't hold back again, I was sure. It was a dangerous game I was playing. But after tonight, the confessions we both made to each other, the vows we made for our future? I couldn't allow Jessica to keep me under her thumb any longer.

I drove through a lovely subdivision of newer houses that had been built recently. It seemed our small town was expanding more than I realized. Finally, I pulled up in front of a lovely two-story brick house and parked. I sat in my Jeep for a minute before turning off the engine. I had put the top and doors back on this morning since the weather was calling for a thunderstorm later tonight and into tomorrow.

As I opened my door to climb out, I saw the front door open, and Reid came out and started down the front walk. He was smiling his big smile, and I felt myself warm inside.

Last night when he brought us here to his house to pick up my Jeep, he kissed me goodbye. That goodbye kiss turned into another and another until he finally broke it off to tell me I had better get home before I got into trouble. Not that there was any trouble to be had since no one was around, though that wasn't a big shocker.

Reid met me on the sidewalk as I walked around my Jeep and pulled me into his arms. I had expected him to go straight for a kiss after last night, but he just held me as close to him as possible, like he missed me so much he wanted to make up for the time we were apart.

When he finally pulled back from me, his hands still on my waist, he looked me over, head to toe. Once he was satisfied that I was still in one piece, he grinned at me and said, "Hey, buddy," then he kissed me. It wasn't a soft peck on the lips, but it wasn't a complete mauling either. I wasn't sure if I was disappointed, but then I looked around at the neighborhood we were in the middle of and was glad for his restraint.

"Come on, let me show you around." He grabbed my hand, linking our fingers together, and walked me into the house. It was much smaller than mine, which was to be expected, but it immediately felt like a home to me. My house, my Uncle's house, was always cold, sterile. We had housekeepers and groundskeepers. It had more rooms than was needed, including entertainment rooms. But it was always...emotionless. Here there was sound and color, pictures and knick-knacks—treasures from favorite places. There were magnets on the refrigerator with names of beaches on them, holding up pictures from vacations. It looked like my house used to look before my parents died. Oh my god, how I missed being a part of a real family.

He continued to lead me around the house, stopping to say hello to his parents and getting a hug from his mom that I tried to take without tearing up. Eventually, we ended up in a wide hallway that obviously led to the bedrooms. Nearly every wall space from waist height up was covered in family photos, portraits, awards, medals, and certificates.

It didn't take me long to see the pictures of a younger Reid also had a little girl in them. A very unhealthy-looking little girl.

I turned to Reid with the one question in my eyes.

His voice was soft, revenant when he started speaking. "Her name was Margaret, named after our grandmother. We all called her Maggie." He ran his finger over the glass of the nearest photo of the little girl that couldn't be anything other than his sister. "She was born with tricuspid atresia. It's a condition where the valve on the right side of the heart that sends the blood into the lower right side doesn't develop." He turned and looked at me with a self-deprecating smile. "That's the easiest way to describe it. It's how they explained it to me when I was little." He looked back at the picture and then at the others. Though it was apparent when Reid aged and there was no longer a little girl next to him, there were many of her holding his hand or smiling with a missing front tooth.

"She was always so sick. Some times were better than others, and when they were good, our parents took us on as many vacations as possible. They wanted memories." He wiped a tear away from his cheek, and I wrapped my arms around him. He held me so tight I felt like he would crush me if he hugged me any tighter, but I wouldn't dare say a word. "I was so excited when my parents brought home this tiny, little baby. I swore I would be the best big brother in the world. I would protect her from all the monsters. I was five and ready to slay dragons for her. I didn't understand why she always had to go to doctor visits and why she had to stay at the hospital so much."

He held up his wrist where the black leather cuff and the beaded bracelets always were. "When she was seven, she made these for me while she was in the hospital." He turned the cuff and showed me where his name was tapped out in dots in uneven lines. "Craft day was her favorite while she was there. She was always making everyone things, a painted flower pot for mom, lots of ornaments or picture frames that she painted. This," he tapped on the cuff, "is the last thing she made. She didn't come home after that last trip. She developed an infection that her body couldn't fight."

We stood there quietly for several minutes as muted sounds came from the kitchen and a tv played in the family room.

He pulled back, his eyes rimmed in red, and looked at me apologetically. "I'm sorry I didn't tell you."

I was already shaking my head before he even finished the words. "Reid, when, exactly, in the last week would you have had a chance to break such a heartbreaking story to me?"

"Well, I want us to always be honest about everything from here on out, no matter how hard it is to say or hear." He took me by the hand and led me back towards the kitchen. "My parents always say: the key to any successful relationship is good communication."

The last word was heard in surround sound as all three of them said it together as if it were a common phrase in their house, and I giggled. His mom smiled and winked at me as she handed Reid a stack of plates.

"Go set the table, boy, before I set your dad on you."

His dad looked up from where he was trying to covertly sneak bites of mashed potatoes out of a bowl with a masher still in it. "Huh? What?"

Mrs. Johnson smacked his hand that was reaching for another swipe of potatoes and shoved a handful of silverware into his hands. "Get out of my food and go help your son set the table."

He was grumbling as he walked out, and I saw him give the bowl one more lingering glance before leaving the room.

"Johnson men!" She said with exasperation. "You'd think they were raised by wolves some days." But she was smiling as she said it.

"Is there anything you'd like me to do?"

"Oh, no, sweetheart. Today you are a guest. Next time I will put you to work. Do you like meatloaf?" She asked as she opened the oven door and used potholders to pull a delicious smelling meatloaf from the oven.

"It's been years since I've had any, but yours smells so good I can't wait to try it!"

———————

THE MEATLOAF WAS EVEN BETTER than it smelled, and I was finally able to understand why Mr. Johnson couldn't stay out of the mashed potatoes. They really were that good.

After dinner, we all watched a movie together in the family room, and they all gave me hugs when it was time to head home. Well, Reid walked me out to my Jeep, and out there alone in the dark, he gave me a kiss that I would be dreaming about later.

"I'm sorry I'm not inviting you to dinner at my Uncle's house tomorrow," I said softly as I played with the necklace he was wearing. It was a Celtic knot hanging on a black string. I kept tracing the lines as they wove around each other.

"Believe me, baby; I completely understand why you don't want me over there."

I winced at his words and glanced up at him before looking back at the knot. "It's not that I don't want you there. I do. It's just that they are all so…"

"Hey, hey." He put his finger under my chin and tilted my head up. "I said I understand, and I do. It would be a nightmare for both of us. I would never be able to handle it if I had to sit there and watch the evil twins say or do anything to you that would cause you pain." He gave me a soft peck on my lips. "That being said, if you need me, I will be there for you. Day or night, no questions asked. You are the most important thing in my life, and until we get older and get married, I have to be content with you keeping me up to date with what is happening when I'm not around."

My breath hitched. "Reid…"

"I told you, baby, this is it, for the both of us. Always. Remember?"

My breath stuttered out of me, but I nodded and then whispered, "Yeah."

"Yeah," he repeated and put our foreheads together. "Call me when you get home, okay?"

"Yes, Reid."

"Good girl," he said and gave me a wink that made my whole body shiver. He had to have known his effect on me because his smirk turned into a delighted grin. "Soon," he growled against my lips and helped me into the Jeep just as the first raindrop fell.

As I pulled away and started back towards my Uncle's house, I looked in my rearview mirror at Reid, who was still standing there watching my tail lights, drenched from the sudden rain shower.

I entered the house, unsurprised to find it quiet and dark but noticed the light coming from my Uncle's office. I hesitated before knocking quietly. He looked up from his paperwork, reading glasses perched on his nose, and caught my breath at how much, in this moment, he looked like my father. My heart hurt as I was hit with a memory of my dad in much this same position, pouring over contracts and other work I had no desire to learn about at the time. He would always sit back in his big leather chair, though, and open his arms to me. I was never a bother to him, and he made sure that my mother and I knew we always came first.

"Yes, Paige?" His sigh was tired, and he took off his glasses and rubbed the bridge of his nose. I didn't know if it was from irritation of being interrupted or if he was just tired from working so late.

I stepped further into the room hesitantly. It was as intimidating as the man was, with the dark wood cabinets filled with thick books and a giant desk facing the door. If I had an office, I think I would turn the desk to face the window so I could watch the trees and flowers. With the rain and lightning, a night like tonight would be beautiful, but I suppose it would also be distracting.

"I wanted to talk to you about possibly moving into the pool house." I started talking faster before he could cut me off. "I'm almost 18 and thought it would be good to start learning to live on my own, you know, baby steps before I moved into my own apartment in a couple of months." It was a bullshit excuse. I only wanted more space and more than a deadbolt between my cousins and me. It wouldn't be any different than the room I have here, just further away, which would be amazing to my peace of mind. I couldn't tell him the real reason. My cousins had already made sure that their parents thought I was a crybaby.

He didn't let me go any further with my semi-rehearsed request, though. "Jason already asked and is moving in this weekend. He might be done already." He put his glasses back on and picked up a paper in front of him. He had already dismissed me in his mind.

I took one more step forward. "Can we talk about me moving out when I turn 18? My trust says I will receive a monthly stipend for living expenses until I can fully claim the whole thing. I think…"

"I don't think it's proper for a young lady still in high school to live on her own. I think you should stay here until you leave for college."

"But Uncle-"

"No, Paige."

"The trust doesn't-"

He slammed a hand down on his desk, making me jump in surprise. He sighed heavily before looking back at me once over his glasses and then looking back at his papers. "My brother trusted me with your care, Paige. I will do what I feel is necessary to keep you safe and healthy. Living on your own while in high school is not something I think he'd want for you. Now, please go to bed."

"Yes, sir," I said quietly and quickly left the room and trudging up the stairs. I knew it was a long shot, but I'd hoped he would at least have listened to me before shutting me down.

I spent the rest of the night talking quietly to Reid on the phone, sharing my secrets until I had none left, telling him about my parents, my baby sibling that never got a chance, and watching the lightning light up the sky.

CHAPTER 20

Paige

Sunday was always the day of family dinner. It was the one time when the entire Anderson family was together in one room. We often spent it quietly in between answering questions about how our weeks had gone. Usually, there wasn't much to tell, but since it was the beginning of the school year, there would be more to say.

We sat around the large formal table with the gleaming silverware and the cut crystal glassware that caught the light of the multitiered chandelier hanging above the table. The food was always delicious, prepared by the cook that came in a few times a week to prepare and portion food that sat in labeled, personal-sized containers in the refrigerator. Sunday's dinner was always freshly prepared, though.

The family sitting around it had to be just as put together, and we were all dressed up. We were just shy of formal, though my aunt did expect the men to wear ties, and we women were expected to wear dresses—no denim and t-shirts for Jolene Anderson's Sunday night dinners.

The conversations were typical, with questions and answers about classes and coursework. There were the obligatory questions about football and cheerleading, grunts of approval about the recent win.

My uncle toasted his glass to Jason, "I hear the scouts are paying close attention this year. Good job, son."

I wanted to snort in disbelief. Those scouts weren't there because of anything Jason had done. Everybody knew there was only one person they truly wanted to recruit.

It was a few minutes later that my aunt set down her fork and picked up her wine glass. "Anyone catch your eye this year, Jessica? Make sure he is worthy of you. Only the best for my beautiful girl."

My heart picked up, and my fork trembled as I held it in my hand. This is what I had been dreading the most. I looked over at Jessica, hoping that I didn't look as scared as I felt. If I thought pleading with her would work, I would beg her not to say anything about Reid. But, instead, I was surprised to see her hesitate and saw her glance quickly at me before picking up her glass to take a sip of her water.

Jason was the one, though, that I should have been afraid of. He snorted and slapped the table as if he had the funniest story to tell.

"Jason," his mother snapped, "manners."

"Mom, if only you knew." He picked up his fork and shoveled a piece of meat into his mouth before quickly chewing and pointed his fork in my direction. "Your perfect little niece over there decided she wanted to steal the guy that your daughter had been crushing on for months."

My mouth dropped open in shock. Why that little shit! "I-I-" I stuttered out, but he interrupted me.

"The new wide receiver? The one that's being scouted that's supposed to help me take the team to state this year? Yeah, Jessica had been talking to him all summer long, and then on the first day of school, Paige over here..." his fork was still pointed in my direction. I looked over at my aunt and uncle, and they both had frowns on their faces. Jessica's was slightly red. I didn't know if she was embarrassed by the story or angry about the whole thing. "Started talking to him, and now he won't have anything to do with Jessica anymore." He started cutting another piece of meat on his plate. "Who knows what she's said to the guy. Probably all lies. I mean, what else could she have done in order to steal the guy from her cousin." He smirked at me and popped the steak into his mouth.

I sat there, sure that my face was flaming. I set my fork gently down next to my plate and placed my hands in my lap, where I balled them into fists. He'd made me out to be the bad guy, of course. It didn't matter what Reid wanted, or what I wanted for that matter.

"Is that true, Jessica?" my aunt looked at Jessica with surprise and anger on her face. Why wouldn't she ask Jessica instead of me? I meant next to nothing to her when her own children were involved. I was just the offspring of a family member she'd been saddled with.

Jessica took another sip of water and cleared her throat. "Well, I had been interested in him, yes."

The truth that was also a lie. She didn't want him for who he was; she wanted him for what he was.

I felt my aunt's eyes on me, but I couldn't look away from Jason's smirking face. He continued to gleefully shovel in his food, content to watch my world implode around him, knowing that he was the one that lit the match.

"This is absolutely appalling, young lady! How dare you! Couldn't you find your own young man? You had to take the one that your cousin liked? No! I won't have it. You are no longer allowed to see this boy. And if Jessica brings him around this house, you are to make yourself scarce. Do I make myself clear?" Her venomous tone was harsher than I had ever heard it. She was never warm with me, but she was looking at me like she hated the sight of me right now.

"I didn't steal Reid from anybody," I whispered. I looked at all the faces around me. Jason with his smug smile, Jessica with her oddly subdued demeanor, my aunt with her glare, daring me to continue. My uncle with his disappointed frown.

"Reid and I met and became friends. We like each other, and we decided that we wanted to be more than friends. But, he didn't want to be with Jessica, and he barely spoke to her all summer." My voice steadily rose from a whisper until it had turned emphatic, almost pleading for everyone to hear me, to believe my words.

"It doesn't matter what you want! You can not take a guy that Jessica liked and then rub it in her face. I will not allow it!" My aunt looked like she wanted to strangle me for daring to cause her precious daughter an ounce of pain.

"It doesn't matter what I want?" I looked at her in total disbelief.

"No, it does not. Not when what you are doing is hurting Jessica. You will not see this boy anymore, and that is final!" She set her glass down hard enough to make some of the wine slosh over the rim of the crystal glass. I watched as the red seeped into the white linen table cloth and spread out like blood. It made me wonder if that's what my heart would look like bleeding out into my body if I had to follow what she said.

I looked up at my uncle for help, but he just continued to stare with a frown on his face as if he wasn't sure what to say, who's side to be on, who it was worth to make angry or who to placate.

I stood up on shaky legs and pushed away from the table. I wiped angrily at the tear that I couldn't hold back.

"There goes the cry baby, again." Jason laughed and shrugged his shoulders before going back to his eating when his dad glared at him.

"Reid and I are together, and," I took a deep breath and let it out, "I love him. They," I pointed at Jessica, "were never a thing, not even friends. She wasn't in love with him. She just wanted him because he was the next best popular guy in order to keep up her image as the top female in school."

My aunt stood up and yelled, "Sit down!" It was the first time I had ever seen her lose control of her temper, and I was slightly in awe while I shook my head at her.

"No. I won't sit down, and I won't stop seeing Reid. If they had been romantically involved, of course, I wouldn't have started seeing him as more than a friend. But they weren't, and they would never have been. He's mine, and I am his." I turned to walk out of the dining room.

"Don't you walk away from me, young lady. I will ground you! I will take away everything you own!"

I was already up the stairs and unlocking my bedroom door. I grabbed my phone and keys off my dresser before re-locking the door and running back down the stairs. I could hear my uncle's voice, too low for me to hear the words and my aunt's "She's out of control, you have to do something about it!"

I walked out the front door and ran to my Jeep through the rain that was still coming down as hard as it had been last night. I was drenched by the time I got into my driver's seat and laid my head back for a minute so I could take a few deep breaths.

I plugged in my phone and started my engine, and had the call dialing Reid before I made it around the circular drive.

"Hey, buddy, how was dinner?" His tone was cheerful, happy to be hearing from me, and I let out a strangled sob. "Baby? Paige? Are you okay? Hang on," there was a rustle, some footsteps like she was stomping down the stairs, and some talking that sounded like he was asking for permission to take one of his parent's cars. "Paige? I'm coming to you. I need your address." He sounded worried and angry all at once.

"Reid," I whimpered, "I need you."

"I know, baby, but I need to know where you are." I heard him run outside and climb into a vehicle, shutting the door and starting the engine immediately.

"I'm actually in my Jeep. I was coming to see you." I whispered.

"Okay, baby, that's fine, but I don't want you driving if you are emotional. It's too dangerous, and I don't want you in an accident. So pull over and tell me where you are, and I will come to meet you, okay?"

I looked around and saw I had already gone past all the big, stately trees that lined the street leading to our house. Instead, I saw lights up ahead through the rain.

"I'm on River Road, and I see the gas station up ahead. The one with the burger place in it."

"Okay, I think I know where that is. I want you to park under a light and keep your doors locked until I get there. It will only be a few minutes, okay?" He still sounded worried, and I realized how hard it was raining.

"Please be careful, Reid. I'll park, but I don't want you getting hurt coming to me, either."

I pulled into a spot away from the doors but under a light and put the Jeep into park. I sat there and watched the rain pounding on the hood. I couldn't even remember how I got here. He was right; I shouldn't be driving right now. I just couldn't stay in that house any longer.

I rested my head back against the seat and closed my eyes. "I'm parked, Reid. Please be careful. I'm so sorry." I ended with a sob. The emotions were finally crashing in on me, and I couldn't hold back the flood. I could hear Reid talking to me, but I couldn't make out the words while I cried for everything, all the pent-up anger, all the sadness. First, I cried for my parents because they weren't here. If they were here, none of this would be happening. And then I cried because if they were here, then I probably would never have even met Reid. Next, I cried that no one in my family stood up for me. My uncle just sat there as his wife yelled and threatened me. While his son laughed at my weakness. The only person I had on my side was Reid, and if my family had their way, I wouldn't even have him.

A knock startled me, and I heard Reid through the window and looked dumbly at him as the same words came through my phone, asking me to unlock the doors. I quickly hit the locks, and he pulled open my door before undoing my seatbelt and picking me up. Then he sat in my seat with me in his lap and reached towards the floor, fumbling for the lever to scoot the seat back. Once he could fit behind the wheel comfortably, he shut the door and held me against his chest.

For several long moments, we both sat in silence while I took deep breaths, trying to get my emotions under control. I just closed my eyes and sank into the warmth and comfort of Reid's safe embrace.

Gently, he pulled my face away so he could look into my eyes. "Do you want to talk about it?"

I shook my head but let out a big sigh. "No, but I need to."

"Okay, tell me whatever you need to tell me. I'm here no matter what you need from me." He pressed a kiss lightly to my lips. The gentleness was almost too much for me to take. I had to fight back another round of tears.

"Jason brought you up at dinner tonight. I mean, I knew he or Jessica would, but it was worse than I thought. Jason dropped the bomb that I stole you from Jessica and then sat back and laughed while my aunt went insane. She demanded I stop seeing you." I watched as his jaw hardened and his eyes narrowed.

"What did your uncle do?" His voice was low, and I could sense the dangerous undertone. He was pissed.

I shook my head and closed my eyes, swallowing back a lump that was trying to choke me. "He didn't say anything, I don't think. I'm pretty sure it was all my aunt. Reid, she was so angry. Jessica was quiet, and Jason continued to eat and laugh." I opened my eyes and looked at Reid again. I could drown in his beautiful blue eyes and never need to come up for air. I couldn't lose him. "What am I going to do? I told her I wouldn't stop seeing you, but she threatened to ground me and take away my things." I didn't really care if she took everything away from me. Honestly, it wasn't as if I couldn't find a ride with either Reid or Lisa. Not having a phone would seriously suck, though.

"I don't want you to keep worrying about this." He cupped my cheeks and held me still so he could look deep into my eyes. "Do you still want me?"

"Of course!" I couldn't believe he was even asking me that.

"Do you trust me?"

Did I trust him? I thought so. He hadn't given me any reason yet not to. "Yes," I whispered.

He kissed my lips again, just a slight brush, enough to make them tingle. "Then trust me to handle this, okay?"

I looked at him, really looked at him. His eyes were fierce and determined. His jaw was tight, showing his anger, but he was holding me so gently. "Okay, Reid."

He smiled. Those creases in his cheeks that weren't quite deep enough to be called dimples flashed at me. And then I couldn't see anything because his lips were back on mine, and I was drowning in his kiss again. "Reid," I moaned. I felt myself losing control, and I suddenly needed to feel him everywhere, over me, under me, inside me. Maybe it was because of the emotional night I'd had so far. Perhaps it was because he was becoming my safe place, my every-thing. "Please."

Somehow my hands ended up under his shirt, and I ran them over bumps and grooves of his abdominals. He felt amazing, and I found myself wanting more. "Reid. Please. Please touch me." I groaned into his mouth.

"Baby, there is no way in hell I'm going to let both our first times be in a car."

That caught my attention, and I paused my roaming hands. "Both of our first times?"

He chuckled though it sounded a little strained. "I told you, I never even looked at another girl before you. So why would I want to be intimate with one?"

"But, you're...you," I knew I was gaping at him.

He raised an eyebrow. "Why haven't you had sex yet?"

"Because I've never found anyone I'd want to kiss, let alone get naked with."

"You don't think it can be the same with guys?"

I shifted in his lap and gasped when I realized why it had gotten slightly uncomfortable. His cock was against my inner thigh, and it was long, thick, and hard. I gave another experimental wiggle and gasped when his hands clamped down on my hips and held me still.

"Umm," what were we talking about again? "I guess so. But I've never heard of one not taking a girl up on what they were offering." I squinted my eyes at him. "I know you've had the offers."

"And, once again, I had no interest in getting intimate with someone I didn't have a connection with."

Lucky me.

I tried to discreetly push down on his erection again, but he tightened his grip on me and groaned before dropping his forehead to mine.

"Soon," he whispered. "We will be together soon. I promise." This time he raised his pelvis, and I felt the heat and hardness of him hit me right in my center, and a jolt of electricity raced through me, and I cried out, throwing my head back. I'd never felt it before.

"Fuck," he whispered. "Fuck."

He did it again, his tight control shattering, and shifted his hips as he thrust his pelvis into mine.

"Just this, for now." He kissed me hard and panted into my mouth. "We'll take just this for now. Rub against me, Paige. Let me help you feel better."

"Reid!" I cried out.

Just a few seconds later, lights burst behind my eyelids like fireworks.

I came back to reality to see Reid panting with a drop of sweat dripping down the side of his face. He had a heated look on his face that seared through me. I realized he watched me have an orgasm with nothing more than a couple of thrusts of his hips against my clit. I felt my face heat up in embarrassment.

He cupped my cheeks and whispered against my lips, "That was beautiful. I can't wait to see it when we are both naked and feel it while I'm deep inside of you."

I smiled at his words. I wanted that, too. So bad.

CHAPTER 21

Reid

Last night I followed Paige home and waited outside until I saw a light on the second-floor turn on and received a text telling me that she was safely in her locked bedroom. After I got home, I took the longest shower of my life and ended up jacking off twice. It was amazing that I hadn't come in my pants last night. If it had taken even one more thrust to make Paige come, I definitely would have. Driving home in wet, sticky boxers wasn't something that I was eager to experience.

I texted my little buddy that I would be late for school and talked with my parents at the breakfast table, gaining their approval for this morning's activities.

Now I found myself in a quiet waiting room just a few feet from the receptionist that kept eyeing me skeptically from her perch behind her glass desk. I looked around the room and took in the tasteful but expensive decor and the large plants that dotted the room. It was apparent from their house that Paige's family had money but sitting in an office waiting room that was ten stories up and looked out over the streets of the larger city that were a few miles down from the smaller town of Rocky Hills, Texas, I could admit I was intimidated.

I still didn't know what her uncle did based on the building or the office I was currently sitting in.

"You may go in now, sir." The receptionist startled me out of my musings, and I jumped to my feet, eager to get this over with and to get back to the school where I would have eyes on my girl.

I entered the office through a heavy wood door and immediately saw a guy who looked around my father's age, maybe a little older. He didn't have much resemblance to Paige except for their eyes. He had the same aqua color that she did. It seemed as if she got her blond coloring from her mother then if her dad and his brother looked anything alike.

I walked to his desk and held out my hand. He looked at me questioningly but didn't hesitate to shake my hand and gestured for me to take a seat in one of the large leather chairs in front of the desk. I thanked him and sat down. I knew he had to be curious by this point as to why a teenager was visiting him.

"So, Mr. Anderson?" He raised a questioning brow and waited for me to confirm my name before continuing. "What brings you here to my office. I'm going to assume you don't have a business you are looking to find an investor for."

So that's what he did, interesting. He must be good at his job.

"I'm here about Paige, sir." I waited for my words to sink in and watched his reaction. I didn't know if I expected him to get angry and demand I leave and stop seeing his niece or what but the deep sigh and him leaning back into his seat, sinking into his plush seat. It wasn't exactly the response I had expected to get. He seemed to age ten years in front of my eyes.

"So, you're the young man that's caused all the uproar in my home lately."

What could I say to that? I wasn't responsible, no, but it was me that had Paige and her cousins fighting.

"I'm sorry about that, sir. By coming in today, I hoped that I could help you better understand what is between Paige and myself."

He nodded his head in encouragement, and I took his lack of anger as well as his willingness to listen as a good sign. I had been prepared to get hauled out of his office by security, so this was a pleasant surprise.

"I came to Rocky Hills for better scout opportunities for football." I looked down at my wrist, where I was nervously fiddling with my cuff. "I have never had a girlfriend before." I looked back at him and saw him watching me closely. "I've always been very serious about football, but I am equally serious about my grades. I hope to make it into professional football, but I understand that may not happen, and even if I did, I could be hurt and only get in a year or less of play time." I swallowed hard because this was a real worry that I had. I didn't want to work so hard for my dream for it to only crash and burn with a torn muscle or tendon.

"I have plans to study for a degree in physical education. If I am offered a draft position, I won't accept until I am ready to graduate college."

"That all sounds very admirable, son, but what has this to do with my daughter or my niece?"

"I wanted you to understand what is important to me." I held out my arms before I dropped them back into my lap. "I've never been interested in dating, never had a girlfriend or partied. I've never been to a single party that wasn't a birthday party for a friend or family member. I'm serious about my goals, sir." I paused and looked at him, silently urging him to see my seriousness. "Until I met Paige."

I watched as his eyes widened slightly and saw when he got it... when he really understood.

"You are in love with my niece." He stated it without question because it was fact, and he saw that.

"Unequivocally, sir."

"You and my daughter..."

"We were never even friends. No offense, sir, but I was never interested in Jessica. I guess you could say she isn't my type."

The corner of his lip twitched, so I didn't think he was offended by my words.

"And what, exactly, is your type, son?"

"Paige."

"I see." He steepled his fingers together and tapped his fingers together as he contemplated me. "Where do you see this relationship with her going if you are so dedicated to the game?"

"For once in my life, I find myself thinking about something other than football. She's the last thing I think about when I shut my eyes and the first thing I wonder about when I wake up. I want everything with her, sir. I want to marry her and grow old together. I want to rock beside her in matching rocking chairs and hold her hand while we watch our grandchild playing in our yard."

"That's all very serious. From what I understand, the two of you have only known each other since the first day of school. How can you be sure so soon?"

I knew this was a question we would both be asked a lot over the years. Most people would never be able to understand the depth of my feelings, and they would always wonder at the suddenness of them.

"Yes, sir, it is soon. But I know because I wasn't looking for it and I didn't want it. I couldn't stress enough about how dedicated I am... was to the game."

"And you don't think those feelings will fade, and you will regret letting her in? Why don't you wait until after college? It's only a few years away, and you will know better what path you will take." I didn't get the feeling he was trying to talk me out of my feelings, more like he was trying to verify that I was as sincere as I came across.

"Is it possible things could change in the future? I suppose. But the reason I know Paige is the most important thing in my life is because if I lost football tomorrow and were never, ever able to play again, I would be disappointed, but if I lost Paige..." I stopped and swallowed before continuing, "if I lost Paige it would destroy me."

We both sat there in silence, me daring him with my eyes to scoff at my words and him with a stoic look until a small smile tipped the corners of his lips.

"I like you."

"Uh, thank you?" Hope expanded in my chest. I had expected a lot of arguing and hoping to convince him before he dismissed me or sent me away with security, but I hadn't imagined him accepting my words so easily.

"I think you will be very good for my niece." He sighed and looked over to a shelf that held a picture of a younger Paige with a smiling couple. The woman was gorgeous, and it was very easy to see that Paige was her mini-me. Every part of Paige came from her mother except her eyes. Those clearly came from her father. The man was a younger version of the man sitting in front of me. The family resemblance couldn't be denied.

"She lost more than her parents in that crash. My family... we aren't warm and loving like her parents were. I love my family, and I would do anything for them, but we aren't close the way her family was." He sighed and rubbed his hand over his brow. "My kids didn't make her feel welcome at all, I'm afraid."

"No, not from what I've heard." I hedged. It wasn't my place to tell her secrets, but he needed to do a better job protecting his niece.

He nodded, "I suspected they were being little shits to her. I made a promise to my brother, that I would protect her and take care of her, but I missed what was going on under my roof." He shook his head and frowned. "Last night at dinner, Jason was positively gleeful when he saw her get upset. And my wife," he clenched his jaw, and a nerve jumped near his eye, "she won't be talking to Paige like that again. Paige is a good girl, the best. Her grades are amazing. I've been assured by the principal that it would take an act of God to keep her from being valedictorian this year. But she isn't happy. I didn't realize until last night that I couldn't remember seeing her smile."

He looked back at the family portrait on the shelf and back to me. "At first, I thought it was because she was sad about her parents, but it wasn't until I saw her on the security camera Friday night coming home." He looked down at his desktop, and I turned my head and studied a young Paige to give him privacy when I saw him discreetly wiping a tear from his cheek. "She was happy. No, she was glowing." He paused, and I turned to look back at him. "I believe that is because of you."

I cleared my throat, "Yes, sir."

"You'll take care of her? Treat her like the princess she is? Always put her first?"

I breathed deeply, wanting him to see my sincerity, "All of that and more, sir."

He nodded and stood up. "Please keep me in her life. I can't lose her or her connection to my brother."

"I will leave it up to her, but I will make sure she knows how much you care."

He cleared his throat and nodded, sticking out his hand for a shake. I quickly stood up and took his hand as he held on for an extra second. "I'd like to threaten you and warn you off, but you really are perfect for her, I think, damned if I'm wrong about it."

"You aren't wrong."

"Good. But know, if you ever hurt her, I will end you."

"Good."

He laughed and walked out from behind my desk to escort me to the door. He turned the knob just as his desk phone started to ring and paused to look at it.

"Go ahead, sir; I've taken up too much of your time already. I appreciate you squeezing me in this morning."

"I'm glad my assistant was able to get you in."

I pulled open the door and walked towards the bank of elevators, nodding to the receptionist as I passed. I was eager to get back to school and felt like I needed to get my eyes on my girl as soon as possible.

I pulled my phone out of my pocket that I had on silent during our meeting and checked to see if any of my teammates had sent any updates. They no longer fucked with Paige. No, now they were in my network of spies. They helped me keep an eye on her and reported if anyone tried fucking with her. A few have stepped in to stop assholes that hadn't gotten the memo that Paige was now off-limits to any bullying. Unfortunately, they couldn't always have eyes on her. The restroom was obviously out of bounds, but they also couldn't follow her while she was doing her job as an office aide.

I was clicking on the first text when I froze in my tracks. I couldn't stop reading each text over and over. My heart stuttered in my chest, and all I could hear was a whooshing sound rushing through my head.

Chad- **Dude! Where the fuck are you, man?**

Sam- **Paige is hurt, man**

Sam- **answer your phone**

Chad- **The ambulance is here**

Chad- **she's asking for you**

Brett- **Someone hurt your girl. They are going to send her to the hospital**

A HAND on my shoulder shook me, and I snarled, lifting my head.

Her uncle nodded towards my phone. "I see you already know. Come on, and I'll drive us. The hospital is only a few blocks away. We'll probably get there before she does."

I numbly followed, scared to breathe.

CHAPTER 22

Paige

I was disappointed when I woke up this morning and saw a text from Reid that he would be late for school. He had become my rock to lean on so quickly I was starting to wonder if I was relying on him too much. I never thought I'd be the type of girl who needed a man to be happy, but I was starting to see that a world without Reid in it would be lonely. Just thinking about it made my heart lurch painfully. So what did I do about it? Did I give in and let him consume me?

I shook my head as I looked at myself in the mirror. I was tempted to leave my hair down, but I just couldn't bring myself to do it. I could leave it down when I was with him but not at school, not yet anyway. Baby steps.

I put a little more effort into my makeup than I usually did, but I still didn't do much more than eyeliner and mascara. I did choose a sparkly lip gloss, though. See...progress.

I kept with a tank and denim shorts with a lightweight hoodie. The heat was just too much to do more. I wouldn't be comfortable going out in a t-shirt, so a hoodie was necessary in order to stay within the dress code.

As soon as I parked in the lot, Lisa jumped on me. Literally. Her arms wrapped around my shoulders, and her legs wrapped around my thighs.

"What the fucking fuck, bitch!"

"What, Lisa?" I slapped at her legs, trying to dislodge her.

"You never called me on Saturday!" She slipped off and stepped over to lean on my Jeep. She was looking at her fingers, studying her nail polish.

Oh, shit. She was hurt. "Oh my god, Lisa! I'm so sorry! I didn't think."

We always talked on Saturday while she cleaned her room and I did homework. Our conversations usually led to Chad and why she was irritated at him or what he had done that was so wonderful. I missed our call because I was excited and nervous about going over to Reid's house and then spent quite a bit of time with him and his parents.

"I am such a horrible friend. I am so sorry." I hugged her, truly sorry I had forgotten about our weekly ritual.

"Honestly, it's okay." She shrugged and grinned. "I'm glad that you have someone else now, to be honest. I always felt bad if I spent time with Chad instead of you, leaving you all alone."

"Well, maybe we can go on double dates sometimes," I suggested grabbing my bag and making sure to lock my doors now that they were on. Together we started walking towards the doors.

"I think that would be amazing! We can go to the bowling alley or to the movies, or...wait!" She came to a halt and yanked on my arm, so I spun towards her, and I started laughing. "Do you mean a real real double date or friends hanging out together double date?"

I bit my lip, trying to hold in my giant grin that was trying to pop out. My cheeks started hurting from holding it in. She screamed then, and I saw a bunch of faces turning our way. I pulled her arm to get her to start walking again as I felt the eyes of the other students burning a hole in my back.

"Shhhhhh!" I hushed her and then let my smile finally break free. "We are officially a couple."

Her shriek was nearly deafening, but I didn't have a chance to cover my ears because she grabbed my arms and started jumping up and down. I didn't jump with her, I just didn't have it in me to let go that much in front of students that had actively hated me for so long, but I didn't stop the smile this time.

"My baby girl is all grown up and finding her a man!"

I lightly punched her shoulder. "Stop it! You're going to embarrass me."

She ignored me, but we did start walking again. "Before you know it, you're going to be lip-locking and giving each other orgasms." She snickered at her joke, trying to embarrass me. My silence must have clued her in but not for the reason she thought I'd be. She looked at me, and then her eyes widened comically. "Holy shit! You already got the big O from your guy. Go, Reid!" She fist-pumped the air and threw her arm over my shoulder while I was actively chanting that the universe, please, please, please allow me to disappear into the floor. "How was it? Did he give you the D, or was it only third base action? Come on! A girl gots to know!"

Her dramatic self was killing me and making me smile. "Ummm, the second one?" I mumbled, hoping she would get the hint. I loved Lisa, but, damn. The girl had no filter and no volume control at the best of times.

She sounded disappointed but tried reassuring me with her wisdom. "Well, I doubt a guy like Reid will let you keep your flower for long. He'll have that thing plucked by next weekend. I'd bet my coupe on it." She loved her Mini Cooper more than her boyfriend of 4 years, and that was saying a lot since she loved Chad fiercely.

She must have noticed my wide-eyed shock at her words because she thought I needed more words of wisdom. The whole time she talked about what to expect and what to do in certain scenarios, I chanted in my head for Chad to come to my rescue by taking his clearly insane girlfriend away. Maybe to an asylum.

"You've been taking those pills that your aunt got you and Jessica, right?"

I breathed out a sigh of relief at the simple, normal question. "Yeah, they really helped with my cramps."

"Good, don't want to be a high school preggo case, amiright?"

I laughed awkwardly but noticed Jenna at her locker as we passed turn a sickly shade of green before turning and darting to the nearest bathroom. I felt bad for her. It was pretty obvious that she was pregnant. I hoped I was wrong, but she gave off all the signs. It also seemed like the baby's father wasn't in her life. It also explained why she tried so hard to get Reid. A young pregnant girl was going to be desperate for a support system, not to mention a man willing to play daddy to someone else's kid. Reid was the kind of guy that would step up and be whatever was needed for someone he loved. Internally I snarled. I felt terrible for her, but she couldn't have my man. Reid was mine. Period.

I was finally given a reprieve from Lisa's incessant chirpiness about my love life when Chad turned the corner, and she abandoned me for his arms which she promptly jumped in to. I loved how happy he made her. They rarely fought, and when they did, they got over it quickly. They definitely had it together for being as young as they were, and it made me wistful for that kind of connection with another person. I was more sure every day that Reid was right and we were meant to be together. I may never be as open with PDA like Lisa was, but I missed Reid at that moment and wished I could feel his arm around my shoulder and his kiss on my head as he always did when we were parting for our separate classes.

I stepped into the office, smiled, and waved at Mrs. Walker, who talked to a student. I dropped my bag at my chair and dropped down into it. I pulled out my phone to check my messages. Reid had already texted earlier, so I wasn't really expecting anything new from him but smiled when I saw a new text from him.

Reid- **Did you make it to school okay?**

Reid- **text me when you are in the office.**

I GRINNED when I typed back that I was, indeed, safe in the office. Then, after a few seconds of waiting and he didn't reply, I shrugged and tucked my phone back into the pocket of my backpack and pulled out my latest romance novel. This one was about a family member of the pirate from the last book.

After a few minutes of getting lost in Regency England, I was startled when Mrs. Walker held out a yellow slip of paper with a classroom number on it. I stuck a ripped piece of paper in my book to save the spot and stood up, taking the piece of paper.

"That's a good one, hun. Gotta love them Mallorys, am I right?" Mrs. Walker laughed when I nodded eagerly, went back to her seat, and immediately started typing something into the computer.

"I'm going to stop by the restroom after I drop this off, okay?" I called out as I was leaving, and Mrs. Walker nodded her head, not looking up from her computer screen, her reading glasses perched at the end of her nose.

"Sure thing, sweetie."

I looked down at the classroom number and headed in that direction. It was in one of the classes nearly at the opposite end of the building, close to the art room.

My footsteps echoed in the quiet halls as I walked through, listening to the quiet hum of the teachers in the classrooms as I passed each one.

When I reached the room, I opened the door as quietly as possible. This was the part I hated the most, interrupting the teacher mid-class. I knew it irritated the teachers, and no matter how quietly I tried to move, it never failed that every single kid would stop what they were doing and stare. At least they haven't been making any rude or derogatory comments like they used to. They always thought they were clever, acting like they were coughing into their hands, making everyone laugh. It was juvenile but effective and never failed to make me turn red with embarrassment. Most of the time, the teachers would just ignore it. A few would bark at the student or the entire class to get back to the work they were doing. But they never stopped the snide comments, and the kids never got in trouble.

I didn't know what kind of magic Reid managed to pull off, but I rarely heard those comments anymore, and if I did, there was usually a football player that put a stop to it immediately. Who knew that I'd actually appreciate any student at this school, let alone a football player? They used to be the worst of the bunch, after the cheerleaders, that was. The cheerleaders hadn't really changed any except to be a little more sly when it came to their taunts. At least they were predictable.

I left just as quietly as I had entered after dropping off the note on the teacher's desk when he gave an irritated nod to it instead of making me walk further into the room to hand it to him. As I was walking out, I saw a football player smile and wave. I was so confused and surprised that I just gave an awkward wave back and slipped out the door. That was strange.

I headed back to the office but stopped when I saw the sign for the girl's restroom. I had almost forgotten that I needed to go after the shock of seeing a football player being nice. Maybe it was a joke or a setup of some kind. I shook my head and pushed open the door noting how quiet it was. I walked to the first stall and tried to open it but jumped when a hand from the other side shoved against the door.

"Sorry," I mumbled and went two stalls down. I hated peeing when there was someone right next to me. It made me uncomfortable.

I covered the toilet seat in the thin toilet paper the school provided before being satisfied I wouldn't pick up any cooties and quickly did my thing. After putting my clothes back together and shoving all the toilet paper into the toilet, I raised my foot to push down the flusher.

Public bathrooms grossed me out. I tried not to touch anything if I could help it. Unfortunately, the school only had hand dryers, so I usually used the bottom of my hoodie to open the door when leaving. I didn't want to think about how many people touched the door without washing their hands.

I had almost forgotten about the person in the stall until I was in front of the sink and looked in the mirror. I could still see their shoes under the stall door. I thought it was strange that they would sit there so quietly.

"Ummm, is everything okay? Do you need me to get you anything? Maybe the nurse?"

There was no answer to my awkward question, but their feet shifted further back as if they could hide themselves. I didn't know why they were hiding out in the bathroom; it could be for any number of reasons. They could be sick, had a fight with a boyfriend or girl-friend, hiding from a test. I wasn't sure that it was really my business. I would mention it to Mrs. Walker when I got back to the office. I shrugged my shoulder and glanced at the black shoes one last time before rinsing the soap off my hands. The sinks had push down faucets, so at least I didn't have to use my clean hands to turn it off.

I moved over to the hand dryers and stuck my dripping hands under the sensor, and started rubbing my hands together, urging the warm air to dry a little faster. I already knew I would get impatient and just shake off the moisture, but I always gave it at least a few seconds.

I didn't hear the stall door opening or the footsteps of the person wearing the black shoes walk up behind me, but I did sense them in my periphery. I started to turn my head but didn't get a chance as I saw a flash of green and felt what seemed like a brick wall slam up against the side of my head.

I immediately saw stars and felt myself tip to the side as pain exploded behind my eyes. I reached out to steady myself but stepped onto the water that was on the floor from my dripping hands and felt my foot slide out from under me.

I landed on my back hard, the breath leaving me, and I felt panic bloom in my chest as it refused to expand. My eyes squeezed in pain and terror. The last thing I remembered was one of those black shoes kicking me right in the side of my head where the first blow had landed.

CHAPTER 23

Reid

As Mr. Anderson pulled into the emergency room parking lot, we saw an ambulance pull under the awning at the emergency entrance. He didn't even try to find a space, just pulled up to the curb and shut off the car, jumping out seconds after I did. We both ran to the entrance and watched as two paramedics opened the back of the ambulance. One jumped inside as the other one waited. It seemed like a lifetime, but it probably wasn't more than 2 or 3 seconds that the gurney started moving out, and the guy waiting outside the ambulance reached in and helped guide the gurney out.

They worked smoothly together as they got the rolling bed settled on the ground and moved it past the ambulance doors, and I was finally able to get a good look at the person lying on the bed.

My heart clenched when I saw Paige lying there, but relief hit me so hard I almost stumbled when I saw she was awake. I couldn't stop myself from taking a step towards her. A hand on my shoulder stopped me, and I turned to snarl at the person keeping me from my buddy when I looked into the eyes of her uncle. His reflected the relief and held the same questions mine did.

"I'm going to park my car before that cop over there," he tilted his head in the direction of the cop that was eyeballing his car. He'd left his car almost in the middle of the road, "tickets me. We'll go in together and find out what is going on, okay?"

I nodded numbly and turned back to see the paramedics disappearing inside the sliding glass doors, taking the girl I was in love with through with them.

I paced back and forth, glancing towards Mr. Anderson every few steps, trying to judge how much longer it would take him to get rid of the cop and park his car properly.

I had finally myself talked into staying calm until I found out what had happened but as soon as her uncle walked up with a determined look in his eye and his jaw clenched in anger, my own anger started flooding back. What the fuck happened to her? Was it an accident, or had someone purposely hurt my girl? Did someone think that since I wasn't there this morning, she was free to bully and torture again?

Mr. Anderson led the way inside the E.R. and I followed him to the window where a nurse sat in bright purple scrubs. She smiled, though it looked wary after she noticed two large men storm up to her. I was sure she had to deal with some interesting situations working here.

"My niece was just brought in by ambulance. I am her legal guardian."

The nurse nodded as her expression changed to one of sympathy and understanding. She turned to her computer screen and started typing.

"Can you give me her name and birthdate, please?"

"Paige Anderson, December 10th. She came from Rocky Hills. Do you have any information on what's wrong or what happened.?" His tone was impatient and demanding, but it was easy to hear the plea.

"I'm sorry, sir. I don't know what happened, but it does say here that she might have a head injury. If you wait in the waiting room right over there, I will go back and find out who is taking care of your niece and get them out to you right away." She pointed towards the grouping of red and orange vinyl seats that only had a few people huddled in them. A couple of them looked like they were on the verge of passing out, and one was holding a towel wrapped around his hand. I guessed that Monday mornings weren't really heavy traffic times for the emergency room.

"Thank you," he said, and we both walked towards a couple of seats that were side by side. "I need to call my wife." He mumbled and fished his cellphone out of the inner pocket of his jacket. It was probably a good idea to call my parents since they would be wondering why I wasn't in school since I had promised I would try to keep my tardy to only one class if I could help it.

I heard Mr. Anderson speaking in a low tone before hanging up and immediately hitting more buttons. He probably had to report to work.

I tapped the button on my own phone and called my dad.

"Everything go okay, son?" My dad sounded busy. Monday's at his job were obviously a lot more hectic than it was in the E.R. I was sitting in.

"Yeah, actually. It went really well."

"That's excellent. Are you back at school yet?" I couldn't blame him for sounding distracted, but I needed him to know that my girl was hurt, and I wasn't leaving until I knew she was okay.

"Actually, dad, I'm at the emergency room. When I was leaving, Paige's uncle got a phone call that she had been picked up by an ambulance and taken to the city. He brought me with him." I paused, "I don't want to leave until I can talk to her and see for myself that she is going to be okay."

It was now silent in the background; whatever he had been doing now stopped as he gave me all his attention. "Damn," he whispered. "Reid, I'm so sorry. Of course, stay as long as you need. I will cover with the school. I'll call your mom and let her know."

His easy acceptance had me choking up. I always loved my parents, but they were amazing when I really needed them. "Thanks, Dad. I appreciate it."

"Don't worry, Reid, you just take care of our girl, understand?" Yeah, I had the best parents ever.

We hung up and sat in silence for a few minutes.

"She's a good girl."

Her uncle's quiet words broke into the panic that had been slowly crawling into my gut. The tension was still there, but the terror eased back. She was awake, and that was a good sign, the best sign.

I cleared my throat. "The best."

"My brother loved his family." He started, gazing into the distance as if seeing his brother sitting there across the room with his wife and daughter. Probably like he'd seen him many times over the years. "Paige was his little princess. He spoiled her rotten." He laughed. "Her favorite thing to do when she was little was have tea parties with her stuffed animals and her daddy. Those tea parties always included crowns and feather boas. Pinkies out." He shook his head. "He loved every second of it."

The picture of a little Paige with missing front teeth and blond hair in pigtails brought a smile to my face. I could easily picture that little girl as my own daughter. Mine and Paige's. I would give anything to be in her father's place in that vision. I would wear as many feather boas as my daughter wanted me to wear as long as I got to sit there drinking tea with her, pinky out.

"You're picturing it, aren't you?"

I looked over to see him looking at me. I chuckled. "Yeah, I am."

"You'll be a good dad, I bet." He looked down into his lap. "Just don't do what I did and let work consume you. I spent too much time in the office and lost touch with my family. I love my kids more than my life, but I've had my priorities lopsided for more years than can be easily fixed." He looked back at me, head tilted as it still hung down. "My kids did this to her, didn't they?"

I cleared my throat and shifted uncomfortably. Did they do this in particular? I had no idea. Did they do other things in the past? Yeah, they did.

He looked back at his hands folded together between his knees at my non-answer. "Shit," he whispered. "I promised my brother I would always take care of her, but I allowed her to be abused in her own home."

I hated that he was clearly in pain, but I was also glad that he was finally opening his eyes. His non-attention had allowed his kids to take advantage of and hurt Paige.

"There were signs, but I ignored them. And my wife," he shook his head, "she has been just as absent as me. Maybe because of me." He sat back in his seat and straightened his tie. He clapped his hand on my shoulder. "Don't worry, I will make sure things are different, and our girl is safe from now on."

Our moment ended as a door was pushed open, and a male nurse in dark green scrubs called out, already looking towards us expectantly. "Paige Anderson's family?"

We both nodded and stood up. I was worried that I wouldn't be allowed to see her since I wasn't family. Unfortunately, boyfriends didn't count when it came to hospitals and HIPAA laws.

The guy looked at me, dark eyes taking me in. "Reid?"

I nodded.

"Good, she's been asking for you." He smiled and turned to Mr. Anderson. "If it's okay with you, I'll take you both back to the room we have her in. I'm afraid we haven't had a chance to do a C.T. scan yet, so she'll have to be taken back for one as soon as we can. I think she's next in line for the machine."

We were walking briskly, occasionally turning corners.

"Can you tell us what happened to her?"

"She was brought in because she was still unconscious when the paramedics arrived. Apparently, someone found her in a bathroom at her school. She came to shortly after they got there, but there is always a reason for concern anytime there is a head injury with unconsciousness. Right now, she has a pretty bad headache, and bruising has started developing around her temple. More than likely, she has a mild concussion."

We were stopped outside an open door with a curtain closed around the bed inside.

"Go ahead inside. Remember, she has a headache, so loud noises and bright lights will probably not feel good right now. Don't over-whelm her, or we'll have to send someone out." He looked at me, "Unfortunately, that'll probably be you since the family has priority."

I wanted to growl and dare him to remove me from her side, but I swallowed it back and nodded instead. I would do what was needed to take care of my girl.

We walked in together and moved around the curtain to see Paige attached to a couple of wires, a heart monitor, blood pressure cuff, and pulse ox monitor. Her eyes were closed, and from my position, I could see a dark bruise at the side of her head, spreading to the top of her cheekbone. She looked small and fragile in the big hospital bed, wearing a light blue gown with darker, tiny blue flowers patterned over it.

We hadn't said anything, just stood there taking in the sight of her hooked to the machines, but her eyes fluttered open, and she turned her head to glance at us. She blinked a few times before she seemed to realize that we were actually standing there.

"Oh! Reid! Uncle James." Her eyes started tearing up. "You're here." She blinked. "Why are you here, together?"

I looked at him, and he nodded at me, so I turned back to her and stepped forward so I could take her hand that didn't have the oxygen monitor on it. "I went to see him this morning. Remember how I told you last night I would take care of everything?" She nodded. "Well, I had my dad make an appointment for me first thing this morning with your uncle, and we came to an understanding." I kissed her hand.

"Understanding?" She looked towards her uncle, who was standing there looking awkward with his hands stuffed in his suit pockets.

He stepped forward and took his hands out, and reached over to squeeze her knee.

"Yeah, squirt. Your guy here wanted me to know how serious he is about you."

Her eyes teared up again, and she whispered, "You haven't called me that in years."

He nodded. "I know. I'm sorry I haven't been there for you. I know you're almost an adult, hell, you're more mature than most adults I know, but I promise I will always be here if you need me from now on, okay?"

She gave out a watery okay just as the nurse came back in the room pushing a wheelchair, and pulled open the curtain. "Your chariot awaits, ma'am." He bowed and swept his hand towards the seat, making my girl giggle. I wanted to push him out the door and lock him out to keep him away from her, but he made her laugh, and I wasn't quite a barbarian, so I clenched my teeth and ignored it. Then, when she looked over at me and gave me a sweet smile and held out her hand, and asked, "Help me?" my jaw relaxed, and I moved forward, ready to do anything she needed.

CHAPTER 24

Paige

I didn't have to stay in the hospital for more than a few hours, thank goodness. I hated the uncomfortable beds and the scratchy gowns with the open backs. I hated the feeling of vulnerability while as a patient.

We were sitting in my uncle's den; somewhere we rarely spent time since we all usually stayed in our own rooms or the dining room on Sundays. The den was usually reserved for Christmas morning while we quietly passed around gifts and anxiously awaited the time we could be dismissed to go back to doing our own thing.

It was a big room with a huge fireplace that was rarely used. The furniture was updated every couple of years even though they only got sat on a few times a year. Large arrangements of live green plants gave the room the only feeling of life. If one thing could be said about my aunt, it was that she had an amazing green thumb. All of her plants thrived under her care. It was one thing I envied and hoped to develop when I got older and kept my own home.

Reid and I were sitting on a loveseat holding hands while his parents sat on the couch next to us. My aunt and uncle sat in armchairs across from us. We had just finished discussing the incident at school and moved onto the topic that was sitting heavy in the room when the front door opened and a pair of footsteps entered the house.

"Jason and Jessica should be in here, don't you think?" My aunt murmured to Uncle James. He looked over at me. As much as I wanted to hide away from my cousins, it was probably best to address the issues we had, especially while I had a room full of support. Everyone except Aunt Jolene. She seemed almost closed off from me. Maybe it was embarrassment over the way she had yelled at me. Perhaps it was resentment that she had been told in no uncertain terms by my uncle that I wasn't to be punished and no one was to try to keep Reid and me apart.

"I actually think that is an excellent idea," he said and called out for his children to join us in the room.

Jason entered first, a cocky smile on his face and a swagger to his steps that made me think of a rooster strutting around. Jessica followed behind him, quietly walking in and standing near her mother's chair, a questioning look on her face as she saw Reid's parents sitting together, though she seemed to resign herself to the situation as she stared at mine and Reid's hands clasped together on my leg.

My head was beginning to throb again as the pain medication they had given me at the hospital started to wear off. Hearing Jason start to chuckle as he, too, took in the room and its occupants didn't help as it made me tense. I fought back a wince as I began to dread how the conversation we were about to have would go.

"Our practice was canceled because of your little incident today, cousin. We have important games coming up. We don't need to be missing practice just because you decide to be clumsy." Jason tilted his head and gave me a mocking smile. I heard a low rumble coming from next to me. I turned to Reid and whispered to him.

"Did you just growl?" I wanted to giggle even though it wasn't the time or the place, but Reid was adorable when he was in protective mode.

"Jason!" my uncle barked out, making me jump. I saw my aunt nervously reach up to grab her pendant. "Paige was attacked in the bathroom. Can you not show some concern?"

Jason shrugged and waved a hand in my direction. "She looks fine to me. It seems like a big overreaction to call in an ambulance and cancel after-school activities. I heard that the police were called in, too."

My uncle looked like he was trying to control his anger and disappointment simultaneously. He shook his head and pinched the bridge of his nose, and took deep breaths. Jason ignored him and looked at his mom, who looked defeated, sitting there as her family couldn't hide their dysfunction for once. It probably felt even worse to her that it was happening in front of strangers.

"Is it alright if I go out to my room since the cry baby seems to be just fine?"

"Jason!" Aunt Jolene looked mortified as she glanced quickly at Reid's parents apologetically.

Reid squeezed my hand, and his parents had frowns on their faces. His mother looked like she wanted to jump up and smack Jason.

A loud smack made me jump, and we all looked over to Uncle James. His hand was resting on the wooden arm of his chair where he had just slammed it down. "How long has this been going on?" He looked between Jason and Jessica, who had backed up against the wall and was leaning against it, her face closed off, not letting on to what she was thinking or feeling.

Uncle James swung his head in my direction. "Well?" His tone was sharp, making me tense up.

"Don't talk to her that way," Reid growled and tightened his grip on my hand. I rubbed my other hand over our clasped hands to calm him. My uncle didn't mean anything by his tone; he was just frustrated by the situation.

Uncle James glared at Reid for a long moment before his face dropped, and he let out a deep breath and rubbed a hand down his face. "I don't really need an answer, though, do I? The bruises, the hair, the stairs. You've been abusing your cousin since she came to live with us."

Jason scoffed. "You think I am the only one? Little orphan free-loader came along, and your little princess decided to put her in her place." He shrugged and turned to Jessica, who was still doing her best impression of being a statue. "I was just following orders, right, sis?"

Aunt Jolene gasped. "Jessica would never…"

Jason laughed so hard he was doubled over. "Are you kidding me?"

Before he could say anything else, the doorbell rang, and a flustered Aunt Jolene jumped up out of her chair and rushed to the front of the house. Quiet voices were heard while we all sat quietly, Jason leaning a hip against his mother's chair. I saw Jessica straighten further when the new people entered the room.

Two uniformed police officers trailed after Aunt Jolene and looked around the room. Reid's dad stood up along with his mom, and they both shook the officer's hands before gesturing to the end of the couch before moving further down the end closer to the love seat we were sitting in. Uncle James stood up and leaned over the marble coffee table.

"Officers." There was no need to ask why they were here.

My aunt was wringing her hands. Distress was written in every line of her body. "Can I get anyone anything to drink?" She looked at the officers and turned to Reid's parents, who shook their heads.

"No, ma'am, we won't take up much of your time. We just came from the school." Then, they turned to me, "We do need your official statement before we leave."

I nodded. I had been warned that I should expect a visit. The principal had told Uncle James when they called him that they had contacted the police.

The talkative one of the duo turned towards my uncle after everyone was comfortably seated, while the quiet one sat a large metal writing tablet/clipboard on his lap and picked up a pen.

"You're the guardian?"

"Yes, me and my wife." He gestured towards Aunt Jolene.

"Right." He turned towards Reid's parents. "And you are?"

"Our son is Paige's boyfriend." Mrs. Johnson patted Reid on the shoulder.

Before it needed to be asked, Uncle James spoke up and waved to indicate Jason and Jessica. After saying her name, the cop stared at her for an extra moment until Jessica flinched. It was the first physical reaction that she'd had since walking in the door.

"The first thing you should know is that we conducted several interviews today. No one knows anything, including the student that found Ms. Anderson. That isn't to say that the students we talked to didn't have a lot to say. It seems the student body has been led to treat Ms. Anderson poorly over the years." His eyes went to Jessica. "There was one name that was brought up repeatedly."

"Why does everyone keep accusing Jessica of being mean to Paige?" Aunt Jolene demanded.

The cop just stared her down. Yes, Aunt Jolene was in denial that her precious girl could be a bully.

"At this moment in time, we have one suspect for the attack on Paige."

"It wasn't Jessica."

Everyone in the room turned to look at me. I looked at Jessica's shoes. She was wearing sky blue ballet flats that perfectly matched her flowy blouse. The blue that perfectly matched her eyes. Those eyes were staring at me in challenge. She hated me and didn't want me to have Reid, but she hadn't kicked me in the head. I knew that sometimes she wanted to hurt me more than she already had. But in this case, it wasn't her.

"The girl that attacked me in the bathroom was wearing black shoes. I didn't get a good look at them; I just know they were probably sneakers. They definitely weren't dress shoes." Everyone glanced at the shoes Jessica was wearing.

The cop cleared his throat, "There is something else." He pulled his phone out of his pocket and touched the screen before turning it and placing it on the table. Mr. Johnson was the first one to get a good look. He sucked in his breath.

"What does this mean?" His voice was angry. He picked up the phone and passed it to Reid, who held it so I could see. The picture of me lying on the floor unconscious had me swallowing hard. It was difficult to see.

Then I saw the caption above the photo.

I warned you

"WHAT DOES THAT MEAN, PAIGE?" Reid's hand was shaking. I didn't know if it was from anger or fear. Probably both.

"I-" I closed my eyes and took a deep breath. "I have seen a couple of other messages over the last week. One was in the bathroom on Friday when I went to clean off the pudding." I looked up at Reid. "Remember? I went to the bathroom with Lisa, and she helped me get cleaned up. On the mirror was a message that said to stay away from you." I glazed quickly over at Jessica. "I thought maybe it was from Jessica. That maybe she had a friend write on it knowing that I would go in there to clean up."

"And the other message?" I could hear him trying to control his emotions.

I touched the screen and scrolled so he could see the other message and was surprised to see three others. "Oh my god!" I cried out. "I didn't even know there were more!" Below the most current post was several more. Most were of Reid at the school. One was during the football game, and one was after the game when he was dirty and sweaty and smiling big. Each of the captions were similar.

He is mine

Reid is too good for you

We will be together soon

"THIS IS RIDICULOUS!" Reid nearly shouted. He looked up at Jessica, glaring at her. "Is this you? Are you behind all this?"

Jessica still didn't say anything, just stared at him before shaking her head.

Uncle James spoke up then. "Jessica, if you know what is going on, if you know who is behind this, you need to tell us."

She looked at her dad for a long moment.

"I don't know anything. Yeah, I wanted Reid, okay?" She looked around at everyone, stopping on Reid. I gripped his hand tighter, wishing I could make her look away from him. "But I didn't do any of this." She looked at me then. "I didn't attack you in the bathroom." There was something in her eyes, a slight flinch maybe, a second of regret possibly. Because even though I didn't believe she was behind the attack today, it didn't mean she hadn't attacked me a week ago right here at home.

Uncle James looked up from the officer's phone before handing it back to him. "Is there a way to trace the account?" he asked the officer.

"Unfortunately, the account was made with a dummy email address, and that was made at the school. The account has only been accessed at the school. It is impossible to tell where or by whom."

Both officers looked at me. "Do you have any other enemies? Do you know of anyone who might want to hurt you?" Then they looked at Reid. "Do you know who might be posting these things? Who might be trying to warn off Paige? Have you noticed any other girls trying to get your attention?"

Jason laughed then, and we all looked at him to see him shaking his head. "He's the fucking wide receiver and the new guy at the school. What bitches don't want on his jock?"

"Jason! That's enough!" My uncle's face was red with anger. "I think you need to head out to the pool house. But you and I are going to be having a serious conversation tonight, do you understand me?"

"Yeah, sure, whatever."

It was silent as he walked out of the room, and it wasn't until we all heard the back door open and close that I let out a breath of relief.

"I honestly don't know who might be behind these posts. I wish I did." Reid let out a frustrated breath.

I hesitated, "What about Jenna?" I asked quietly.

It was quiet for a minute, and I chanced a peek over at his mom. I knew she liked Jenna, that she thought she was still that sweet girl that had grown up next door to them. Her face was sad, but she didn't look angry or even like she didn't believe it was possible.

"I don't know." Reid shook his head. "I would have said 'no way' until I saw the way she's been acting lately." He looked down at his lap. "I just don't know." I squeezed his hand. It had to be hard to think your childhood friend could end up being so cruel, so different from the person you thought you knew.

"Well, if either one of you think of anything else, give us a call right away." The officer laid a business card on the table. "We will be monitoring this social media page as well, watching for new activity."

"You aren't going to take it down?" Aunt Jolene asked, shocked.

"It's best that we don't right now. The perpetrator might do or say something to help us figure out who they are. In the meantime, we will interview Jenna, but according to the records, she went home sick before the first period even started." I thought about how she ran to the bathroom and my thoughts about how she might be pregnant. "We already got a list of students that had hall passes during the time of the incident. Unfortunately, there were only 2 of them, and they were both males, and neither one fits for this."

They stood up and shook hands with everyone. "Keep your eyes open, especially you, Reid. The person doing this seems to have a fascination. If you can figure out who it is, it will help us put a stop to this." Reid nodded, and we both sat back down while Uncle James led them back through the house and to the front door.

Mrs. Johnson reached over and patted my hand. "Are you okay, Paige? You look like you are in pain."

I smiled back, but I was sure it looked more like a grimace. "I'm okay. But I think my medicine has worn off. My head is hurting a little more than it was."

Reid glanced at his phone, "It's time for another pill. I'm going to stay with you tonight and take care of you. The doctor said you need to be watched."

"I don't think that is appropriate." Aunt Jolene sniffed.

"I'm not leaving her side." Reid pushed.

Uncle James walked back into the room and looked at me, and smiled. "I don't think there is a better person suited for keeping an eye on our girl." He looked over to Reid's parents. "As long as your parents agree, you are welcome to stay."

They smiled and agreed. As everyone was headed towards the front door to see them out, I saw Mr. Johnson pull Reid to the side to talk to him quietly and watched as Reid nodded his head. I looked around and realized that Jessica was already gone.

"I'll be back in a little while with an overnight bag, son." Mr. Johnson clapped Reid on the shoulder and shook hands with my aunt and uncle. I felt my eyes sting when both of his parents hugged me tightly before walking out the door, telling me to get some rest.

"I don't like this." Aunt Jolene started the moment the front door closed.

Uncle James took her hand and started leading her away. "It's done. Let's go to bed." He looked back at us, "If you need anything, let us know. I will call the school tomorrow to let them know you won't be in."

Reid and I stood there for a minute just looking at each other before I took a deep, shaky breath and said, "Come on, I'll show you to my room."

CHAPTER 25

Reid

Last night I carefully tucked Paige into bed, making sure she had a pain pill and was comfortable having me with her. If she wasn't ready for me to actually stay with her in her room, in her bed, I would have asked for a guest room or would have at least slept in her chair. I just needed to make sure that she was going to be okay. The doctor had said there was no need to wake her through the night, but it was important to keep an eye on her.

All through the night, I checked on her. I didn't need to wake her, but I did need to wake myself, so I set my alarm for every four hours, only waking her once for a new dose of pain medication.

Last night was hard for her, I knew. Seeing the social media page with the multiple posts on it was shocking to see. I had been thinking about it most of the night, and I still couldn't think of who could be behind the posts and the attack.

Laying there thinking about it all night in between dozing off and making sure Paige was resting okay without pain, I thought of the incident with the pudding cup in the cafeteria. It had to have been the stalker- because that's what she obviously was at this point, since she had already had the mirror ready, knowing that Paige would head in there to clean up.

The person was taking a lot of chances, though. I frowned. Anyone else could have seen the message. Maybe they did see it. But what would they have thought about it? Probably just excuse it as more bathroom graffiti, most likely.

Could it actually be a guy? It wasn't out of the realm of possibility. But since the person was in and out of the girl's restroom, that seemed very unlikely. These speculations weren't helping and were starting to give me my own headache.

I glanced over at Paige, who was still sleeping peacefully. Spending the night with her, holding her in my arms, was a dream come true. Since I had no experience with another girl, never wanted any until Paige, I found myself staring at her sleeping profile most of the night. This girl had struck me hard from the second I laid eyes on her. But now that I have gotten to know her? Now that I have tasted her lips, held her against me, I never wanted to sleep alone again. My parents probably wouldn't fight me on it, but I was sure to face a battle with her family.

I carefully got out of bed and made sure the comforter was tucked in around her. I went into her attached bathroom, noticing how tidy it was, just like her bedroom. My overnight bag was sitting on the counter where I had left it last night. I rummaged inside until I found a change of clothes and quickly brushed my teeth while the shower water heated. Once I was done, I stepped inside the glass enclosure and washed up quickly, not wanting to leave my buddy for too long. I ignored my hard on. It was a permanent state I was in since I met Paige. She never noticed, or was too innocent to realize, that I was almost always in some state of arousal around her. I had jacked off, of course, I was a teenage boy, but I would be embarrassed if anyone found out just how often I had been jacking off in the last week or so.

I dried off and got dressed in the sweats and t-shirt my dad had packed for me, grateful for the comfortable clothes since I didn't plan on letting Paige go anywhere today. When I cracked open the bathroom door, I was relieved to see that my time in the bathroom hadn't disturbed her.

I had to feed her, so I left the room and made my way into the kitchen. On my way, I looked around. The house was lavishly furnished but didn't look like it was actually lived in. Everything was spotless without even a speck of dust. I couldn't imagine Mrs. Anderson walking around with a rag and can of Pledge, so they must have at least one maid. I shook my head. It was mind-boggling how the rich lived. My parents made really good money and were definitely above the middle-class tax bracket, but we didn't live like this.

When I stepped into the kitchen, I let out a low whistle. My mom would probably move in and permanently camp herself right in the middle of the kitchen floor if she saw the gleaming appliances that were all oversized and could hold enough food to feed an entire house full of partiers. You could probably run a catering business from that stove.

I opened the refrigerator and perused the contents before selecting a carton of eggs and a stick of butter. I continued to rummage around the kitchen until I found a bag of bread and the toaster. It didn't take me long to scramble up a bunch of eggs and make a few slices of buttered toast. I was about to fill up two glasses with orange juice until I remembered with a grimace that I just brushed my teeth and grabbed out the milk instead.

Satisfied with my small meal offerings for my buddy, I made it back to her room after putting everything away where I had found it. My mom would have my ass if I left a mess in anyone's kitchen. I balanced the plate of eggs on top of the plate of toast and carefully held both glasses of milk in one hand with the plates in the other. I was gaining an appreciation for waitresses and their talent for carrying so much at once all day.

Once I managed to get the bedroom door opened without spilling anything, the first thing I noticed was that Paige was no longer in bed. I could hear the shower running, so I carefully put everything down on her desk and picked up a piece of toast while relaxing in her desk chair while trying to ignore the fact that my beautiful girl was one wall away from me. Naked. Slippery. Covered in soap. I groaned and ran a hand over my erection.

I did my best to ignore the sounds of water and ate a few bites of scrambled eggs. I was doing great until the bathroom door opened, and Paige exited in a cloud of steam and humidity. She was using a towel to squeeze the excess water out of her long hair that was several shades darker while wet but was still very clearly golden. What made me almost choke on my tongue, though, was her naked body that still had droplets of water covering parts of her body. I wanted to lick every single drop as I watched her large breasts jiggle with her movements.

My groan must have been loud enough for her to hear because she yelped and turned to face me. She dropped the towel from her hair and used it to cover the front of her body and almost made me whimper at the loss.

"Oh my god, Reid! I thought you had left!" Paige's entire body was beet red, and I was sure it wasn't all because of the heat from the shower she'd just stepped out of.

I couldn't answer since my mind could only repeat one phrase over and over inside my skull - MINE!

"Baby," I choked out, "if you aren't ready to lose our virginities in about 30 seconds, then I'm begging you to get dressed. Right. Now." The last of my words ended in a growl I hadn't realized I was capable of. Apparently, my girl turned me into a caveman.

Paige's eyes widened dramatically as she stood frozen. When her eyes dropped to my lap where I had been absent-mindedly rubbing my erection, she swallowed audibly. She took one step backward, and I bit back the sound that I was making in the back of my throat. She must have heard it anyway because her eyes snapped back up to mine, her eyes still wide.

I was mentally scolding myself for scaring her until I looked closer and saw she was breathing hard. She was licking her lips and squeezing her beautiful thighs together. My girl wasn't scared. No, she was turned the fuck on.

I was about to jump out of my seat and lunge for her when she took a deep breath and dropped the towel at her feet. My body practically melted back into the chair. I thought seeing her body only moments ago was amazing, but seeing her purposely showing me all of her, it ratcheted my arousal from a 10 to outer space. Seeing her nipples tighten into small little points, seeing her thighs rubbing together, her lips wet from her tongue, I finally broke.

She squeaked adorably as I jumped up and took the few steps needed to reach her in a second flat. I wrapped one arm around her lower back and yanked her body into mine, and grabbed a handful of her wet hair with my other hand. Then, I tilted her head back to the perfect angle and proceeded to devour her mouth. She tasted like mint, smelled like strawberries, and felt like heaven.

She whimpered, and I was about to let her go until I realized she was pressing herself into me, rubbing her bare belly into my clothed cock. Now it was my turn to whimper. I hoped it came across as a moan or a groan, though, because I didn't want to lose my man card before I even managed to get inside her. It would be a miracle if I managed to hold back my release until I was finally deep inside her.

"Reid, please," she whispered against my lips. I pulled back and ran my eyes over her flushed face and her already plump lips even more swollen from our kisses. She was beautiful.

"Tell me," I demanded. I wanted her more than I needed my next breath, but I wouldn't touch her if she weren't ready. I would wait forever for her as long as she needed me to.

"Please," her whispered plea was full of desperation.

"Please, what, buddy? I need you to spell it out for me."

"Reid!" She whined, continuing to rub herself against me, and I felt her hands sneak under my shirt and rub across my back before sliding towards the front.

I squeezed my eyes shut tight. I wanted nothing more than to toss her onto her bed and shove her legs apart so I could get a taste of the wetness between her legs. Then, after eating her out for a few hours, I would finish up the day going through every single condom in the box that my dad had stashed in my bag. He was a smart man, and I would have to thank him later. I wouldn't tell him why I was thanking him, though. Awkward.

"Baby, what do you want? Do you want me to touch you? Do you want me to suck on your clit and tongue your little hole? Do you want me to spread you out on your cute little purple comforter and shove my fat cock into you until you can't tell where I end and you begin?"

Her breaths were fast and hot against my mouth. "Yes! All of that, yes! Reid, please. I can't stand it. It hurts."

And that's what did it. She broke me, my control officially gone. I was nothing but hunger, hunger for her. Lips, tongues, teeth, our kiss was frantic, and I quickly backed her up until the backs of her thighs hit her mattress, and a soft push was enough to have her falling backward. I didn't try to catch her. By the time she stopped bouncing, I was already on my knees and spreading her legs wide.

I pulled her hips to the very edge of her bed and came to a complete stop, barely even breathing. My first look at her pussy was more than I could have imagined. Her pinkness was glistening with moisture, her short, trimmed hair not able to hide the treasure of her pussy.

I couldn't have stopped myself from leaning forward and licking her from asshole to clit if there was a bomb dropped on my head. She was all I saw and tasted and smelled. She was everything. She had been my everything since we met, but this moment was all I needed to cement my claim on her. For the rest of my life, I would be her slave. I would do anything to keep her happy and satisfied.

I had to hold down her hips with my arm before she ended up falling off the bed. She was doing her best to drown me in her pussy, rubbing herself against me. I stuck my tongue into her tight as fuck little hole and groaned at her tightness. The last thing I wanted to do was hurt her. I wasn't small. I wasn't even average. I wasn't blind, and I had spent a lot of time inside locker rooms and knew I was bigger than most. I also knew that the female body was a fantastic thing. She would stretch and accept me into her, but that first thrust was going to hurt.

I slipped one digit slowly into her hole while I sucked on her clit, once again having to put weight into my arm across her hips. I felt her fingers run through my hair and start pulling with every suck of my lips and thrust of my finger.

"Reid!" she screamed before letting out a deep, painful-sounding groan. At the same time, her thighs stiffened before squeezing tightly.

I took my time to lick up as much of her release as I could until her pleas to stop made me lift my head and look at her blissed-out expression. I stood up and leaned over her, and kissed her softly. "Are you okay?" I asked.

"Ummm, I'm amazing." She stretched her arms above her head and stretched languidly. I watched her breasts move and bounce with her movements, and that was when I realized that I had yet to get my mouth on those spectacular tits. I'd had some fun dreams of those tits. I'd also woken up just as wet as I was currently. It didn't stop my cock from getting just as hard as it had been before, though.

I gave in to the temptation so prettily displayed before me and sucked a nipple into my mouth. Paige immediately arched her back deeply and brought her hands to my hair again. She could pluck me bald as long as she never stopped letting me feast on her body.

I had barely switched to the other nipple when she was back to begging. "Reid! I need you now! Please fuck me!"

I grinned against her breast. It hadn't taken her long to get over her shyness. My girl knew what she wanted. I reluctantly let her nipple go with a pop and looked longingly at the other one before lifting my body off her to head into the bathroom for that box of condoms I had found in my bag last night when I was getting ready for bed.

"Where are you going?" She looked confused but didn't try to cover herself up.

"I'm not going anywhere," I promised. "I'm just going to grab a condom."

She turned redder than she had before when she had been trying to hide her body with the towel. "I, ummm, I'm on birth control. I have been since I was 15. Aunt Jolene put both Jessica and me on it so we wouldn't become 'teenage statistics.'" She quoted with her fingers in the air. "I don't mind taking it because it keeps me from getting bad cramps. So, yeah, ummm, I'm protected." She finished in a whisper.

I leaned back over her and kissed her lips softly. "That's good, baby. But I will still use condoms because I will never put you at risk. You have dreams of becoming a pediatric nurse, and I won't take any chances of ruining that by accidentally getting you pregnant. When you're ready, after we've been married and you get your nursing degree, then we can have as many children as you want."

By the time I was done talking, Paige's eyes were watering. She flung her arms around me and squeezed me tight. "I love you, Reid. So much."

I hugged her back and kissed her head, basking in the warmth running through me at hearing her words. "I love you, too, buddy."

She giggled and pushed me back. "Are you ever going to stop calling me that?"

"Nope," I grinned and got off her, and headed into the bathroom.

CHAPTER 26

Paige

I lay there staring at my ceiling, reliving the feelings that had been coursing through my body. I never knew it was possible to feel that way. I was eager to learn more.

I lifted my head to look at Reid as he came back from the bathroom and about swallowed my tongue. He had stripped his clothes off while he'd been in there and was now just as bare as I was. He was magnificent. I hadn't really thought much about the male body before, but now, while looking at Reid's grooved abs and that V I kept hearing so much about in books, I was fascinated. But what really took my breath away was the massive cock that was more than I could have imagined. I had equal feelings of eagerness and dread while looking at it.

"How is your head?"

I jerked my head up to look at his concerned face. "What?"

"Your head? Do you still have a headache? We can wait to do this."

He waved in the direction of his dick, bringing it back to my attention.

As I watched, a bead of liquid formed at the tip and slowly slid over the side and rolled along one of the large veins that were practically pulsing. The whole thing was red and angry-looking. It looked painful, and I wondered how he could stand it.

"Paige?" There was an unmistakable hint of humor in his tone that time.

I swallowed hard, but the heat that was flooding through me didn't go away. If anything, it kept rising until I thought I would self-combust. "I-I," what had he asked me again? Did my head hurt? I couldn't tell over the beating of my heart that matched the throbbing between my legs. He had just given me a massive orgasm until I had to push him away, but it was as if I hadn't just had a release. The need inside of me was bigger than anything I had ever expected it to be. Stronger.

"Reid, if you don't fuck me soon, I might die from need."

He groaned and chuckled at the same time, a sound that made my nipples harden even more than they already were. I had gotten a taste of what he could do to my body, and I was already addicted. I needed to know what else there was. "Baby, you can't say things like that."

"Why?" I tilted my head questioningly.

"Because," he growled as he prowled over to me and then put one knee and then the other on the bed until he was caging me in with his body. I could feel his large erection rub against my skin as he settled himself over me. The wetness was making a trail over me, sending goosebumps all over my body. "You'll make me lose control again. I already came in my pants at the taste of your pussy. If you say things like fuck from these soft lips, I don't know if I'll be able to control myself." His thumb brushed over my bottom lip, pulling it down, exposing my teeth. I leaned up slightly, closing my lips around his thumb, and sucked it lightly against my tongue.

"Fuuuuck."

There were no other words, and things turned frantic from that second on. He pulled his thumb from my lips and slammed his mouth on mine, and thrust his tongue against mine. He pulled away, and I watched in rapt attention as he brought a condom to his mouth and ripped the package open. I couldn't see anymore as his mouth skimmed over my cheek and down to my neck, where he nipped and sucked.

I could feel him between our bodies. The thought of what he was doing there had more wetness dripping out of me. I had a brief moment of thought that I should have moved my comforter off the bed, and then all rational thought left me as I suddenly felt the tip of his cock brush over my clit.

He pulled back from my neck, and we both looked down at his cock as he used one hand to hold himself up by my shoulder and used the other one to guide his cock over me.

Up and down, over my folds, bumping against my clit, down to my entrance, and back again. He was teasing us both until the condom was coated in my wetness. Then, finally, when neither one of us could handle any more of the anticipation, he looked into my eyes and paused right at my entrance.

"Are you ready?" I'd never heard his voice so deep and guttural.

"Yes," I whispered. My eyes begged him to do it, to push through and take both of our innocence.

His eyes never left mine as he slowly started to push inside me. Inch by inch, I felt myself being stretched open. It was uncomfortable, but it didn't hurt. He was being so careful, taking his time with me when I could see the strain in his muscles. He was shaking from the effort of holding back, and I fell even deeper in love with him. He must have seen it in my eyes because his face got softer and some of the tightness I could feel in his shoulders left him.

He lowered his head and kissed me softly, sweetly. By the time he was fully seated inside me, I had forgotten all about the uncomfortable feeling of being stretched by something so big for the first time and was able to relax enough to make it easier on both of us.

He held still for a long minute, just kissing me and rubbing his large calloused hand up and down my side and over my breast, teasing my nipple. His hand stopped there, and he ran his thumb over my nipple and lightly pinched it, making me gasp at the sensations that action brought. I had no idea that my breasts were so sensitive or that having Reid touch them could be so erotic.

"How are you doing, baby?" He whispered.

I thought about it and wiggled my hips lightly to test the feelings inside me and gasped when the movement caused his cock to slide a bit. "Good. I'm good. Please move."

I heard him groan and then watched as he slowly pulled out. It felt like it took him forever to slide that massive cock out of me, and we both looked back down where we were connected, and I gasped at the sight. It was a shocking sight seeing him stretch me so wide around him. I felt myself get even wetter.

"Fuck. Look at that beautiful pussy stretched out around me. You have me drenched, baby."

He started sliding back in just as slowly, and once he was fully inside me again, I felt him bump against something deep inside me, making me gasp, and Reid groan. He pulled out slightly quicker and slid back in at the same speed. I still felt overfull, but it was a good feeling. It was erotic and had feelings I didn't have words for running through my whole body.

The next time he slid out, he pushed back in fast and hard, and I couldn't have held in the gasp of shock and pleasure if I'd tried.

"Baby? You okay?" His voice was strained, and I had the feeling he wouldn't be able to hold on much longer. I didn't think I wanted him to anymore.

"Yes!" I screamed when he did it again. "More! Please!"

His slow in and outs sped up until he was going so fast I was out of breath. All I could think was that I needed more. He slid his hand down from my side and over my hip until he reached my thigh. When he had my thigh in his hand, he slipped his hand around it and brought it up until my leg was touching my breast. The new position let him go in even deeper at a different angle. Every time he thrust in and out, he moved over a spot that made stars dance behind my eyes.

"Look at me!" His demand had my eyes flying back open and staring into his beautiful sky blue eyes that were filled with a seriousness I had never seen in them before. "I want your eyes on me when you come, Paige. I need you to show me how much you love this. Do you know why?" He punctuated his question with a harder thrust that made me gasp. "Because you're mine, Paige. You will always be mine. I will never let you go." And if I thought he was going hard and fast before I found out how wrong I was.

He was dripping in sweat, and drops were falling on my chest. His long hair was sticking to his cheeks. He looked almost feral moving above me. His eyes were focused on me like I was the only thing in his entire world.

I had been feeling something building inside me, a pressure that threatened to destroy me. It was different from how I felt when he had eaten me out. This one was bigger, and I was scared that I would never be the same.

"Reid..." I whimpered.

"Let it happen, baby. Fuck! I need you to come, baby, please." His words were pleading, but his tone was a snarl. He adjusted his hips, and each time he bottomed out, his pelvis ground against my clit.

Suddenly that tightness inside me exploded, and all I saw, all I felt, was blinding flashes of light. "Reid!" I screamed. I couldn't keep my eyes open anymore. As much as I wanted to keep them open for him, I just couldn't.

I lost track of what was happening around me. I could feel Reid's pace stutter and then stop as he thrust in deep and stayed there, his grinds against my clit, making my climax extend with aftershocks that were not as strong but no less pleasurable.

When the aftershocks finally ended, I found myself cradled in Reid's arms. We were lying face to face, his big hand stroking my face and hair. I blinked at him and tried to make my brain work again.

"Hi," I whispered.

He didn't answer. He just grinned at me, those almost dimples flashing at me, and leaned forward to kiss my nose and nuzzled his cheek against mine.

I must have fallen asleep for several hours because the next thing I knew, I heard Jessica walking down the hallway and closing her bedroom door down the hall. I looked over and saw Reid lying next to me, his blue eyes watching me closely.

"How are you, buddy?" He looked concerned. He brushed my hair back and rubbed his thumb over my jaw.

"I'm good, I think?" I shrugged my shoulders. I honestly didn't know since I hadn't moved yet. I was kind of scared, to be honest. He was pretty large, and he hadn't exactly been gentle. Not that I would have wanted anything less than what he gave me.

He looked like he was feeling remorse for what we had done, and I never wanted him to feel that. I leaned up on one arm so I could lean over him and get his attention for once.

"Listen to me, Reid Johnson. Don't you dare tell me you are sorry for what we did! It was perfect—the most amazing experience of my life. I loved every single second of it. You've ruined me for any other man." I declared.

I immediately found myself flat on my back and a snarling Reid in my face. "There will never be another man!" His declaration made me laugh. "Why are you laughing?" He questioned, but I noticed his eyes get snagged on my breasts as they shook with my laughter. I snickered —such a guy thing to do.

"You're adorable when you're jealous." I kissed his cheek and then shoved him and slid off the bed. I groaned with my first step. Yep, I would be feeling him for the next few days. I squealed when he snatched me up in his arms and carried me into the bathroom, and stepped into the shower, turning his back to the shower head when he turned it on, taking the brunt of the cold water until it heated up.

I wrapped my arms around his shoulders and kissed his cheek. "Awwww, my hero!"

"Anything for you." He winked and set me down in the warm water. I watched as he picked up my bottle of body wash and popped the lid, and sniffed it before pouring some into his hand, then proceeded to wash every inch of me, paying particular attention to my boobs.

CHAPTER 27

Paige

Reid spent the night with me again but left early in the morning to run home for a shower and a change of clothes.

We hadn't made love again since I was so sore from the first time, but that hadn't stopped us from exploring other aspects of our new love life. Both of us had ideas about how we could entertain each other and were eager to do so as two recently deflowered virgins. Reid turned red and made me promise to never call him that again by tickling me until I couldn't breathe.

I was pulling into the school parking lot and didn't see Reid's motorcycle, so I sat in my Jeep until I finally heard the rumble of his engine. My smile spread over my face, and my whole body grew warm at the promise of being near him again in just a few minutes. I was getting as bad as Lisa was when she acted like she was having Chad withdrawals. I may have owed her an apology for giving her a hard time. I finally understood.

I grabbed my bag and hopped out of the Jeep and locked the doors since I still hadn't taken the doors and top off yet, and practically skipped over to where Reid had backed his bike into a spot. I stopped and watched as he pulled his helmet off and shook out his hair. I watched the way his jeans clung to his muscular thighs and how his ass-kicker boots were flat on the ground as he sat on his motorcycle while he stowed his helmet on the back of his seat.

His head turned, and his eyes met mine, a sensual promise in the depths of the blue.

"Get over here, buddy." He demanded.

I grinned and got over there.

He wrapped his hands around my waist and hauled me across his lap until I was sitting across his legs and didn't waste two seconds before he had his hand in my hair that he had convinced me to leave down for the first time in years, and was kissing me deeply.

I sighed into the kiss and held on to his shoulders while he showed me how much he had missed me in the short time we'd been apart that morning.

"How's your head?" He asked me after he broke the kiss and rested his forehead against mine.

I couldn't help the giggle that broke out of me. "You do realize that's approximately the tenth time you've asked me that since we woke up, right?"

He kissed my bruised temple lightly and looked into my eyes, searching for some sign of pain, I guessed. "Humor me?"

I sighed, "I'm not going to lie, there is a bit of an ache, but the pain pills are keeping it very manageable."

"You'll tell me if it gets worse." It wasn't a request, and I didn't think he intended for it to be one. But, I knew it came from a place of worry and even love, so I just nodded. He looked at me for another long minute before he seemed satisfied and then surprised me by smacking my butt and growled, "Alright, buddy, get your cute butt up and let's get going."

I yelped and slipped off his lap and onto the pavement. I reached down to pick up my bag, and mock glared at him. "I'm going to get you back for that," I warned, rubbing a hand over the barely-there sting. He didn't hurt me. If anything, he lit a small flame in my belly.

He snickered at me and winked, "I'm looking forward to it."

He took my hand and led me towards the doors. It wasn't until we were halfway across the parking lot that I noticed all the students staring at the two of us. I could feel my cheeks turn bright pink. I hated being the center of attention and being on these kid's radars never ended up being a good thing for me.

I was seconds from running back to my Jeep when something flew at me from the side and collided with me, making me yelp in surprise.

"You dirty little bitch!" Lisa glared at me and then turned to Reid. "If you hurt her, I will castrate you." She looked back at me before Reid could say anything at all. "I'm sad you didn't call me after you got hurt, and I'm sad you didn't tell me about this little development between the two of you." She waved her hand between Reid and me, and I felt my nose start to sting because she was right; she was my only friend for years, but I hadn't even thought to call her to reassure her after the attack. I felt like shit because I had obviously hurt her, and that was never my intention.

She surprised me when she sighed heavily and then hugged me hard. "I understand, and I don't blame you. I've been a shitty friend to you for such a long time. I'm not surprised you didn't think to call me." I watched as a tear slowly slipped down her cheek before she brushed it away. "I've been so wrapped up with Chad that I haven't made any time for you in months." She laughed bitterly. "I can't even remember the last time we went to a movie or out to eat together. Are you okay, babes? Can we have lunch together, please? We can double date in the school cafeteria, and then we can make plans for a girl's night." Her eyes were pleading.

"Lisa, I love you! I don't blame you for spending time with your hot boyfriend."

"Hey! No calling other guys hot!" Reid growled from behind me.

Both Lisa and I started giggling and looked at each other before hugging again. "Did you forget we eat together at lunch every day?" She snorted at me. "We'll talk later, okay?" I whispered just as the warning bell rang out, and Lisa nodded and gave me a half-smile, just tilting up one side of her mouth. She still looked so sad, and I hated that I had put that look on her face. But, she was right. I loved her, but somewhere along the way, we stopped hanging out, and she spent all of her time with Chad. I guess I stopped thinking that she was the first person to share things with.

She put her arm through mine and started dragging me through the doors with Reid on our heels. We got a lot of looks from all the students, and I remembered what most of them had seen outside in the parking lot, and I felt my cheeks grow hot again. I was going to have to get used to being on display if I hung around Reid. He was as popular as I was an outcast; we made an interesting pair that people would love gossiping about.

I kept my eyes down, trying to avoid seeing the sneers on the faces of the cheerleaders that we were passing. I squeezed Lisa's arm as tight as I could just as I heard her take a deep breath. I just knew she was going to go off on them and had to head her off at the pass before she could get started.

"We don't have time!" I hissed. "You guys need to get to class. The bell is going to be ringing in just a minute."

She huffed and crossed her arms. "Those trophy wives in training need to be taught a lesson."

"Yeah, well, now isn't a good time. Maybe schedule it in when you don't have 30 seconds to get to class."

"Yeah, yeah. Love you bitch!" she yelled as she walked off, and then she suddenly squealed when she saw Chad and, predictably, jumped in his arms.

I turned to Reid, "You need to get going, too." I said, looking up at his handsome face. It suddenly dawned on me that I now have the right to touch his fantastic hair and reached up to brush it back from his face and tucked it behind his ear.

He grinned down at me, his cheek crease making my heart pitter-patter slightly quicker than it had been a few seconds ago. "A lunch double date, huh?"

I shrugged my shoulders.

"I'd love to get to know your friend better." He leaned down and softly brushed his lips against mine. "But we've both got to run to not be late." He kissed me one more time, just the quickest smooch before backing up. Right before he turned around, he called out, "Love you, buddy!" Then he was gone, disappearing in the sea of bodies all rushing to first period.

I walked to the office in a daze, practically floating on a cloud of warmth and fuzziness. I walked in and sat in my usual chair, and just stared at the wall in front of me. I thought of the last 24 hours and sighed. It was amazing. He was amazing. And he loved me. And the things he did to my body. I felt goosebumps cover my arms and smiled wistfully. I wondered when I could get him to do all those things again.

"Ahhhh! I know that look!" Mrs. Walker called out.

"Wh-what look?" I questioned as I spun my chair to face my favorite person in the whole school. Okay, my favorite adult. "I don't know what look you're talking about." I reached into my bag to pull out my book and realized I hadn't read at all since before the incident.

"Oh, honey pie, you are just too precious. That man is just like my Reggie, and Reggie was never the kind to let moss grow under his feet. Nope, that boy put his claim on you."

I just looked at her over the top of my book and hummed my agreement.

"Honey, you let that man show you how serious he is about you." She paused until I looked at her again. "But you make sure he knows you want to take care of him, too. If you let a man like that, he will get lost in his need to be everything he thinks you need and will forget that you two are a team. You aren't a weak girl."

I closed my book and looked down at my lap.

"No, don't you look like that! Other girls, they might have crawled into themselves after everything you've gone through. You lost your parents and were moved across the country to a place that has been less than welcoming. You don't think the administration doesn't see what the students do to you here? We see it. Those little bastards are smart, though, and we can't do much about it. But instead of crawling into a hole and trying to disappear, you've made yourself strong in your own way."

I shook my head. "I'm not strong, Mrs. Walker. I could probably tell you where every stain and crack is in the floor in this entire school because of how much I've stared at the floor as I walk."

"Avoiding conflict doesn't mean you're weak, honey. It means you're smart. No, what makes you strong is that while everyone else was doing their best to tear you down, you were building your future. You are going to be valedictorian, and when you are up on that stage and standing behind that podium giving all those students that tried to hold you down a speech about their future, you look them in the eye and tell them that you made it. Not despite them, because of them. They pushed you and gave you the strength you needed to become the amazing young woman you are."

"I kinda don't want to give them any credit." I gave a watery laugh.

"Nah, I think you would have been at the top even if you were the most popular girl, but wouldn't it be a kick in the teeth for them to think it's their fault that you are better than them?" She winked and turned back to her computer.

I wasn't sure what to think. I liked the thought of rubbing it in their faces, but I also really didn't want to give the bullies a single bit of credit for my success. They didn't deserve it.

I opened up my book and immersed myself back into the world of pirates and dashing London gentlemen that weren't really gentlemen at all.

CHAPTER 28

Paige

When Reid and I walked into third period hand in hand, we had the entire class staring at us. But, of course, that was nothing new since every step we'd taken since walking into the school was being watched. I didn't know how long it would last, but I had a sinking feeling that I needed to get used to it.

"Mr. Johnson, Ms. Anderson, good to have you both back in class. We started a new assignment that you are already two days late for. I think that in order to get you caught up, you should be paired up with students that are already caught up." He waved to a couple of students. "You two can pair up with Suzanne and Charles."

Reid and I had been sitting in our usual seats, but when he heard that we wouldn't be working together on this project, he sat up and looked like he was ready to jump to his feet.

"Mr. Rhodes, I think I need to object. I'm sure these students are lovely people and would make great study partners, but I'm afraid it just wouldn't work with my or Paige's schedules. You see, between football and all my other AP classes I have to study for, my time is already pretty stretched. I wouldn't be able to make time for another partner when my study buddy here," He put his hand over mine that was resting on my notebook, "Are already spending all our time studying for those other classes together. It would be a terrible shame to fall behind because I would have to cut my other studying short."

Mr. Rhodes sighed heavily and rubbed the bridge of his nose. "I'm not sure if that was the most persuasive or most ridiculous reasoning I've ever heard."

"Whichever works in my favor, sir," Reid said with a grin.

Mr. Rhodes sighed again and looked at me. "Ms. Anderson, do you believe that you would do better staying partnered with Mr. Johnson, or would it be better to get caught up with a different student?"

"Honestly, sir, Reid is right. We already spend so much time studying our other subjects that it would actually take time out of the day to switch partners when we are already together."

"And you believe you can get caught up?"

I looked over to Reid. Spend even more time with him over the next couple of days? "Yes, sir," I said without taking my eyes off of Reids. He grinned at me, and I couldn't hold in my returning smile.

"Alright then, I'm trusting you to get the assignment done. Don't make me look bad." Mr. Rhodes walked over to his desk, picked up his heavy course guide, and pulled his reading glasses out of his pocket. "Let's all turn to page 152 and start reading out loud. We'll start with Ryan.

As all the students flipped open their books and looked for the spot, I looked up and saw Suzanne staring at Reid with a sad look on her face. The poor girl was probably looking forward to working with him and got her hopes crushed. I felt bad even though she looked like she was in love with him.

Same, girl. Same.

THE GUYS INSISTED that us girls get comfortable at our table in the cafeteria while they did the heaving lifting. I could have argued that I didn't need a big strong man to take care of me, but I noticed that, while Reid was being overly demanding, the look in his eyes was almost pleading. He really wanted to do this for me so I wouldn't have to. That's when I realized that he wanted to take care of me, and by letting him, I was taking care of him, too. It didn't make me weak to allow him to get my food tray. I was giving him something he needed.

But we would have to talk about the way he demanded I sit while he did his thing.

"I really am sorry about abandoning you, Paige." Lisa was quiet, more than I think I had ever seen her. She was my loud, boisterous friend with the beautiful dark skin and the long braids that I wished I could pull off. She also had the tall, muscular boyfriend that she'd been with since forever. Yet, she was the one that never stopped standing up for me. Even while she spent almost all her time with Chad, she still never stopped.

"Lisa, I know. Seriously, it's okay. I didn't take it personally."

"I'd like to change things. I want to hang out more, spend time on double dates and have girl time, just the two of us."

"I'd really like that."

"And it's not just because he's a hotty either." She looked at me, her face turning serious. "I mean it. I don't want things to change just because you have a guy, and it will make it easier to hang out, like on double dates. I don't want you to think that's all the reason for my change of heart. Honestly, when I'd found out you'd been hurt at school, I realized how much I had pushed you away."

I reached over and hugged her to me, hard. "Lisa, I don't think that at all. I love you. You're one of the only people in the world that I can say that to. You never made me feel like you were pushing me away. I knew you needed alone time with your boyfriend."

She leaned back and looked at me. "Yeah, I did. And I still do, so don't be trying to take my sugar time away." We both giggled. "But seriously, we will figure out how to balance everything. You have a lot of studying, and the guys have their sports. Even though Chad isn't currently playing, they still have conditioning twice a week. The coach wants to keep them ready and at the top of their game once the season starts."

"Well, we can make sure we have lunch together every day, which is something we pretty much have already done for the most part. And we can plan to eat after school every Monday or something. Then, maybe on Saturday afternoons, we could all go see a movie?"

Lisa nodded, "Those all sound like good ideas. But we still have to fit in girl time somewhere. So why don't we do girl time every other Saturday or do girl time Saturday afternoon and then do couple time Saturday night every other week so we could have sugar time, too."

"When are we having sugar time?" Chad asked as he dropped a tray in front of Lisa and kissed her cheek when she grinned up at him. "You better not be taking away my sugar time, woman."

"You hush!" She swatted him with a french fry before sticking it in her mouth. "Paige and I are just trying to come up with a schedule that will work for all of us. Where's Reid?" She asked when she realized I hadn't started eating and handed me a fry.

Chad sighed and opened up one of his three milk cartons. "That Jenna chick stopped him."

We all three looked over where we could see Reid holding a tray that was loaded down with food and cartons of milk. He looked irritated but was trying not to just push Jenna out of his way, who was blocking his path to our table.

I made a strangled sound in the back of my throat. That girl was relentless. "I think she's pregnant," I said without thinking.

"Wait. What? Really?" Lisa leaned forward as if she'd be able to look through her skin and see the fetus that may or may not be there.

"Shit, forget I said that. It's none of my business."

"Uh uh, girl. Spill it."

I sighed and watched as Reid shifted from foot to foot and glanced over to me, and gestured with his head to go over and save him. I popped another fry in my mouth and wished I had ketchup. Lisa never got ketchup.

"If you watch her, she touches her stomach a lot, and the other morning she turned green before running to the bathroom."

"Maybe she's got irritable bowel syndrome."

I laughed out loud as Reid scowled at me. "Maybe." I swallowed the dry french fry and sighed. I need to go save him so I can get my lunch."

"You just want the ketchup. I told you, you should just keep a bottle of it in your bag."

"I tried that once, but someone stepped on my backpack, and ketchup got on everything inside. I had to redo all my homework."

"Well, go save your man before preggo decides that he would make the perfect baby daddy."

"Yeah, I'm afraid that ship has sailed." I got up and started walking towards Reid. How could she not see how irritated he was. And that my food was getting cold. Well, colder. It wasn't as if cafeteria food was ever hot and fresh.

I tapped her shoulder, interrupting her pretty much begging him to have dinner with her family tonight. "Excuse me?"

"What?" She snapped and turned to look at me. She must not have realized it was me because her irritation shot straight to anger. She shoved past me and shot out over her shoulder to Reid, "Never mind. I'll just tell my parents you don't care about them anymore!"

Reid stared after her as she stormed off. I watched as his expression changed rapidly. I caught a hint of anger, sadness, frustration, and determination. He looked down at me. "It's not as if I was close to her parents. I only ever saw them when my parents had the occasional dinner party." He shrugged and reached out with one hand to pull me back towards the table.

When he pulled me down to sit next to him, I looked over at Lisa, who was still arguing about, making sure they had enough sugar time. They made me giggle at their antics. I remembered when they first started having sex. Lisa made sure to relate every detail of the experience, and I was sure, looking back now since I finally had my own experience to go off of, that the time had been pretty magical for her, too. He had rented a hotel room and set up the whole cliché of rose petals and candles. She had complained about having rose petals stuck to her ass afterwards, but she had done it with a dreamy look on her face.

I looked down at the tray that Reid and I were apparently sharing and noticed the massive pile of empty ketchup packets and the lake of ketchup he had created next to the fries. I gave him a huge grin. Awww. He knew me so well already.

"Personally, I think if we are creative, we'll manage to get in plenty of sugar time." Reid imparted.

I started choking on my fry and looked up at him with big eyes as I took a big drink of the milk he had pushed into my hands.

"Seriously?" I choked out.

"Of course, buddy. Now that I've had you, you don't think I'd be able to resist your cute little body? Honestly, I think it would be a great reward for studying, don't you think?" He smirked at me and took the milk carton back, and handed me another fry that was perfectly covered in ketchup. "Work first, then reward. Am I right?" He winked and picked up his hamburger, and took a huge bite.

"Uh-huh," I mumbled as I watched him lick his lips.

"You go, girl!" Lisa whooped and stuffed a carrot stick in her mouth, crunching down.

"Oh, god, you guys!" I facepalmed. "Can we not talk about sugar at the lunch table?" I mumbled under my hand.

Everyone laughed, and we finally went back to eating since our lunchtime was already almost up.

"So, what are we doing this afternoon?" I asked once my ketchup lake was emptied and there were six empty cartons of milk littering the table.

"Well, I have practice after school, and the coach already sent out a message to the team that he was going to work us extra hard today due to taking two days off. But we have to get caught up on the English assignment. So I could come over afterward, and we could go over everything. Between the two of us, we could have it caught up tonight or tomorrow at the latest."

I nodded my head. "Yeah. I could go through the work and then give you the cliff notes version as soon as you get to my house." I looked at him. "Or would you rather I go to your place?"

"It will probably be easier for me to just go to yours, so you don't have to pack everything up. Why don't I bring you something to eat? I can go home and take a shower and then bring you whatever my mom made for dinner?"

I blinked up at him. "Your mom won't mind?"

He put his arm around me. "Baby, my mom loves you. If I told her I was going to take you some of her food, she'd make something special just for you. But I won't because when she gets excited about cooking, it takes her all day to make a feast, and I want to be able to get to you sometime tonight."

CHAPTER 29

Reid

For the rest of the week, we spent several hours working on our English assignment along with the other studying that we already had to do. We didn't just have English to get caught up on. Having so many AP classes and missing two days of school really pushed us behind. But it was Friday now, and we were finally caught up.

We hadn't had a chance to make love again since we were exhausted by the time we were done studying. I would leave her with a hot kiss and drag myself back home for some much needed sleep before my alarm going off and starting the next day with the same shit all over again.

I had started following the page that was posting pictures of me. It was disturbing, to say the least. Times, when I hadn't even realized I was being watched, were being documented by pictures and posted by some anonymous person. I was starting to believe that Paige was right; it wasn't Jessica. For some reason, as strong as she had come on to me since the summer months ago, she had barely even looked at me since Paige had been attacked.

I thought about Jenna, but it didn't fit for me for her either. I mean, yeah, she was still trying to get me to talk to her, and I often found her staring at me, often with tears in her eyes, but I had a gut feeling that she wasn't the person taking the pictures.

Paige called the person a stalker, and I had to concede that was pretty much what the person was. No one had approached me. Well, that wasn't true. Every day before, during, and after football practice, I had a gaggle of cheerleaders trying to get my attention, but I didn't even look at them, let alone talk to them. I wasn't happy to let anyone get in my way when all I wanted to do was get back to my little buddy, even if all we'd been doing was studying until we nearly passed out.

I looked in the mirror, and straightened my red tie. I made sure the sleeves of my black shirt were neatly rolled up to my elbows. No way was I going to wear a white shirt in this heat. Black may be hot, but at least it didn't show sweat stains.

I skipped down the stairs and kissed my mom on the cheek, who was standing at the sink in her big robe. She smiled at me and handed me a breakfast burrito wrapped in a paper towel. I thanked her and took a giant bite as I put on my backpack and grabbed my helmet and keys from the table by the front door. I'd have the burrito gone before I even reached my bike. My mom was an angel, and it made me want to give that to my little buddy, too. I didn't think her aunt had much of the maternal gene. But I was willing to share my mother with my girl if she'd let me.

If I could, I would move her in with me, but I didn't think her uncle would even consider it. At least not before she turned 18. I guess I could understand that. But, until I could have her with me every night and morning, I was going to do my best to spend as much time with her as I could. If I could manage to spend a night here and there with her at either of our houses, I thought I might be able to hold back my need to kidnap her and hold her hostage.

I roared my bike down the road. My house wasn't too far from the school, so my drive was pretty short. I thought about taking my girl on a long ride in the country. I'd have to plan that out soon. I was sure she'd love it.

I pulled into the parking lot and wasn't surprised to see the majority of the students wearing red. The usual cheerleaders were grouped in the lot wearing their cheer outfits, and the football players were like me, wearing ties and dress shirts under their jerseys. It was hot as fuck, but the coach insisted that we showed school spirit. He said it would get the other students excited for the games. I honestly didn't think there was anything that could actually hurt their school spirit. My last school was nothing like this one. No one cared about football. The visitor's stands held more people than our home stands ever did in California.

I continued to scan the lot and finally saw my girl pull up in her red Jeep. She looked hot as fuck riding around in that thing with the doors and roof off. Of course, now that she had started wearing her hair down, she had to braid it back while she drove so it wasn't a mess by the time she got to school. I smirked, thinking about every time I had the pleasure of taking that braid out and running my fingers through it.

I stowed my helmet and hefted my bag higher on my shoulder as I made my way over to my girl. I heard a whistle and looked over to see one of the fuckers from the JV team. I grunted when I saw he was whistling at someone other than my girl. He still had a fat lip from when I punched him two days ago. He'd run his mouth during practice, asking me if the ice queen had given my cock frostbite. After I'd shut his mouth for him, I was pretty confident that he'd think twice before making shitty comments about girls in the future.

I leaned into her Jeep, her seat putting her almost to my level, making it easy to grip her braid and tilt her head at the perfect angle. I kissed her until she was moaning, and we were both gasping for much needed oxygen.

"You're riding with Lisa to the game, right?" I double-checked with her. The game was an away game, but luckily it was only one town over, and the drive was relatively short, but I still didn't want her driving that late at night by herself.

She smiled at me. "Yep! We are riding in with Chad in his truck."

"I would ride back with you if I could, baby." I leaned my forehead against hers, hating that it would be even longer until we could be alone, but school rules said we had to ride back on the bus.

She touched my cheek. "I know, Reid. It's okay. We will wait here in the parking lot for you so you and I can leave as soon as you get back."

"And then we can have sugar time," I smirked and winked.

She laughed and pushed me back so she could hop down. "Maybe if you win." She gave me a sassy grin before reaching into the back seat for her bag. I had to bite back a groan and the urge to adjust my hard-on at seeing her confidence. Seeing her in those short shorts and my jersey didn't help my cock situation either.

She had changed so much since I met her in such a short time. She was like a flower that finally got the sunlight it had been craving and had its chance to bloom. I knew I had something to do with it, but it was mostly her. She had finally found her self-confidence. I was just glad that I was a part of that and had a front-row seat to watch it happen. I vowed never to let her lose that confidence again. As long as I was alive, I would do anything to keep her in the sun.

I put my arm around her and pulled her into me, and kissed her head. "Come on, let's hit the locker. I'm actually curious to see how they decorated it this time. Do you know if Jessica is still my assigned cheerleader?" I didn't care who it was as long as they didn't try anything with me or try to get between my girl and me.

Paige frowned. "I don't know if she is or not. But, honestly, I hope it is."

That surprised me. "Why?"

"Because she knows that we are together, and I think she respects that now. After everything that happened and her parents finding out what she's done in the past has really made her change, she doesn't glare at me so much anymore. The rest of the cheerleaders wouldn't have a problem trying to break us up, though. So, yeah, I hope it's still Jessica."

I grunted. She was right, but I was holding my opinion on Jessica in reserve for now. I wasn't so sure she had made that much of a change, but at least she wasn't trying to hurt my girl anymore.

We passed several kids that wanted to talk, but I just shook them off with 'hellos' and 'laters' until we were in front of our shared locker. Then, we both just stood there, neither one of us knowing what to say. Or think.

The decorations were pretty much the same as last week's. I wouldn't be surprised, really, if it was mostly just recycled. But what was new were the pictures that covered most of the locker over the hideous red glitter. They were mostly the same pictures that were posted on my stalker's page, all the ones of me in my jersey at practice or from last week's football game.

The largest one in the center was of me catching a football. It was a pretty good picture, actually, one my mom would probably have liked to frame, but it had a note written on it in red marker and a big red heart.

I love you, Reid
Your #1 Fan

"WHAT THE FUCK." I mumbled.

"Okay, this is creepy and out of control," Paige said. She turned to me. "I think we need to let those police officers know. The ones that came to my house. This is getting bad, Reid."

"Yeah, it is. Do you have their card with you?"

She shook her head. "No, I think my uncle has it, though."

I sighed. "Alright. You call him. I'm going to take a picture of it before someone takes them off. I don't know if the cops can dust them for prints or whatever, but we probably shouldn't touch them."

She didn't say anything next to me, so I looked down at her. She was holding her phone in her hand, but she was still staring at that center picture with wide eyes and a white face that made her bruise stand out even more. I couldn't hold in my growl and grabbed her to my chest, wrapping my arms around her.

"We will find out who did this is and make them stop, I swear." She nodded her head but didn't say anything. I didn't think she believed me. And truthfully? I didn't believe myself, either.

"What are you guys doing?" Lisa walked up beside us and then let out a breathy, "What the fuck?"

The hall was getting pretty crowded since first period would be starting soon, but mostly everyone was beginning to crowd around our locker. There were some murmured conversations I couldn't make out, but it was easy to tell most of the students were freaked out. Everyone knew what had happened to Paige the other day right here at school, and the police had interviewed several of them. Everyone was aware of the social media page as well, and it was evident between the two that whoever was behind this infatuation was a little unhinged.

I looked around the crowd, and my eyes snagged on Jessica. Her face was almost as white as Paige's had been and she looked about as freaked out as my girl. Her eyes darted from the locker to Paige, and her eyes grew concerned. I watched as she pulled her phone out and pressed a couple of buttons, and brought her phone up to her ear. Before she turned to walk away, I heard her say, "Hey, dad..."

My girl was right. It wasn't her cousin. So if it wasn't her, then who the hell was it?

CHAPTER 30

Paige

My knee wouldn't stop bouncing as I sat on the visitor side of the football stadium. It was just as packed as last week had been. But, at least this week, we had some shade to help cut down some of the heat from the blazing sun. The sun wouldn't go down for another couple of hours, so I was incredibly grateful for that shade.

"Here, girl." Lisa passed me a large soda cup and a tray of nachos and cheese. If there was one thing I liked almost as much as ketchup and french fries, it was chips and hot, spicy nacho cheese.

"Thanks, Chad." I smiled over Lisa at him as he waved off my thanks and took a large sip of his soda.

"How are you doing?" Lisa whispered in my ear. I shrugged. I didn't know what to say. I was nervous and couldn't stop looking at everyone, wondering if they were the one that was stalking Reid and trying to hurt me to get to him. She squeezed my knee.

I swept my eyes over the crowd again and tried to spot anyone that could be responsible. There were several people with cameras and even more with their phones out taking pictures. I counted at least ten people with jerseys that had Johnson on the back. I cursed under my breath. It was going to be next to impossible to figure out who it was.

The morning had been long and hectic. Jessica had called her dad, and he called the police in charge of the case. They came out and bagged the photos and interviewed several of us again. Jessica had spent the longest amount of time in the office. So when it was my turn to be interviewed, I made sure to insist that it couldn't have been Jessica. I just didn't believe that she would go that far. And I was convinced that there was someone else she was interested in.

Jenna could have done it, maybe. I wasn't ruling her out completely, but she didn't show up to school until after ten with a doctor's note. So, unless she snuck in the school after hours last night, it couldn't have been her either.

I sighed and took a bite of my chip, barely able to enjoy the spicy goodness of the cheese sauce. It couldn't be ruled out entirely that it was a guy, but it was highly improbable.

I had finished my nachos and took a big drink of my soda when the announcement was made that the teams were coming out. I stood up with everyone else when our team came out onto the field, running through the giant banner that the cheerleaders had stretched out. When Reid's name and number were announced, I cheered for him as loud as I could. I didn't know how he could have heard me over the racket that everyone else was making, but he somehow looked right up at me where I was sitting in the crowd and pointed at me, tapped his finger to his heart, and pointed back at me again. If I weren't worried about falling and rolling down the metal bleachers to my death, I would have swooned.

Then I heard behind me some squealing and excited screeching. "Did you see that?! He pointed at me! Oh my god! I can't believe Reid Johnson pointed at me! I have to see him after the game!" Lisa and I looked at each other and snickered. Chad looked back at the girls that were sitting behind me and snorted before shaking his head and looking back at the field.

Lisa leaned over and whispered to him, and he responded. Then she leaned back over to me. "He said they look like they're in middle school." We both giggled. It was cute. We both remembered what it was like to have a crush on an older guy at that age. They were harmless.

By the time the game was half over, it wasn't quite as cute.

The girls hadn't stopped going on and on about how hot Reid was and about how much they were in love with him. The one who believed Reid had been looking at her throughout the game was insistent that she would marry him and have lots and lots of his babies. She had already named about 5 of them. It was getting on my nerves. Though I wasn't opposed to stealing a couple of the names she had picked out. They were pretty good ones.

By the time the game was over, I was on the verge of laughing until I cried. Or, ready to smack a middle schooler.

She had their wedding planned and where they were going to live. As a pro football player's wife, they'd be rich, of course, and have a giant house and fancy cars. I had to grit my teeth to stop myself from turning around and had to hold on to Lisa. Chad ended up putting his arm around her shoulders and held her tight to him. Her eyes were looking a bit murderous.

When the game was over, we waited our turn to walk down the bleachers to make our way onto the field. Somehow those girls ended up staying right behind us until we made it to the bottom of the stairs. They must have finally lost their patience because they pushed their way through Lisa and me.

"Excuse me!" The future Mrs. Johnson said to us. Then, she turned around and looked at me. "You know, you really shouldn't wear another woman's man's jersey. It's disrespectful."

I cocked my head to the side and studied her. She was already as tall as I was with at least a couple more inches left to grow. She would be a tall, beautiful girl one day. She had stunning green eyes and curly black hair. She was definitely going to break hearts. "Is that so? What if they are fans?"

She shook her head and smirked at me. "As his woman, I would have the final say, and I say that no one else should wear his name or number."

I nodded my head at her logic. Sure, when he was pro, it would totally be up to the wife and not the commissioner, coach, or team owner. "Okay." I shrugged.

She was about to say something else, I could see the spark of something mean just growing in the depths of her eyes, and I couldn't wait to hear what it was, but it was interrupted by the cheering of the crowd.

I stood up on my tiptoes to try to see over everybody and noticed the girl trying to do the same thing. Chad raised his hand and waved, then pointed down at me. My heart rate picked up, knowing that Reid was about to come through the crowd and sweep me up in his arms.

Seconds later, the crowd parted, and Reid smiled huge, flashing his straight white teeth. He was exactly what I expected him to be, completely soaked with sweat and covered in dirt and grass stains. He never looked hotter.

He started towards me, and the girls started towards him. I almost snickered when he went around the girls and came straight for me. He picked me up, and I wrapped my legs around his hips as well as I could with all his gear on and let him kiss me breathless. When he lifted his lips from mine, I managed to say, "congratulations" in a shaky voice.

"You're mine tonight." He growled against my lips, making my toes curl.

Lisa laughed and cleared her throat. "Hey, Reid? You have a couple of fans that want to say hi."

Reid turned around but refused to let me slip down his body. Instead, he kept one hand under my ass and held out a hand to shake the girl's hands.

"Did you enjoy the game?"

Neither one of them seemed able to speak and just nodded their heads. Surprisingly, neither one of them seemed upset that they were no longer in the running for future Mrs. Johnson. Instead, they just seemed to be excited to meet a high school football player that had a high chance of going pro one day in the near future.

The girl with the black curly hair looked at me in awe, and I winked at her. She blushed in embarrassment, but I lost sight of her when Reid pulled my head back to his and took my lips in another searing kiss.

"Meet me in the school parking lot in about 45 minutes?"

All I could do was nod my head.

He nipped my bottom lip and then ran his tongue over it to soothe the slight sting. "Good," he whispered and then placed me back on my feet. He turned to Chad and shook his hand while thanking him for looking out for his girl. I internally squealed just like that middle school girl had. He was talking about me! I was his girl.

"WHERE ARE WE GOING?" I yelled over the sound of the wind.

We were on his motorcycle, driving through the dark. I had my arms wrapped tight around him, and my hands gripped tight to his abs, my head resting against his back. I didn't care where we went. Nothing mattered at that moment except him and me and the motorcycle that carried us into the night.

He squeezed my leg and ran his hand up and down my thigh before putting his hand back on the handlebar without answering.

We started slowing, and I realized he had brought us back to the same lake that he had brought me last week. I couldn't believe that it had only been a week, even less that we had made the steps to make our relationship official. Yet, it seemed like it had been so much longer. And somehow, as if it had been only seconds.

He rode slowly towards a glow that could I could see cutting through the darkness. I squinted my eyes so I could see better and then lifted the visor on my helmet. I had to wait until we rolled closer to finally see what the lights were.

In the little clearing next to the water with its own shoreline, strands of fairy lights were in the trees giving off a gentle glow of light. A blanket was already laid out on the ground. There was another folded up on top of that one and a small cooler sitting next to the blanket.

I continued to sit on the bike and watched as Reid climbed off and shook his hair out after removing his helmet. Then he walked over to the blanket and picked it up, shaking it out before laying it back out onto the ground how it was.

He turned to me and shrugged. "I wanted to make sure it was still clean." He walked back to me and removed my helmet. "Come on, baby." His voice was husky. When he took my hand to help guide me off the back of the bike, I realized that my breaths were coming out quick and choppy.

"You did this for me?" I whispered.

He gave me a small crooked smile and looked at the ground before looking back at me with that smile. "Yeah. Is it okay?"

I cleared my throat and tried to speak over a whisper, but it wasn't happening. "It's perfect."

"Good," he whispered back at me and pulled my body into his. "I love you." His kiss was full of everything I had ever dreamed of. He was everything I had ever dreamed of and everything I never knew I wanted.

"I love you, too, Reid." I stepped back from him, and his eyes grew heated as I reached down to my shirt and lifted it over my head. I stood in front of him, baring more than just my body to him. I let him see what was inside me, my scars, my fears, my hopes, wants, and dreams. "Don't hurt me," I whispered, knowing he knew I didn't mean physically.

He took the step needed to be back in front of me and dropped to his knees. "Baby, I could never hurt you. It would be like cutting off a limb. You are more vital to me than the air I need to survive. Without you, I don't exist."

"Reid," I choked out.

He wrapped his arms around my hips and buried his face in my stomach. "I know, baby, I know."

We stayed there like that for a long minute until I ran my hand through his beautiful hair. He looked up at me, and I placed my hands along his jaw. "I need you, Reid."

"I'll always give you what you need." He got to his feet and swept me up into his arms and carried me over to the blanket, and gently laid me down.

Silently, to only the sounds of the frogs and the nighttime insects, Reid stripped me of the rest of my clothing and then his own. He took his time worshipping every inch of my body until I was writhing and crying out his name.

When he slid inside of me, both of us were breathing with heavy, shaky breaths. He held our hands linked together above my head on the blanket, and I felt wholly surrounded by him. His eyes told me how much I meant to him, and just to make sure I understood, he whispered the words in my ear.

CHAPTER 31

Paige

All four of us were laughing our asses off as we walked out of the theater. It was probably the best night I'd had, maybe ever. We watched an action film that was fun and a little bloody. It definitely kept me on the edge of my seat.

Reid had paid for the large popcorn combo, and between the two of us, it had been demolished. Now my stomach was uncomfortably full with all the greasy goodness that was movie theater popcorn.

I hugged Lisa goodbye and laughed when Chad picked her up, hauled her over his shoulder, and shouted about it being time for sugar. As he walked off, I watched Lisa smacking his butt with her palm shouting back at him, "I'll show you sugar, you big brute!"

Chad smacked her ass right back, and the last thing I heard was, "That's the point, woman!"

I was laughing so hard I had tears in my eyes. I grinned up at Reid when he pulled on my belt loop and tugged me to him. He lowered his face and nuzzled my neck, making me groan...right before he blew a raspberry on my skin. I squealed and pushed away, but he didn't let me get far before he was tugging me right back and wrapped his arms around me.

"What do you want to do now, buddy?" He growled into my neck, taking a nip at my skin and soothing it with a lick of his tongue.

I rolled my head, giving him better access, and then hopped up, using his shoulders as leverage. I wrapped my legs around his lean waist and took his hair in one of my hands, and tugged his head back.

"I think it's time for some sugar," I whispered before lowering my head and taking his lips. I could feel his hardness at the juncture of my thighs. I wiggled my hips, making my clit rub just right against his cock. "Mmmmm. Definitely need to go somewhere for sugar," I groaned.

His big hands were under my thighs, holding me tight, and I was conscious of his fingers and how close they were in proximity to my pussy. I didn't even look when he started moving. I knew he was headed towards my Jeep. I would have told him to hurry, but my mouth was busy kissing his neck.

I expected him to stop, and I even expected him to set me down but what I hadn't expected was the heavy curses coming from him.

"What?" I asked and turned around, feeling my eyes grow wide.

My Jeep. My beautiful cherry red Jeep that was less than two years old was utterly and completely trashed. The headlights and taillights were smashed, the windshield was gone, the leather seats were slashed. Dents covered the hood. It looked like someone had taken a sledgehammer to every inch. There was too much damage to list individually.

I stood there for I didn't know how long and just stared, not comprehending what I was seeing. I vaguely heard Reid making a phone call but didn't hear the words. All I could hear was the rushing of blood through my head.

I jumped when I felt hands touch me, but I knew immediately that they were Reid's. He wrapped me up in his strong arms. I wasn't sure what to think. It was just a car, but it was my car. I was also sure this had to be related to the other things that were happening. This is what law enforcement called escalating. I just knew it. And if it had jumped to this, what else was the person capable of?

Flashing lights broke through my musings, and we both looked towards the police cars headed our way. We continued to stand there holding each other while the police asked questions and looked at all the damage. It was only a few minutes later that my uncle and Reid's father pulled up in their cars. I guessed that while I was spacing out, Reid had been busy informing everyone.

"Paige!" Uncle James exclaimed, looking from my Jeep to me and back again. "Are you okay, squirt?" I think his words and that nickname I hadn't realized I missed until he said it the other day is what finally broke the dam on my shock.

I burst into tears and held out my arms to Uncle James, needing to be comforted by the closest thing I had to a parent.

"I-I d-d-don't know what ha-happened!" I wailed.

"Shhhh, it will be alright, squirt. We'll get you a new car." He rubbed my back and continued to shush me. "What's most important here is that neither one of you is hurt. We'll let the police figure out who did this. Hopefully, soon they will catch the culprit, and all this will be over."

I sniffled and nodded my head. I looked back at my destroyed Jeep and took a deep breath. "I'm scared, Uncle James."

He hugged me to him a little tighter. "Me too, squirt, me too."

I looked over and saw Reid talking to one of the police officers and watched him pull the business card the detectives gave us from his wallet. I watched as the officer looked at it, nodded his head, and started talking into his microphone. Then we heard footsteps coming our way.

A group of girls who looked like they were in their early twenties held to-go boxes from the restaurant next door to the movie theater. They looked apprehensive and gave each other looks, but as one, they moved closer.

"We, ummm, we saw what happened if you need a witness."

All of us stopped and stared at the girls, waiting to hear more information. If they saw the person that did this, then maybe everything could finally be over. I wouldn't have to worry or be scared anymore.

The police started asking questions and the girls nervously started to answer. "We parked over there," the girl pointed to a cute red coupe a couple of rows over. "There was a girl that walked up out of nowhere. We didn't see a car or anything, but she was carrying this metal bat, you know? And she came straight to this car." She pointed at my poor, abused Jeep. "Then she just took the bat in both hands and smashed the hell out of one of the headlights. We all asked her what the hell she was doing, and she said that she caught her boyfriend cheating on her."

She stopped and looked at her friends. "We've all been there, you know? We've all had a boyfriend cheat and always talked about what we would do if we were able to get revenge." She stopped and took a deep breath. "We kind of cheered her on for a minute. Then we decided that we probably shouldn't be witnesses, so we left to have dinner."

I was disappointed, but I guess I could understand. Maybe. It made me wonder what I would have done in their situation. I looked at Reid, and he looked livid. I didn't think that I had ever seen him look so angry.

I turned and looked at the girls. "That's my Jeep." I wiped my eyes, walked over to Reid, took his hand in mine, and smoothed out his clenched fist. "This is my boyfriend. He didn't cheat on anyone. He has a stalker that has fixated on hurting me."

All three girls looked sick. The one in the back hung her head. "We're so sorry we didn't stop her or call the police."

The officer that had been taking the statements asked her, "Do you have a description? Can you tell us anything about the girl?"

They all three shook their heads. "She was wearing all black and had a hoodie on with the hood covering her. She kept her head down while we were talking to her, and we couldn't see anything at all." She looked over at me. "We're really sorry."

All I could do was nod. I turned into Reid's chest and let him hold me.

"What about cameras?" Reid's dad asked. We all looked up at the light posts in the parking lot, but not one of them had a camera.

"We'll ask the businesses if they have cameras that reach out here, but I'm afraid it looks like we won't get any luck there."

The officers took the girl's information and let them leave.

"I don't understand why no one else saw her?"

"People tend to be in their own worlds. Sometimes they just don't want to get involved when they see someone commit a crime, so they pretend they never saw it." One of the officers answered my question.

A tow truck pulled up just as another police cruiser came into the lot. The same officers from the other day walked up and started talking to the ones that had arrived to take everyone's statements. They all shook hands, and the first officers left. We watched the officers that had been helping us before walk up.

"Looks like your trouble has gotten a little worse now."

I snorted, and the officer winked at me, making Reid growl.

"Unfortunately, and fortunately, we are going to have to turn your case over to detectives at this point. Before, you had a crime happen when you were attacked, and that was something that we could handle. But now that the perpetrator has escalated to this degree, it's best that a detective take over. We will still be involved, but their training and skills will be a better choice for this case."

We all shook hands, and the officers promised that a detective would be contacting us tomorrow, and I watched mournfully as my beautiful baby was loaded onto the back of a tow truck and driven away.

Reid and I stood in the parking lot with his dad and my uncle quietly for a few minutes.

"Reid," my uncle began, "we'd love to have you at our family dinner tomorrow night if you'd like to come."

Reid shook Uncle Jame's offered hand. "I'd be honored, sir."

"Good, we will see you at six sharp then." He nodded his head and turned to me. "I'll be waiting in the car."

I sighed and turned to Reid. "You don't have to come…"

"I'll be there," Reid interrupted. "I'm sorry our evening was cut short."

"Me, too," I whispered and went to my tiptoes and gave him a quick kiss.

"Call me when you get to your room, okay?"

"Okay."

"I love you." He said softly, smoothing the hair back from my eyes.

"I love you, too." I backed up until his arms fell from me. I smiled at his dad, "Bye, Mr. Johnson." I waved and turned to walk towards my uncle's car. When I climbed in, and we were driving away, I saw Reid still standing there watching me, his dad waiting for him patiently.

"He's a good young man." My uncle murmured.

"He is," I whispered back.

We were quiet the rest of the drive home. When we got out and were walking in the front door, Uncle James stopped me. "Are you sure you want to continue with this relationship right now?"

My mouth dropped open, and I stared at him in shock.

"I thought you liked him?"

He sighed and ran his hand over his face. "I do, I think he's a great kid, and he treats you well. If I had to choose a guy for you, he would have been at the top of the list." He dropped his hand and looked at me, his face looking like he'd aged ten years overnight. "I'm worried about you, Paige. This person is escalating, and I'm scared of what she will do next. You've already been hurt once. What if she goes after you again?"

He looked so distraught that my heart ached for him. For so long, I had been living in my own private world, no one cared about me, and I didn't get close to anyone. Lisa was my only friend, and even she spent so much time with her boyfriend that we weren't very close. Now I was seeing that I had someone that cared all along. I only wished he would have shown it when I needed it the most.

"I need him, Uncle James. As cliché as it makes me sound." I laughed weakly. "I love him. For so long, I felt that I had no one. Then, he came along, and without even trying, he showed me how much I meant to him."

Uncle James lightly brushed his thumb over my cheek. "Okay, squirt. I understand. But I'm here for you. Do you hear me? We are here for you. As your family, we failed you but no more. We all have to make changes in order to make things right, and I am going to lead by example."

I hugged him tightly. "Thanks, Uncle James."

"You got it, squirt. Now get up to your room and make your phone call before your young man starts pounding on my front door."

I gave a small laugh and turned towards the stairs. I was unlocking my bedroom door when I heard Jessica open her door. She was standing there in a tank top and a pair of sleep shorts, her arms crossed over her chest. Her thick dark hair was pulled up into a messy bun on the top of her head. All of that was what I would have expected from my cousin. What I didn't expect was her face. She looked worried. About me.

"Paige, are you okay? Dad ran out of the house so fast." She looked around her. It seemed she wasn't really seeing the hallway we were standing in. When she brought her eyes back to mine, they were full of concern. "He yelled to mom that something had happened to you and that he needed to go. Did something happen again?"

I stood there with a hand on my doorknob and a key in the dead-bolt that I had felt I needed to install in order to feel safe in my own bedroom, thanks to my cousin, who was currently showing concern for my well-being. I swayed on my feet a little bit and closed my eyes. I was mentally exhausted, and I wasn't sure how much more I could take.

I opened my eyes back up and gave Jessica a small, brittle smile. "A bit of car trouble. Everything will be fine, I'm sure." I twisted the key and pulled it back out of the lock. I turned my head to look at Jessica one more time to see she was biting her lip and wringing her hands. Her eyes were suspiciously glassy. I turned the doorknob and swung open my bedroom door. "Goodnight, Jessica."

I stepped into my room and was about to close the door when I heard her speak once more, quietly. "If you need anything...to talk, maybe. I don't know, whatever... I'm here."

I didn't turn to look at her. I couldn't. Her words would have been welcome years ago. Right now, I just needed to hear from the one person that had yet to let me down.

I closed the door and locked it.

CHAPTER 32

Paige

I hated Sunday dinner.

Every week it was the same thing. We dressed up and pretended to be a family. Every week Aunt Jolene would ask what her children had been up to and acted like she was listening while she drank wine and nibbled on the food that the cook we rarely saw prepared.

If she actually acted like a mother, she would already know how her children's week had been. But that was just my opinion.

It was tedious and often full of passive-aggressiveness. I hated every second of it.

It wasn't unheard of for someone to invite a guest. Jason often invited a friend and occasionally Jessica. Unfortunately, those times were the worst. Since their friends went to our school, they were always a part of the bullying I was subjected to. Having one of them sit across the table from me, sneering at me without anyone making them stop, was often torturous.

When Uncle James or Aunt Jolene had a friend or associate over, it was more tolerable since everyone stayed on their best behavior - meaning I could sit quietly until I could make my escape back into my safe haven.

Tonight would be the first time a guest came to our family dinner that was one of mine. I hadn't invited him, but there was no doubt that he would be there for me. I only hoped everyone would act like normal human beings for once.

I paced back and forth across my room, the skirt to my dress swishing around my legs as I spun to make another pass across my carpet.

Reid had texted about fifteen minutes ago to tell me he was on his way, and I knew he would be arriving any minute.

My phone dinged a message, and I ran to grab it off my desk and saw the expected text from Reid letting me know he had arrived. I slipped on my flats and rushed out of my bedroom door to let him in the house. I didn't want him to be subjected to my aunt all alone if she was the one to answer the door.

I took the stairs quickly, nearly slipping on the bottom step in my haste. I practically ran to the front door and opened it. My heart finally started to slow down when I saw Reid standing there with a bouquet of flowers and wearing a similar black shirt and red tie to the one he wore at school. However, this time his sleeves were rolled down and the cuffs buttoned. His leather cuff and beaded bracelets peaked out from underneath, though.

"Are those for my aunt?" I breathed out.

"They are. I was hoping to make a good impression. Do you think it will work?"

I laughed quietly. "I have no idea."

He leaned down and kissed me softly. "Are you okay?"

I nodded and said, "Yes." lying to us both.

I wasn't okay. I was nervous about dinner. I was still upset over my poor Jeep, and I was scared that the stalker would do something else to hurt me. Or worse, she would turn on Reid and hurt him instead.

He studied my eyes and shook his head. "You aren't okay. But you will be." He gently brushed his thumb over my cheek.

We heard the backdoor open and turned towards the sound of footsteps coming our way. Jason appeared dressed similarly to Reid, and he was smiling.

"Hey, wide receiver! Welcome to *mi casa*. Better not stand in the doorway all night. Mother keeps a strict schedule for dinner and doesn't like it when people are late to the table." He continued on his way, whistling.

Reid threaded our fingers together and gently squeezed my hand, letting me know that he was there to support me. We followed behind Jason and entered the dining room, where the table was decorated elaborately in the lavish dining room. A feast was already laid out with roast, salad, and rolls. The glasses were already full of sparkling water for us teenagers and dark red wine for the adults. Aunt Jolene was already seated, and her glass was in her hand. What remained in her glass was hardly more than a swallow.

Jessica came in, followed quickly by Uncle James, and we all took our seats.

"Finally! We are all together again!" Aunt Jolene laughed and tipped up her glass, finishing the last of her wine. She didn't set it down, though, merely held it out to my uncle for him to dutifully refill.

"We have a guest tonight." My aunt gave Reid a big smile. "So nice to meet you, young man. Tell me about yourself."

Reid had sat down with the flowers still in his hand, which he looked at and then held up. "I, uh, brought you flowers, ma'am, as a thank you for inviting me."

"Well, isn't that thoughtful! You can just lay them down on the chair next to you for now. I'll have the housekeeper take care of them later, so we don't let our lovely dinner grow cold."

"Yes, ma'am," he said and awkwardly did what she asked. I inwardly cringed because, what the hell? Isn't the hostess supposed to show more appreciation than that?

"So you're the young man that has my daughter and my niece

fighting over you." It wasn't a question, and it made my already high tension ratchet up another degree.

"If that were so, ma'am, I apologize. It was never my intention to cause any trouble between your girls."

"Enough of this ma'am business. Call me Jolene."

I could tell Reid was already feeling uncomfortable with the way things were going. I felt so much relief the moment Uncle James stepped in and ordered everyone to start serving themselves.

It was silent for a few minutes while everyone got situated with their plates and started eating until Aunt Jolene started her usual questions.

"So, Jason. How was your week? I heard that you won another game. It must feel nice to be champions."

"Well, we are currently 2-0, so we have a long way to go until we are the champions, but I am confident that we will be able to pull it off." Jason buttered a roll, took a large bite and pointed to Reid while still chewing. "He's the one that is helping me the most, though."

"Oh? Are you the one making all the goals?" Aunt Jolene took a dainty bite of her salad.

Jason snorted. "Touchdowns, mother, and yes, he is the one that catches all my throws and gets us into the end zone."

My aunt waved her fork around and said, "Touchdowns, goals, who can keep all those sports terms straight. It all means the same thing in the end, right? You're winning, and that's all that matters."

"Yeah, mother, winning is all that matters," Jason grunted and stabbed at a chunk of roasted meat on his plate. He didn't seem thrilled that his mom had lessened his entire football experience down to nothing but winning and losing. Even I knew that a lot went into playing a good game of football. These guys went through so much training and conditioning to be the best team they could be, and it showed. I wondered if Jason wished his mom was more involved. Reid's mom went to all his games and held on to his bracelets for him. She made sure he got them back afterward. She told him how proud she was. I don't recall ever hearing about Aunt Jolene going to one of Jason's games.

"And what about you, Jessica? How did your week go?"

Jessica raised her head briefly to look at her mom. "It went well, mother. I have nothing new to report, I'm afraid. This week was pretty much the same as last week."

Aunt Jolene stared at her for a minute before saying, "Hmmm, and any new young men since this one seems fully taken by your cousin?"

I watched as Jessica's knuckles turned white as she clenched her fork and said quietly, "No, mother, nobody new."

"What a shame. A beautiful girl like you deserves to have a handsome young man like this one on her arm." She waved towards Reid.

"Jolene." My uncle growled under his breath at my aunt.

"What? A mother can't wish for more for her daughter?" She picked up her glass and waved it around the table. "Look at my children, doing so well in school and their sports. They need to start looking forward to their futures now. Especially my daughter. She needs to find a nice man to take care of her before she's too old."

Oh god, it was even worse than usual. I didn't know what was happening or why now. I thought maybe it was because Reid had settled on me instead of Jessica, and she was trying to embarrass me. Or perhaps she was trying to embarrass Reid and scare him away. I didn't think it would work, but why would he want to hang around for all this crazy?

Jessica didn't say a single word. She was smart enough to know when to back off and let her mom exhaust herself. Without fuel, her fire would eventually smother itself out.

"Jolene!" Uncle James glared at her.

Aunt Jolene just huffed and rolled her eyes. "Fine!" I watched as her eyes came to me and narrowed. "Paige, dear. It's nice to see your hair down for once and out of that hideous bun that you always kept it in. I almost forgot that you inherited your mother's hair."

I looked down at my plate and tried to ignore the words. It would have been a beautiful compliment if it hadn't come from someone I knew who had disliked my mom since they both married into the family.

"Were you able to catch up on your schoolwork since you took so many days off of school this week?" She tsked. "You know you can't afford to let your grades drop."

Actually, my GPA was so high that I would probably still make valedictorian even if they did drop slightly. I didn't say that, though. Her words had made it sound as if I were failing school instead of excelling, but everyone at the table knew that wasn't true in the least.

"Actually, I was able to get caught up quickly." It was best to try to keep my answers to her questions short and to the point.

"That's good, dear. You want to be accepted into a halfway decent school, right?" She laughed as if she said the funniest thing in the world.

"Right," I muttered.

"My husband told me last night that you got into a bit of trouble with your car last night, Paige. I'm really disappointed. He said he was going to take you car shopping for a replacement, but I think that it's important to teach young people responsibility and to take care of their belongings." She pursed her wine-stained lips and shook her head. "No, I don't think so. I think you need to go without for a while so you can learn to appreciate nice things."

"What?" I whispered, unable to believe what she was saying. "You think my Jeep being vandalized was my fault?" I asked in disbelief.

"Well, if you had parked it in a well-lit parking lot and kept the doors on it instead of rolling around town like it is perfectly acceptable to drive with half your vehicle disassembled, then maybe it wouldn't have been targeted." She huffed.

"Jolene, her car was a Jeep, and it is expected to remove the doors and roof. It's part of the appeal of even owning one." My uncle gritted out. "And that had nothing to do with why her car was vandalized. It was parked in a perfectly well-lit lot. The person that did it is the same one that attacked her at school on Monday and put her in the hospital."

She waved her hand dismissively. "Regardless, I still don't think she needs a brand new car. Perhaps a used one would be more suitable."

"I will not punish her for the acts of a crazy person."

"If it is a crazy person responsible for all of her problems lately, then maybe she should stop associating with people that bring that type into her life." She actually pointed her fork in Reid's direction, and I felt him tense beside me. "We should be worried that her issues will spill over onto our children. It is our responsibility to protect them. I knew bringing her here was a bad idea, and now she's finally proving me right."

"Mom," Jessica whispered. Even Jason had stopped eating and was staring at his mother in disbelief at all she was saying.

Uncle James slammed his fist down on the table, causing his untouched wine glass to tip over and spill onto the pristine white table cloth. I watched numbly as the stain spread out quickly. I remembered thinking last week that her wine that had sloshed out of her glass looked like blood, but this stain was so much worse.

"That's enough!" He yelled. "That is my niece! My brother's only child! He trusted me with her, and this is what I've brought her to?"

"Oh boo hoo. The poor little orphan that lost her perfect parents." She stumbled to her feet. "Don't worry, dear husband, I'm done." She winked and left the room in silence.

We sat there for several long minutes until Uncle James started speaking, and when he did, we just sat and listened.

"I'm sorry. I'm sorry to all of you. I had no idea, and that is on me. I should have noticed that your mother wasn't paying attention. I should have noticed that she had lost all interest in being a mother long ago. We-we have been having marital problems for years now and haven't been close in quite a while. I stayed away from the house to avoid our problems, but all that did was make it to where you stopped having both a mother and a father present."

He looked at me. "Paige, I knew she was jealous of your mother long before any of you were ever born. She had no reason to be. I loved her and only saw her, but because your mother was so beautiful, it ate her up inside, and she was convinced that I was secretly in love with her. I never thought she would take that hatred out on you."

He stood up. "Reid, I'm sorry you had to see all of this tonight, but I'm glad my niece had you by her side." He looked at both Jason and

Jessica. "I'm tired of saying I'm sorry already, but I need to say it one more time and warn you that things are going to change even more than they already were. We'll talk more just the three of us tomorrow evening." With that, he nodded at us all and walked out of the room.

Jessica left immediately, and her steps could be heard running up the stairs. Jason stood up and nodded at Reid, "See you at school tomorrow, Johnson." and walked out of the room. The backdoor slammed a minute later, making me jump in my seat.

I turned to Reid. "Did that just happen?" I whispered.

"Yeah, baby, it did." He helped me to my feet and held my hand as we walked to the front door. "Do you want to come to my house tonight?"

I really thought about it, about sleeping in his arms, in his bed, in the safety and comfort of his house, but I shook my head. It would feel too much like I was abandoning my family. I just couldn't bring myself to leave when there was a large, gaping wound in the heart of it right then.

He kissed my head. "Okay, baby. Call me if you need me, okay?" I nodded. "Good. I will see you in the morning. I'll be here to give you a ride to school."

"You don't have to do that," I protested. "I could ride in with Jessica."

"I won't be happy until I can see you again, buddy. So first thing in the morning, it is. Got me?"

"Yes, caveman, I got you." I snarked back.

"I'll show you caveman the next time we get alone time." He leaned down and bit lightly on my neck, making me shriek and wriggle.

"Call me when you get home?" I asked quietly.

"Always," he replied. "I love you."

"I love you, too."

He kissed me softly and then turned to go. I watched from the doorway as he powered up his motorcycle and drove away.

CHAPTER 33

Paige

The house stayed quiet all night. I had almost expected to hear yelling, maybe things being thrown and broken, but there was nothing but silence.

I had decided to call Lisa, something I wasn't used to doing, but since we had agreed we were going to work more on our friendship, I was going to make the effort. She was horrified to hear that my Jeep had been destroyed while we had been together in the movie theater. She sounded genuinely sad for my family that there was so much drama blowing up all at once.

We talked for several minutes until exhaustion became too much for me. Even though I had assured her that nothing was likely to happen, I had to let Lisa go with a promise to update her if anything else happened between then and morning. After Reid and I texted our goodnights, I dragged myself into the shower and washed quickly and then regretted it since I would have to blow dry my hair, so I didn't get my pillows sopping wet.

By the time I was finally able to, I was literally crawling onto my bed and dropping face down. I half-heartedly pulled my purple comforter over my body. I must have passed out and slept pretty hard because when my alarm went off at the regular time, I woke up in the same exact position I had been in the night before.

I still didn't feel rested, though, and had to splash cold water on my face to wake up more fully. I figured it was more mental exhaustion than physical with everything that had been happening in my life lately.

I was ready to go and about to head downstairs to wait for Reid when I heard a soft knock on my bedroom door. I cautiously opened it and peeked my head out. Jessica stood in the hallway with her designer school bag over one arm and held her Porsche keys with her other hand.

"Umm, hey, Paige. I was wondering if you needed a ride to school or if Reid was going to pick you up?"

I stared at her. "Really?" I asked dumbly.

She frowned and looked down at her shoes, and took a heavy breath. "Yeah, I just wanted to make sure you were able to make it to school okay."

"That's very...nice of you, but Reid is on his way. I was just about to head down to wait for him since he should be here any minute." I couldn't believe we were having that conversation. It was probably the most words we'd had together since we were kids.

She nodded and took a step back. "I figured, just thought I'd ask." She turned and headed to the stairs.

"Hey, Jessica?" I called out.

She stopped and looked back at me.

"Thanks for the offer. I appreciate it."

She smiled at me, the first genuine smile she'd ever given me, and I gave a small smile back.

I went over to my desk, picked up my cell phone, and slung my backpack over my shoulder. When I left my room, I closed my door and pulled out my keychain but paused with the key hovering just outside the keyhole. I closed my eyes and then let my head drop. I put my keys back in my bag and turned away from my bedroom door without locking it.

ONE WOULD THINK that the student body of Rocky Hills High School would have been used to seeing their starring wide receiver and resident outcast together by now. When we arrived at the parking lot, though, it seemed as if every student was standing still and staring at us.

Reid parked his bike and removed his helmet while I swung my leg over the back and worked on removing my own helmet. Once he had them both stowed away, he took his book bag from me since I'd worn both of ours during the ride over.

I watched his muscles flex and bunch as he climbed off and stood up to his full height in front of me and wondered if I needed a napkin to wipe the drool off my chin. No matter how often I saw him or what we had done together, he still had the power to take my breath away and make my heart speed up by just being him. I had a feeling that would never change even if we lived to be 100 years old.

"Do you feel like you are being watched? I asked with a smirk.

"Do you mean by the stalker or by the hundreds of nosy students that have nothing better to do but ogle your legs in those short shorts?" He ran his big palm over my thigh and cupped my butt while I frowned up at him.

"Well, I wasn't thinking about the stalker until you said something. So, thanks for that. And, I'll have you know, these shorts are fully within the dress code!" I declared. "But, yeah, the students. When do you think they will start to get bored of watching the Paige and Reid show?"

He took my hand and laced our fingers together as we started walking to the doors. "Hmmm. I think it should be the Reid and Paige show. I'm bigger than you."

"That's funny. I always hear everyone talking about how size doesn't matter." I grinned at him.

"It's a good thing you don't have to worry about size, so you don't have to pretend then." He winked at me, making my tummy flutter. "Well, I'm older, too. I should totally get top billing."

"If it makes you happy to stay on top, then...." I trailed off, trying to keep from laughing when he realized what I had implied.

"Now, wait a minute. I think I'm okay with taking turns being on top." I giggled.

We were about to go through the doors when a group of cheer-leaders I hadn't been paying any attention to spat at me. "Slut!"

"She's such a whore!" Another one snickered.

My first instinct was to put my head down and scurry away, but Reid squeezed my hand, silently telling me that he was with me. I stopped and turned to them, still holding on to my boyfriend's hand. The only boyfriend I'd ever had. I wasn't a slut or a whore. But even if I had slept with a hundred guys, calling each other names was ridiculous.

"When are you going to grow up. Calling other girls names? As women, we should be supporting each other." I shook my head and looked at each of them. "Haven't you heard? Slut shaming is out."

They all turned an angry shade of red, and one of them stepped forward. I didn't know what she was planning on doing, but several things happened at once.

I lifted my chin and dared her with my eyes to make a move. It was the first time I had ever stood up for myself, and even though my heart was racing, I felt good.

Reid straightened his shoulders and growled at the girls. But what surprised me the most was hearing Jessica come up from behind us and snap out. "Enough! No more bullying. It's time to grow up. God! Isn't there enough crap going on in your lives that you should be worrying about? Leave. My. Cousin. Alone."

She then stood there and stared down her friends, silently daring them to say or do anything else. When they stepped back, they were scowling, but they didn't speak again. They were shocked that their leader was standing up for the outcast, the same one they had been tormenting for years, but Jessica was well established in her role. No one was going to go against her. She nodded and turned back to the school doors. "Everyone get to class! School is starting."

Like magic, the entire group of students loitering in the area started moving, and not one more word was said to either me or Reid.

We were at our locker when Reid whistled low. "That's some power she has."

I sighed. "Yeah. She's used it against me for so long that I'm sure if she uses it for good, she could probably rule the world."

He chuckled. "Maybe." He leaned down and brushed a quick kiss to my lips. "I'll see you after first period."

"Okay," I whispered, and we both separated and started to walk away when he called out.

"Hey, buddy!"

I looked back at him with one eyebrow raised in question.

"I'm proud of you."

I felt myself flush with pleasure. I was proud of myself, too. It wasn't easy standing up to those girls, but I had done it.

"Thanks." I grinned back at him, turned around, and headed towards the office while heading down the hall to his art class.

I had only been sitting in the office for about ten minutes when the phone rang with an internal call. I was only half-listening to the secretary, saying, "Sure, honey, I'll send Paige right over."

I immediately put my book down and stood up, stretching my arms over my head, waiting for Mrs. Walker to hang up and tell me where I was headed to.

"The coach needs an incident form and can't find any in her office. She asked if I could have one run up to her."

"Sure," I replied and walked over to a filing cabinet where all the blank forms were kept. I ran my fingers over the labels on the files until I found the one I needed and snagged a couple of extra so she'd have them just in case. "Be back in a few!" I called out to Mrs. Walker, who was already answering another phone call, and left the office.

The gym was on the complete opposite side of the school from where I was, so it would take a few minutes to get there and get back.

As usual, the halls were eerily silent with just the indistinct murmur of voices behind the closed doors that I passed.

When I started down the last hallway, I noticed that a door was partially opened, which I thought was strange. I didn't think I had ever seen that particular door open before. It was one that didn't have a room number or a plaque outside the door naming what the room was for, so I was kind of curious but didn't really care enough to look.

I had just passed the door when I felt myself suddenly get yanked to the side and let out a yelp of surprise before terror filled my body. I just knew that this had to be the stalker and started to try to pull away, but I was off-balance from the suddenness and couldn't gain the traction I needed against the slick tile floor to pull myself free.

I realized the person had yanked me through the open doorway, and in the few seconds it had occurred, I was kicking myself for being an absolute idiot for not being more cautious. I should have realized that I could be attacked again.

Before I could get my bearings, I felt a hard shove to my chest and threw my arms out wide, wildly trying to reach for something, anything to grab onto, but there was nothing. And there was nothing below my feet as I started to fall backward.

The first bump I felt knocked the breath completely out of me but didn't stop the pain from searing through me as my shoulders collided with what had to be a set of stairs. After that, I felt my world turn upside down as I kept falling, my head making contact before rotating until I was face down, my knees hitting the stairs hard enough to make me cry out, but with the momentum of the fall, I still didn't stop until my body rotated again. Then, finally, I came to a sudden awkward stop, half on and half off the bottom steps.

I could only whimper in pain as I lay there, my head on the floor and my legs on the steps. I tried to move, but there was pain everywhere.

Movement at the top of the stairs startled me, and I immediately tried to scoot as far away from the person as possible, but when I put my hand down to lift my upper body, I screamed out in pain and dropped to the floor again.

The person slowly started walking towards me, taking the steps one at a time. I could feel the menace radiating off the girl. It had to be a girl. Even in my dazed state of mind, with the pain nearly consuming me, I could see the long hair and petite frame, too small to be a guy.

I turned over and tried to crawl away from the girl, terror digging into me like sharp claws. I couldn't use one of my arms without screaming in agony, so I pulled myself away from the stairs with one hand. I was crying uncontrollably from the fear and the pain, both trying to take me over, but I fought the darkness that was calling me. All that was running through my mind was I needed to get away, away, away.

I couldn't have made it far when I felt a foot on my back making me cry out again. She put pressure down until I could barely take a breath. One of my ribs must have been broken, and I hadn't felt that particular pain until her weight pressed my chest harder into the floor.

"Please," I begged, but I knew that she would never show me any mercy. She had set out to hurt me, had already hurt me once, but this time I wasn't going to get away.

I laid my cheek down on the cold concrete floor, thankful for the coldness, and closed my eyes. I didn't want to know what else she was going to do to me, and I was afraid that down here, in a basement that no one knew about, she would be able to do anything she wanted.

Suddenly the pressure lifted from my back, and though I still couldn't take a good breath, it was still a relief. That relief was short-lived, though, when I felt her grab one of my legs and start to drag me away from the stairs.

I could do nothing to stop myself from being dragged. There was nothing to grab onto. The cement floor caused my shirt to roll up under my breasts, and I could feel my skin scraping raw. She grunted as she pulled me several feet. I tried to kick out to stop her, but I felt so weak, and every time I moved, the pain made black dots dance in front of my eyes.

She finally stopped and dropped my leg, making me grunt. After that, all I could do was lay there and try to breathe. I was so nauseous I was afraid I was going to throw up from the pain.

I heard a chain rattle and tried to lift my head to see what she was doing, but she kicked me in the head in the same spot she had kicked me a week ago. I cried out and tried to curl up into a ball as black spots filled my vision.

She grabbed my leg again, and I felt her wrap the chain around my ankle. She was done, and I heard a click before I could even try to fight back again.

In the entire time, she hadn't said one word, had barely made a sound. I lay there sobbing as I heard her footsteps walking away from me.

"Why?"

The word was low and garbled since I could barely catch my breath or even slow down my crying. I could barely even recognize my own voice, but I heard her stop.

"Why? You want to know why?" Her voice was familiar, but in my pained haze, I couldn't think straight to place it. And, honestly, at that moment, I didn't care who it was. But, yes, I did want to know why. She started walking back towards me but stopped a foot away. "Because you took everything from me. You keep taking everything from me. But with you gone, I'll be able to have it back."

With those confusing words resonating in my ears, she turned around and walked up the stairs. I heard the door open and opened my mouth to scream, hoping I would be able to get someone's attention, but before I could pull in enough breath through my burning chest, I heard the door slam shut.

CHAPTER 34

Reid

I made my way down the hall, nodding my head to the 'heys' that were thrown at me and ignoring the looks of the girls that always tried to catch my attention. I didn't stop or slow down, eager to get to my little buddy so we could head to second period together.

I hated the classes that we didn't have together, hated not having my eyes on her and not having her by my side. College was going to be a pain in my ass since we would have to take different classes. But I'd make sure that all of our required classes were together at least.

I had plans that I hadn't discussed with her yet about our living arrangements. Some colleges had rules about freshmen being required to live in the dorms, and I knew that being on the football team, I would be expected to room with most of the players. But I had been doing my research and found out that those rules didn't apply to married couples.

We would be able to live in an apartment off-campus as long as I held up to the rigorous schedule that they kept for the players. I would be willing to do anything as long as I could hold my girl every night. If that meant being married teenagers, then so be it. I knew my parents would be happy for us, and I was sure that it wouldn't be too difficult to convince her uncle as long as he knew I was taking care of her the way she deserved to be cared for.

I didn't see her waiting outside the office door the way she usually was, so I pushed open the door expecting to see her talking to Mrs. Walker. But, instead, when I walked in, I met the frantic, watery eyes of the secretary. I knew immediately that something had to be wrong.

"Where is she?" I demanded.

Mrs. Walker just dropped heavily into her chair and wrung her hands as a tear slipped down her cheek.

The principal rushed into the room with her phone to her ear and pushed past me. I followed her with my eyes and watched as she went to the main doors of the school and pushed them open, letting in the two police officers that had been assigned to our case along with two other men wearing slacks and button down shirts with gun holsters on their chests and badges clipped to their belts.

Seconds later, Paige's uncle rushed through the open doors. His eyes were frantic when they landed on mine.

Blood was rushing through my ears, and I couldn't make out what anyone was saying around me. All I knew is that something was terribly wrong, and it had something to do with Paige.

Principal Nieves ushered everyone into a meeting room a few doors down the inner office hallway, and I followed numbly. No one took a seat after the principal closed the door. The detectives were asking questions, and the principal was talking, but I turned to Mr. Anderson.

"Where is she?" I croaked out.

"Should he be in here?" One of the detectives looked at me.

I turned to snarl at him, daring him to throw me out when Mr. Anderson placed his hand on my shoulder, calming me a fraction.

"He has every right to be here."

"If we are going to find the girl, we don't have time to waste on boyfriends."

I clenched my hands and realized they were shaking. I turned back to Paige's uncle. "Please tell me where my girl is."

He looked at me sadly and pulled out a chair, and pushed on my shoulder to make me sit. I didn't want to sit. I wanted my buddy. Why did he look sad?

Mrs. Nieves was the one to speak up. "About 40 minutes ago, a call came into the office. The student said that the girl's coach needed an incident form but didn't have any. When she didn't return after 15 minutes, Mrs. Walker called the coach, and she said that she never asked for any forms." She rubbed her neck and looked worn out. "Because of the recent problems the two of you have had, we thought it best to call her uncle and the officers that handled the last incident."

"Where. Is. She?" I gritted out between clenched teeth.

"We don't know." She whispered.

I closed my eyes. This couldn't be happening. Why didn't I watch her? Why didn't I make sure she was safe? We knew she was still being targeted. "Fuck!" I roared and jumped to my feet.

The two officers looked at me with understanding, but the two detectives stiffened and inched their hands towards their weapons.

Mr. Anderson put both his hands on my shoulders and looked me in the eyes. "I know, son, I know. We'll find her, I promise."

"But what kind of condition will we find her in?" I asked brokenly.

He shook his head. "All we can do is look for her and hope she's okay. We can't think the worst."

"She's already been to the hospital once because of this psychopath!" I yelled.

"Son, I'm going to have to ask you to sit down and be quiet, or we are going to make you leave." One of the asshole detectives threatened.

"I dare you to make me leave." I sneered.

Mrs. Nieves stepped forward. "Okay, that's enough for now. Reid, we will do everything we can to find her, and she's going to need you to be there for her as soon as we do." She turned to the detectives. "I'm going to have to ask you not to threaten my students. He's upset, and rightly so. You would be just as worried as he is if it were your girlfriend that was missing after already being attacked once."

"Keep a chain on your kid, and we won't have any problems." He growled out and dismissed us by turning to the officers. "We need to know what we are dealing with here."

I wanted to take out my anger and frustration on the asshole, but I knew it wouldn't do any good, so I ignored the police as they discussed the case. I looked back at the principal and asked, "Where have you looked? Did you check the bathrooms? Have you tried calling her phone?"

She sighed. "Her phone is in her backpack, which she left in the office when she went on her run to the gym. She never reached the gym, so we were about to start searching. First, I need to make an announcement to the teachers to check their rooms and the closets. I've already checked the cameras, but we only have cameras at the doors, and no one has been in or out during first period."

I was about to tell her that we shouldn't be wasting time when we could be searching the school instead of talking about it, but I was interrupted when the door to the room flew open. I watched as a worried Jessica stepped in, followed by Jason.

"We heard that the police arrived at the school. Dad? What's going on? Is it Paige?" She looked on the verge of tears as she looked around the room, and her eyes landed on me. "Oh god, did something happen to her?"

I had never seen Jessica as anything other than completely put together. Even when she was dirty and sweaty from cheering, she was still calm and collected, almost stoic. Seeing her distraught almost made me smile because it looked like my girl had more people on her side than she realized.

Jason just stood next to her without saying a word, but he wasn't his usual cocky self. Instead, his hands were held in tight fists next to his sides. I didn't know if he'd ever admit it to anyone, but he was worried, too.

Mr. Anderson opened his arms, and Jessica rushed to him, and he held her and whispered to her. He must have told her what was happening because she cried out and buried her face in his chest.

"At this time, I think it's best if we lock down the school. We are going to have to go room by room and search everywhere. She's probably just locked in somewhere and is just fine, but we won't know until we find her." Asshole #1 said.

I agreed with what he said, but I didn't like his attitude or how he was brushing off her disappearance as if she were just playing hide and seek.

Mrs. Nieves agreed and left the room. The room stayed quiet for a few minutes with just the sounds of Jessica sniffling and the occasional paper rustling while the detectives made themselves familiar with the case. Asshole #1 put his hands down on the table and looked at me with a serious expression.

"Listen, son, if you know where your girlfriend is, you need to speak up now. We don't need to be scaring all these kids and their parents with a lockdown if you know where she's hiding." His tone was commanding, and he looked like he was on the verge of forcing me to give him information that I didn't have.

I took a step to the table and leaned forward with my palms flat on the table, mirroring his pose. "First of all," I growled out, scared that my girl was out there and fucking pissed the hell off that this guy wasn't taking her disappearance seriously. "Don't call me son. Secondly, this isn't some fucking joke! I said she wouldn't do something like that, and I fucking meant it. Thirdly, why don't you pull the stick out of your ass and do your fucking job and find her!"

Mr. Anderson took my shoulder and pushed me away from the table and against the wall where Jason stepped in front of me. He was standing with his dad against the two detectives that had turned red with anger. They were attempting to step around the two police officers that had stepped forward to block them.

"The two of you have already been briefed on the case, and you can clearly see that a very unstable person has targeted my niece and her boyfriend. You are barking up the wrong tree here, and you'd know it if you started taking this seriously. My niece has been missing for almost an hour now, and who knows what's been done to her. I can tell you right now, if your attitudes cause further harm to come to her, I will personally see to it that you lose your badges."

Asshole #2 nodded his head at Mr. Anderson and took his partner's arm, pulling him back. "Understood, sir. We will be taking this case seriously. You can have confidence that we will do everything we can to make sure we find Miss Anderson in a timely manner."

Asshole #1 yanked his arm back from his partner's tight hold and pointed his finger in my direction. "But one more outburst from the kid, I will have him locked up in juvenile hall before he can blink!"

Asshole #2 whispered back to him, "Come on, man, just focus on the case. He's worried and has every right to be."

Yeah, I had a fucking right to be worried.

Seconds later, we listened as Mrs. Nieves made the announcement that the school was on lockdown. Jason sighed and turned to me. "Don't do anything that will kick you out of here. You know she's going to need you once she's found." He turned and dropped heavily into a chair. "So, what's the first step in finding the orphan?"

"Jason!" Jessica screeched at him, and he ran his hand over his face.

"Sorry, sorry, old habit." He looked at the officers, completely ignoring the two assholes. "What is the first step in finding my cousin?"

"Now that the principal has made the announcement and ordered everyone to stay in place, we can sweep each hall until everywhere has been thoroughly checked. It shouldn't take too long if we," he waved to himself and the other officer, "split up. We will ask you to all stay here in this room. It will be easier to search without anyone else walking around."

"You don't think it would be better to have more eyes looking?" Mr. Anderson asked.

"I want to help search," Jessica spoke up.

"I'm sorry, it's best that you all wait here." He walked towards the door, the detectives following. He stopped and looked at me, leaning against the wall and doing my best not to freak out any more than I already had. "I know it's easier said than done, but try not to worry until you have a reason to worry, okay?"

It sounded like the stupidest advice I'd heard. I nodded just to get him to hurry the hell up out of the door. As soon as the doors closed on them, I turned around and put my forehead to the wall and punched once, twice, before Jason jumped up and held my wrist to keep me from hitting it again.

"Dude, don't. You don't want to ruin your football career before it can even get started."

"I don't give a fuck about football right now!"

"I know, man, I know. But once she's found and the bad guy is caught, you will regret destroying your future."

I grunted. I really didn't care at the moment. I wasn't sure if I would ever care about it again if I lost my girl. What if whatever had happened to her scarred her for life? How would I take care of her? I walked to the table and pulled out a chair. Sitting in it, I dropped my head onto the table and just sat there, staring blankly at the wall.

CHAPTER 35

Paige

I didn't know when I had stopped crying. All I knew was that as long as I didn't move at all, my body stayed numb, and I didn't feel the pain as much. Unfortunately, a while ago, I had started shivering uncontrollably.

The cement floor I was lying on was cold. At first, the chill helped and actually felt good against my cheek. However, it didn't take very long for that coldness to seep into my bones. I wanted to curl into a ball to warm myself, but the pain in my ribs wouldn't let me move.

After taking stock of my injuries, I was fairly certain that I had broken my wrist and at least one rib. My knees had hurt for a while, but the pain from those had faded, so I figured they weren't too bad. What worried me the most was the back of my head. I had hit those stairs pretty hard when I'd fallen.

I could barely see. The room I was in was so dark that I couldn't even see my hand in front of my face. I didn't know what room I was in, but I figured it had to be the boiler room. I mean, those do exist, right? I'd read a creepy-pasta that had a boiler room in it. Remembering the story didn't do me any favors, and since then, I couldn't turn my mind off of what could be lurking in the dark. If I survived this, I was afraid that I would end up needing some serious therapy.

I knew that the school would be searching for me. They had to find me. It wasn't as if they would allow a student to disappear inside the school and not try to find her. If I didn't return to the office Mrs. Walker would start to worry. Even then, Reid would realize I was missing, and he would never stop looking for me.

Another round of shivers wracked my body, and I couldn't hold back the whimper of pain.

Please hurry.

Reid

MY MOM REACHED out for my hand and gave it a slight squeeze. "Please, honey, sit down."

I shook my head and continued my pacing from one wall to the other in the small, cramped room. "I can't, mom." I was close to losing my mind with worry. "It's been three hours with no word. Why haven't they found her yet?"

No one answered me. I was the only one pacing; everyone else was sitting around the table. Jason was on his phone. Jessica was staring at the same spot she'd been staring at for the last hour. Eventually, she will give up on that spot and find another one to fixate on like she'd been doing for the last *three fucking hours.*

My mom and dad were sitting together holding hands, mom always looking like she was on the verge of tears. Mr. Anderson would sit down for a few minutes before standing up and walking to the window to stare out at the quad. The only thing to see out there today was empty metal tables and the occasional paper blowing across the grass.

Mrs. Nieves never stayed in the room for long. She had delivered a box of donuts and a carton of coffee about an hour ago, but no one had touched any of it yet. I felt that if I were to put anything in my mouth, I would just vomit it right back up.

Suddenly, there was commotion from the hall, and then the door swung open. The two detective assholes walked into the room. They stopped and looked around at all of us before heading to the table and making themselves each a cup of coffee.

"We've checked every hall and didn't find her." Asshole #1 said as he stirred his cup with a little wooden stick.

My mom sat up straighter. "What does that mean? Are you just giving up?"

Asshole #2 blew on his coffee. "No, ma'am. It just means that we need to look harder."

Mom nodded her head and wiped away a tear.

"We are double-checking the security cameras to see if anyone has left the building. We also need to locate the janitor because there are a few locked doors that no one seems to have a key for. We don't really think she'd be in any of those rooms due to the locks, but we don't want to overlook the possibility, either."

Mrs. Nieves stepped into the room. "The janitor just called. He said he was on his way and said something about having car trouble, but he would be here soon." She turned to look at the rest of us. "How is everyone doing?" She closed her eyes and sighed, shaking her head. "Stupid question, I'm sorry. Can I get anyone anything else? Maybe water instead of coffee?"

My mom shook her head and smiled sadly. "It's okay. We are fine right now."

Mrs. Nieves nodded her head and walked back out of the room. I could tell she was blaming herself. I guess I could understand why she would take the blame. It was her school, and she was responsible for everything that went on in its halls. But no one would have been able to anticipate there being a crazy person. If we had known who it was, we wouldn't all be huddled in this room right now, hoping that Paige was still breathing.

The detectives followed the principal out of the room, and I watched as the door swung closed behind them.

I'd had it with being cooped up in that tiny room without receiving any updates. I stormed across the room and put my hand on the doorknob.

"Honey, what are you doing?" My mom started to stand, looking panicked.

"Sorry, mom. I can't stay in here any longer. I have to go out there and help look."

Jason pushed his chair back. "I'm with you. This sitting here staring at these stupid walls isn't helping anything, and my ass is getting tired of these shitty chairs." He walked up next to me and slapped me on the back. "Let's get out there and see what we can do to end this." I nodded my head in thanks and pulled the door open.

We walked towards the front desk and looked around. I was looking for Mrs. Nieves. I was certain she would allow us to search even if the detectives had said not to. I turned when I heard footsteps behind me and saw Mrs. Nieves rush from her office to the front doors. She looked at us as she passed and headed to the office door, and swung it open.

"Well, are you coming or not?" She asked with a raised eyebrow.

Jason and I looked at each other, and then we both hurried to follow the principal out the door and to the school's front doors.

She unlocked the doors and stepped outside while we followed. We watched as she just stood there staring out across the parking lot. I figured we were waiting for the janitor so he could use the keys to unlock the doors.

"God, I wish I had a cigarette right now." She mumbled as she crossed her arms and watched as traffic slowly rolled by past the school.

"Those things will kill you." Jason snickered.

She nodded without looking away from the cars. "Yep. But so will stress. Thank god, there he is."

I straightened up, and my heart started beating faster. Finally, with the keys, we will be able to find her.

The janitor didn't bother to park properly; he just pulled to the closet curb and jumped out of his car. He was a tall, skinny man. His cheekbones were hollowed out, and his eyes almost looked sunken in. Either he was incredibly sick, or he never took care of himself. Whichever one it was, he looked like a strong wind would be able to break him in half, and I could hardly imagine him being able to do much heavy lifting.

"Jeffery! Thank you so much for rushing. But I really wish you would have left the keys here on the school property where they belong." She admonished lightly.

He bowed his head and turned red with embarrassment. "I'm really sorry, ma'am." He held out the large ring with about 20 different keys on it. "I often don't even think about them being in my pocket when I leave for the night. It won't happen again, I promise."

She sighed heavily and took the keys from him. "Okay, Jeffery. See that it doesn't. Why don't you go into the employee lounge and have a seat in there unless someone needs you?"

He nodded, "Yes, ma'am," and walked past us into the school.

"Alright, boys. Stay with me. And no talking back to the detectives. I won't be able to help you if they try to throw you out again. They've already warned you twice."

I bite back a retort that I'd like to see them try, but she was right. I couldn't afford to get left out. Paige needed me.

We went back into the office and waited while she went to retrieve a walkie-talkie that she had left on her desk. As soon as she came back out, we left the office and headed for the first hallway that branched off from the one we were in.

"I've got the keys. Which door is the first one we need to check? Over." She clicked off the mike, and we waited a few seconds until we heard a staticky answer of 16.

We all rushed to the door marked 16. Jason and I waited while Mrs. Nieves looked through the keyring until she found the one marked with the room number. I think we all held our breaths when the tumblers in the lock clicked, and she pulled open the door. I let out a breath of frustration when the room was revealed to be no bigger than a few feet deep and was nothing but a sink and a rolling mop bucket.

"Fuck, fuck, fuck." Mrs. Nieves started cursing under her breath as she slammed the door shut and started walking quickly further down the hall.

She clicked on the radio, "16 was a bust. What's next?" She ground out. A few seconds later was the reply of 30.

We checked five other locked doors, which were all mostly the same - brooms, mops, shelves with bathroom supplies, one was completely empty.

We turned down the third hallway and saw the four policemen standing in front of the door that was next on the list. One held a map of the school, and another was holding a radio. The two detectives each wore matching determined expressions. We stopped in front of the door while Mrs. Nieves searched the key ring.

"I don't think these boys should be out here."

Mrs. Nieves gave me a warning look but ignored the detective. She found the corresponding key and turned the lock, but it was another empty room.

"Goddamnit!" She was losing her patience steadily as we continued to come up empty. She slammed the door closed and ground out, "What's next?"

The detective huffed at her ignoring him, and we all ignored that, too.

"Room number 210." Said the guy holding the map.

As one, we all made our way past the classrooms and turned the corner to one of the last halls. It only took a couple of minutes to unlock and dismiss that room as well.

"There is a door up ahead that doesn't have a room number. Do you know what it is?" He asked.

"It's a waste of time, is what it is." Griped the asshole.

Mrs. Nieves spun on him and pointed a red-tipped finger in his face. "I've had enough of your nonsense. If you don't want to do your job, then I suggest you leave and reassign yourself to a different case. This girl needs people that want to help her, not complain." Then she turned to the officer. "Where is it?" She growled out.

"It's just a few doors up the way."

We all hurried up the hall as the two detectives hung back while they whispered back and forth to each other angrily. Finally, we stopped in front of a heavy metal door that had no number and no window. Mrs. Nieves looked through the keyring before looking up. Her eyes were glassy with unshed tears.

"I don't know which one it is."

She held up the keys with shaky fingers.

Jason snatched the keys from her hand and said, "Then we try them all."

We watched as he carefully tried each key, but none of them would fit or wouldn't turn.

"It's not here!" He yelled after trying them all. He kicked the door and turned to her. "Where would the key be?"

"I don't know. I just don't know." She wiped her eyes. "We need Jeffery."

He nodded, tossed the keyring to the detectives when they walked up, and turned to run down the hall.

"We'll check the last few doors while you wait for the janitor." One of the officers said.

Mrs. Nieves let out a shaky breath. "Yes. That's a good idea. Reid and I will wait here until you get back."

A few minutes later, the janitor was rushing behind Jason as he ran back toward us. The skinny man who looked a few minutes from death was breathing hard when he came to a stop.

I looked at him, watching him gulp in huge breaths of air. "What room is this?" I asked him.

"It… it's the boiler room."

"Where's the key, Jefferey?" Mrs. Nieves asked him.

"It's not on the keyring?" He asked in bewilderment.

"No! We tried every key, none of them fit."

"I-I don't know." He stammered out.

Jason shoved him up against the wall. "Where the fuck would it be?"

"I don't know! I swear!" He cried out.

"Mr. Anderson! Let him go!" Mrs. Nieves yelled.

Jason pushed away from him and reached up to grip his hair, and yanked. He lifted his head towards the ceiling and yelled, "Fuck!"

"Who has access to the keys?" I looked the janitor in the eye. If he didn't have the key, then someone stole it. Someone knew enough about the school to use the keys to lock her inside. If it wasn't on the keyring, then it had to be this door. "Paige!" I shouted and started banging on the door. If we couldn't unlock it, then I was going to damn well break it down. "Paige!"

Jason started banging on the door with me. We tried pulling on the handle. We tried kicking it and ramming our shoulders into it, but nothing even put a dent in the metal.

I turned back to the janitor. "Who. Has. Access. To. Your. Keys?"

He scooted back along the wall, trying to get away.

"No one! Just my daughter!"

"Who's your daughter?" I gritted out. It took every bit of willpower I had to stop myself from reaching out for his throat.

I heard Mrs. Nieves say, "Suzanne."

I turned to her, puzzled. I didn't know that name, did I? "Who's Suzanne?"

"Suzanne Hinkley. She's a senior here. You probably have some of the same classes."

I looked at Jason, but he just shrugged his shoulders. Mrs. Nieves pulled her phone out of her pocket and dialed a number. "Shiela, I need to know which class Suzanne Hinkley would be in right now." She paused, and we all waited in silence; only our heavy breathing filled the hall. "Okay, I need you to call the classroom and tell the teacher to send her out." She turned and hurried down the hall. She called over her shoulder. "I'm going to get Suzanne and escort her back here."

I turned towards the door that I was sure my girl was behind, leaned my forehead against it, and placed my hands flat against the door. She was in there. I swore I could feel her, and I knew she needed me.

CHAPTER 36

Reid

It took a few minutes, but I finally heard footsteps coming back our way. I pushed back from the door and watched as everyone approached. The officers and detectives were following the principal and a girl with long black hair wearing worn-out jeans, a t-shirt, and black running shoes. She was small, and I knew I'd seen her before, but it took me a minute to place her.

Mrs. Nieves was right; we had classes together, four of them. She was in the same AP classes that Paige and I were in. As she reached the door, she looked at her dad while she twisted her fingers together. I saw her glance at me and then back to her dad.

"Daddy, what's going on?"

Before he could say anything, Jason stepped towards her. "Where's the key to this door?" He ground out.

"I don't know what you are talking about." She looked at me again and gave me a small smile. "Hi, Reid."

Jason huffed. "Really? That's how you're going to play it?" He took another menacing step towards her.

"Son, you're going to want to back off." Asshole #1 said.

"Back off? Are you kidding me? This girl has to be the one that stole the key. Her daddy is the janitor. He takes his keys home with him." He waved to her. "Look at her! She's wearing black shoes just like Paige described when she was attacked last week. Do something!" He thundered.

"Mrs. Nieves," I began, "we need to get inside this door."

She nodded at me. "Suzanne, if you have the key, we need it now."

Suzanne crossed her arms over her chest but didn't say a word, and she just kept staring at me. A shiver ran up my spine.

"Suzanne," I said softly.

She smiled big at me. "Yes, Reid?" Her voice was breathless, like she was turned on. I felt sick to my stomach.

"Do you have the key?" I kept my voice low and calm. I had the feeling we were standing in front of a completely unhinged girl.

"Yes, Reid." She took a step in my direction, and it took everything I had not to step back.

"Did you lock Paige inside?"

She swayed towards me. "Uh huh."

"Why did you do that, Suzanne."

"I did it for us." She reached out a hand towards me, but I took a step back. Just the thought of having this girl touch me was enough to make me want to vomit. She frowned as she watched me retreat.

"What about us?" I asked her as I watched one of the officers reach for his handcuffs.

"She was standing in the way. She's no good for you. She's nothing but a charity case, a nothing. That's what they all say, even her cousins."

I heard Jason groan.

"Did you hurt her?" I asked behind clenched teeth.

"I had to." She cried out as the officers grabbed her arms and pulled them behind her back. She looked to her dad, who was standing there staring at her in horror. "Daddy! I wanted to be valedictorian! You made me promise, remember?" She started crying as the cuffs snapped onto her wrists. "I was the smartest kid since preschool. You told me I was the best."

"Yes, baby girl, you were the smartest." He repeated as he watched his daughter being arrested.

Her face twisted in an ugly grimace. "But then she," she spat out, "came along, and suddenly she took my spot. Nothing but a charity case."

"Fuuuuck." Jason groaned again.

She looked at me and smiled again. "I saw you first. You were in the grocery store over the summer. You bumped into me when we were both looking at the ice cream. There was only one chocolate brownie left, and you let me have it." She had a dreamy look on her face. "You smiled at me. You wanted me."

I shook my head, lost. I barely remembered that. I was just being nice like my parents taught me.

"But on the first day of school, you saw her and never spoke to me again. Don't you see?" She cried out. "I needed to get rid of her so I could have everything again. It was mine first!" She wailed.

I looked at Mrs. Nieves. "You need to check her for the key."

She started screaming and twisting her body to get away. "No! You can't! She has to stay in there, so he forgets about her!"

Mrs. Nieves looked sad as she pulled a key from her front pocket and looked at Suzanne's dad. "I'm sorry, Jeffery." He nodded and wiped his cheeks while he watched his daughter struggling and screaming.

Mrs. Nieves pushed the key in the lock and turned it before twisting the knob. She pulled it open, and we all stepped back to give her room to open it completely.

The only thing I saw was darkness. It wasn't like the other doors we'd opened. Those were small closets, and this looked like it was much larger. I noticed the stairs next. She stepped aside, allowing me to enter first. I slid my hand across the wall, feeling for a light switch. When I found it and flipped it on, the light revealed a steep metal staircase with several large metal canister-looking things attached to a lot of pipes and wires.

I raced down the steps and came to a halt at the bottom when I saw a bit of blood spotted on the floor. I looked at it, my heart racing in my chest. I followed the smeared trail of blood to the back of the room, around a row of what looked like industrial-sized water heaters, and then froze solid. I could feel the room fill up behind me as I blocked the back part of the room from sight. And then I ran to the body on the floor.

I dropped to my knees next to my beautiful Paige. I faintly heard a gasp and a few curses coming from the others, but I ignored them as I looked over my girl. She was lying face down on the cold concrete. Her hair was tangled and wild around her, matted with blood and covering her face.

I gently took a finger and brushed her hair back so I could see her face. Her eyes were closed, but she was breathing. Her body shook with intense shivers every few seconds. I wanted so badly to pull her into my arms and hold her, to get her off the hard floor, but I didn't want to hurt her more without knowing what her injuries were.

She had one arm outstretched as if reaching towards the stairs, the other one was placed close to her body, and I could see it was likely broken. It was swollen to twice its size and was already severely bruised. One of her legs was chained to a large pipe coming out of one of the machines. I couldn't see any other damage, but I still didn't dare move her.

I vaguely heard someone say that we needed an ambulance, and Mrs. Nieves directed Jason to run to the metal shop for a tool to cut the chain off of her leg.

I lay down on the floor next to my buddy and stroked her soft cheek with a shaky finger. I watched as her eyelids fluttered and she cracked open her eyes.

"Reid?" She croaked out.

"Yeah, buddy, I'm here," I whispered brokenly. God, seeing her like this was ripping my heart into shreds.

"You're crying for me?" Her voice was rough, and I wanted nothing more than to find her a bottle of water and help her drink it.

"Yeah, I guess I am," I replied, and I felt a tear drip off the bridge of my nose and fall to the floor under my cheek.

"I don't want you to cry for me." She whispered and made to move her hand towards me but cried out in pain.

"No, baby, don't move. Help will be here soon, okay?" I pleaded with her.

She sighed and closed her eyes as another shiver shook her whole body. "Cold." She mumbled.

I looked up at the adults standing around us, looking sad. "Can anyone get her a blanket? She needs something to cover her!"

The detective shook his head sadly, "I'm sorry, son, I doubt anyone has a blanket right now."

"Fuck!" I yelled and lay my head back down, heedless of the wetness. I continued stroking her cheek with my thumb, watching as her eyes fluttered again. "I'm so sorry, baby. So fucking sorry."

"Not," she shivered violently and whimpered, "not your fault. Cra-crazy."

I snorted out a watery laugh. "Yeah, you could say that." The girl needed more help than a jail cell could give her.

Footsteps pounded down the stairs, but I didn't take my eyes off my girl. Then, finally, Jason and the shop teacher came into view, and I heard more curses as the shop teacher took in the situation.

"Hey, cuz," Jason said as he dropped to his knees on the other side of her. "Looks like someone got you good this time."

"Jason?" Paige's voice was hardly a whisper, but he heard her. He leaned down over her head.

"Yeah, cuz?"

"I-I'm really sorry about everything."

"No," he let out a tormented groan, "don't you dare apologize. Nothing was ever your fault. I was an asshole because I was angry and jealous. You had such a perfect life with perfect parents. My mom had the maternal capacity of a head of cabbage, and my dad worked all the time to stay away from her. I'm nothing but a jerk and a bully."

"Are we going to be okay? Us and Jessica, too?"

"Yeah, cuz," he wiped his cheek, "we will be great."

"That's good," she whispered and closed her eyes again before slowly opening them again to look into my eyes inches from hers. "Hurts." she whimpered.

"I know, buddy, I know. I'm sure the ambulance will be here any second now."

She closed her eyes again, but this time they stayed closed. I watched for the next few minutes as her body periodically shook. Then finally, there were multiple footsteps rushing down the stairs.

"We're going to need you gentleman to back away so we can get to your girl."

I didn't want to move from her side, but I wanted her off the ground, and I wanted her to get the help she needed, so I reluctantly sat up and scooted back far enough to allow the paramedics access. I watched their every move as they carefully put a collar around her neck and quickly and efficiently flipped her over and belted her to an orange backboard. They had her immobilized and lifted within seconds. I stood there for a second, still staring at the floor where she had laid for hours, seeing the blood where her head was. Then, I noticed the chain lying there where the teacher must have cut it off.

I looked up and watched as the paramedics carried my girl up the stairs and the rest of the people following them. I swiped both hands down my face. I wanted to scream and yell, to punch things, to make something or someone hurt as much as I was inside. As much as Paige was hurt.

I let out a shaky breath and looked down at the stained floor one more time before finally jogging to the stairs.

When I entered the hall, there was a lot of commotion as our families had arrived and were asking questions. My mom held on to Jessica; both of them were crying as they watched the paramedics place the backboard on the gurney and secure it. Her uncle looked devastated. My dad put a hand on my shoulder.

"You doing okay, son?"

I nodded, then paused and shook my head. "No, Dad, I'm not okay. I don't think I'll ever be okay again."

CHAPTER 37

Paige

I woke up feeling groggy but warm. It was a feeling I didn't expect to ever feel again.

I looked around the room I was in, blinking my eyes several times, trying to bring the world into focus.

"Reid?" my voice sounded scratchy, my throat dry from not drinking anything for hours. Where was Reid? I didn't think for a minute that he wouldn't have planted himself by my side, refusing to leave.

A nurse wearing purple scrub pants and a top with superheroes all over it bustled into the room and gave me a big smile. "Young lady, I am so glad that you are finally awake." She went straight to my bedside and started checking the machines. "You are probably thirsty." She grabbed a cup and filled it with a small plastic pitcher. And stuck a straw in it. "Here, sip slowly, though. Don't want it coming back up."

I let her put the straw between my lips and took a tentative sip. The cold water felt amazing on my throat, and I probably would have chugged the whole thing if the nurse, Misty, according to her badge, wasn't holding it.

"That's enough for now. We'll give that just a few minutes to settle, and then you can have more, okay?"

I nodded and started looking down at myself. My head was a little woozy, but I didn't really hurt anywhere, just dull aches. My wrist lay next to me on the bed and had a bright pink cast on it, covering all but my fingers and up to half of my forearm.

"You're pretty lucky, from what I understand." I turned my head to look at my nurse as she was typing on the computer in the corner of the room.

"What's wrong with me?" I questioned. What I actually wanted to know is where Reid was.

"Your wrist has a fracture, hence the cast." She waved to my hand, and I looked back down to my right hand. My bright pink-covered hand. It was kind of pretty, actually. "You also have a small fracture to the back of your skull. Since it is so small with minimum swelling, there isn't much to do other than give it time and rest. You might have headaches for a while though you shouldn't have any lasting effects."

She finished typing and pushed the keyboard in on its sliding base, and turned back to me. "You probably aren't feeling the pain of your other injuries right now. However, you have some scrapes on your torso and pretty decent bruising on your knees and legs. You also have a fractured rib that only needs to be taped for a few weeks. Like I said, pretty lucky."

I remembered falling down those stairs and closed my eyes. Yeah, I felt pretty lucky. At the time, I felt like I was dying. I was glad to know that it wasn't as severe as it felt. I opened my eyes back up and finally asked the question I'd been aching to ask since I woke up.

"Reid?" I whispered.

"Oh! If you're asking about the handsome young man that hasn't left your side, you just missed him. He's probably going to be upset once he realizes that you woke up without him. I think his mom made him go home to shower and change his clothes."

Figures. "How long have I been here?"

"You've been unconscious for two days. It's to be expected. The body has a way of knowing what it needs to heal. In the time you've been asleep, the swelling around your brain has disappeared to almost nothing. You do have a couple of stitches back there. I'm sorry to say, but the doctor had to shave a bit of your hair from around the site."

I nodded and immediately felt a wave of dizziness.

"Yeah, I wouldn't be moving my head around very much if I were you. In a couple of days, you will feel a hundred times better than you do now, though, don't worry." She patted my hand. "I'll be back to check on you soon. Just keep resting. I'm sure another wave of visitors will be back in soon." She slipped out of the door.

Visitors? I took another look around the room and noticed the flowers and balloons. A pink teddy bear was holding a small balloon that read 'get well soon'. My eyes started watering at all the get-well messages. The entire windowsill was covered without an inch of remaining space. For so long, I had been so alone, afraid to leave the safety of my room. But seeing all the gifts, I was overwhelmed.

The door opened, and Reid walked in. He took one look at me and rushed over to my bedside, and dropped into the chair there. "You're awake! I knew I shouldn't have left. Why are you crying? Are you in pain?" He was frantic and looked like he was about to jump out of his seat and run for the doctor.

"No," I sniffled. "I'm just surprised by all the flowers and stuff."

"Oh." He smiled and looked towards the window. "Yeah, my mom had to take a bunch of it home because we ran out of room."

"What?" I was shocked.

He stood up and walked around the room, pointing out the different flower arrangements and balloons. "This," he pointed to the teddy bear, "is from Lisa and Chad. Those," he pointed to a large mylar balloon bundle with a cartoon giraffe that told me to keep my chin up, "are from the cheerleaders."

I started to laugh but thought better of it when my side ached. "Now I know I'm dreaming. The cheerleaders hate me."

"Maybe," he said, coming back over to his chair. "But Jessica had a long talk with them and put her foot down." He picked up a stack of greeting cards. "Most of these have apologies written in them. Nearly every student in the senior year has sent a card, letter, or told one of us to tell you how sorry they are for the way they've been treating you for so long."

"But...why?" I asked, bewildered by the abrupt change in everyone.

"Because of me."

I looked up at the sound of my cousin's voice. I didn't remember ever hearing him speak to me in a way that wasn't condescending or angry. Right then, he looked ashamed.

"I asked Mrs. Nieves to hold an assembly, and she let me speak. I told everyone how wrong I was for the way I had been treating you and for urging everyone else to do the same." He shook his head. "I told them that being bullies aren't what we are. It isn't what we should be. And I told them it wouldn't be tolerated anymore. Not in any way, shape, or form."

"Jason," I whispered, feeling the tears sliding down my cheeks before Reid reached over to wipe them away for me.

"I need to apologize to you, Paige. I was an asshole—an unbelievable one to you our whole lives. I was jealous and insecure. I guess I wanted you to feel that way, too." He sighed. "My parents are getting a divorce, and we are all going to go to family counseling. None of us realized how much mom's hatred of your family had rubbed off on us. Jessica already made an appointment." He gave a slight smirk. "We go this afternoon at 3 to talk about our feelings and shit."

I smiled back.

"Knowing you were missing really scared me, you know? I realized that somewhere in this black heart," he pointed to his chest, "there is still some goodness. Some part that wasn't just filled with hate. But seeing you lay there, broken? That gutted me." He coughed a little to clear his throat. "Anyway, I made it clear at the school to stop being dumbasses, and I think they got the message."

"Thank you," I whispered.

"You're family." He shrugged.

Family. It wasn't something I thought I'd have again, and it wasn't until he said those words that I realized how much I needed it.

. . .

OVER THE NEXT FEW HOURS, I started feeling overwhelmed by the number of visitors that came and went through the door. More flowers were delivered, and I had to whisper to Reid's mom to take some to the other patients. I kept the box of chocolates for myself, though, because...chocolate.

Lisa only stayed for 10 minutes before Chad picked her up and carried her out of the room, calling over his shoulder, "We'll try again tomorrow!" Lisa's wails could be heard down the corridor, along with the nurse shushing her.

Around six o'clock later that evening, Reid and I were alone, enjoying the lack of visitors and eating dinner together. We were laughing at an old 90's comedy show when the door opened again. I watched two men walk in wearing suits with badges clipped to their belts. They looked to be in their 30's with neatly trimmed hair. They were both relatively good-looking, I supposed, but someone needed to tell the taller one to shave off his mustache.

I looked at Reid as he went rigid next to me. "What's wrong?" I asked him, looking from him to the men.

"Calm down, boy. We're here to apologize." Said mustache.

Reid slowly put his hamburger down on my rolling tray and growled out, "The first thing you should do if you want to apologize is to not call me 'boy'!"

The other guy stepped forward and lifted both hands in surrender. "What my partner is trying to say is that we fucked up, and we know it."

I tilted my head and looked at their contrite expressions. "How did you fuck up?"

Mustache sighed and said, "When we were handed your case on Sunday, we assumed that it was just teenage angst caused by jealousy and cheating. Not many teenagers are honest when they are caught cheating, so we figured you had lied to your girlfriend - whichever one of the girls was actually your girlfriend. And when Miss Anderson, here, ended up missing on Monday, we figured she found out and had run off somewhere to pout." He turned to me and winced. "No offense."

"None taken," I replied absently.

Actually, when he laid it all out there, it sounded pretty plausible.

"So that whole time you were at the school acting like assholes..." Reid trailed off.

"We thought you had a love triangle, lover's spat going on and wasting everyone's time and resources. Unfortunately, we were too stubborn to see how serious everyone else was taking her disappearance."

Reid was quietly taking in their words, so I spoke up. "Thank you for your apology. From what it sounds like, you wouldn't have been able to do anything in the short time you had the case anyway. But, I appreciate your apology." I would have to ask Reid about what had happened that day because he still seemed tense and hadn't said anything.

"Alright, well, we are glad to see you are doing well, Miss Anderson." They turned to leave when mustache stopped and turned back. "Oh, we also came to tell you that Suzanne Hinkley is being charged with wrongful imprisonment. I believe the DA was going to try for attempted murder as well but wasn't too confident on that one. The imprisonment, though? There probably won't need to be a trial if she pleads guilty. Unfortunately, she'll be going to a mental hospital instead of prison. But, just between you and me and these walls... that girl is looney."

They nodded and left the room. Reid still hadn't said anything, so I stared at him until he finally broke.

"I was so goddamned pissed that day."

Tears immediately filled my eyes. I knew he'd had the worst day imaginable while I was trapped in that basement.

"We didn't know where you were. We waited for hours. *Hours*. For any word. Jason and I finally had enough and decided we would try to help. We just couldn't keep sitting there waiting and wondering. And those assholes," he growled, "kept giving me a hard time through the whole thing. Playing it off like you were hiding."

He turned to look at my face, and he gently brushed a tear from my cheek. "And then I saw you laying there. My first thought was that you were gone for good. I thought you were dead, baby, and it broke me." I let out a sob as I watched a tear fall from his eye and then another and another until he lowered his head onto the side of my bed, and his hand gripped my thigh. I watched as his shoulders shook and all I could do was lift my casted arm and gently comb through his long strands with my fingers.

After several long minutes, Reid stood up and kissed the tips of my fingers before disappearing into the bathroom. I listened to the sink running and thought about how I would have felt if I were in his shoes. I was the one lying there in pain, but I always knew he would come for me. On the other hand, he didn't have any reassurance that I would be alive if I were even found.

I was starting to think that seeing a counselor would be an excellent idea for the both of us. I didn't think I was as traumatized as everyone expected me to be, but what if it hit me later? And Reid might hold onto the fear that I could be taken from him. I didn't want him to worry any time I ran to the grocery store, or if we didn't have the same class, he'd wonder if I was hurt somewhere. So I made a mental reminder to ask Uncle James to help me find a therapist to help us both individually and together.

A few minutes later, he opened the door, his eyes red-rimmed, and walked back to my bedside, and bent down to kiss me.

"I love you," he whispered.

"I love you too, Reid," I whispered back.

Then he sat down and picked up his hamburger, and we both looked at the T.V. to see we'd missed the entire show we'd been watching.

CHAPTER 38

Reid

8 months later

I stood up with the entire stadium full of parents, teachers, students, all kinds of family members, friends, and... hell, half the damn town was probably squeezed into our little high school football stadium.

The field had a large wooden stage at the fifty-yard line. In front and in back of the stage were rows of chairs - one side for the students to sit and wait for their names to be called, and the front side of the stage held the rows and rows of chairs for the parents. Each student was allowed to have two guests sitting on the field, and it looked like every admission ticket had been used. The rest of the spectators filled every seat to capacity in the stands.

The energy levels were sky-high, everyone was excited to be at our high school. But it wasn't just because of the graduating class.

My girl had just finished her valedictorian speech, and the cheers were almost deafening. But no one cheered louder than me.

The entire town had rallied around my little study buddy once her ordeal had hit the papers. The whole story had been written up, including her backstory of losing her parents and unborn sibling and then moving to a new state where she spent more than three years being bullied and ostracized, led by her own family. The story described how instead of hitting back or curling into a ball and trying to disappear, Paige strived to make herself into something she was proud of.

Everyone loves a good story, especially when the underdog becomes the hero, but when Paige requested to make a speech at Suzanne Hinkley's sentencing, she argued for leniency. The girl that stalked and hurt her ended up being sentenced to half the time the DA had initially recommended at a mental health facility because Paige didn't want her life wasted. Suzanne was a very smart girl, and she would probably have ended up being a salutatorian had she not lost her mind.

The story had also included a sincere, heartfelt apology, and very few who read it could do so without shedding a tear or two. I didn't think anyone realized how much Jessica really wanted to be a journalist until that story was released. She decided to stay right where she was and go to a nearby college for journalism. Though, one day, Paige confided in me that she believed Jessica was secretly in love with someone she probably shouldn't be. But after she told me about her suspicions, I started watching too. And I was pretty sure that the defensive coach for the varsity team liked her too. Good thing he wasn't married. Oh, and that Jessica had finally turned 18 years old a few months ago.

Jason was actually coming with us to Michigan State. He stopped partying quite as much as he did and started putting more effort into football and his grades. No one was surprised when the scouts came around with scholarship offers except him. We all sat down to dinner one night with our parents and the scout and listened to his offer. He would make sure we would stay together since we played so well as a team if we signed up with MSU. Jason and I didn't have to discuss it for very long because, yeah, he had turned out to be one hell of a quarterback, and I trusted him to get the ball in my hands.

Paige hadn't really cared as long as the school had a pediatric nursing program, and it wasn't as hot as Texas in the summer.

Lisa was planning to follow Chad to the college he received a baseball scholarship for since they had gotten married the day she turned 18. Not one single person was surprised. But *they* were when we all met them on the steps to the courthouse and insisted we be allowed to witness their wedding. Her mother even brought her a dress she'd been holding for her. Lisa cried so much that Chad had to threaten to postpone their wedding if she couldn't get herself together.

I stood with my row and turned to walk in a line up to the stage. The sun was starting to set, and the air was beginning to cool down a bit. It was still early summer, so we hadn't quite reached the heat that would show up in another month. By then, we would be in Michigan, and the hottest days wouldn't get much higher than mid 80's. Paige was eagerly anticipating the change.

I stood at the base of the steps leading up to the podium where the principal was waiting to shake everyone's hand, but I didn't want to move because I had a perfect view of my girl from where I was standing. She was playing with one of the ends of the many cords hanging around her neck. The setting sun was turning her golden hair into something resembling glitter. I'd never liked glitter, but at that moment, I thought it was one of my most favorite things in the world.

I vaguely heard my name called, and Paige jumped and looked directly at me and smiled her brilliant smile. I felt my heart speed up like it did every time we were in the same room. Every time we came in contact with each other. Every time I heard her voice. I continued to admire her when she covered her mouth and started laughing under her hand. What light that was left from the sun caught on the diamond on her ring finger, and I finally smiled back at her.

She would be mine soon. In another month, she would be Mrs. Johnson.

I felt someone pat me on the back and yell in my ear, and I looked away from my girl so I could ask what the fuck their problem was, but I finally got it. I looked back at Paige and winked while she laughed at me and shooed me towards the stage.

I climbed the stairs and raised my hand to wave at my parents, who managed to get a front-row seat thanks to Paige's uncle since she was valedictorian, and her family had reserved seating. I ignored the laughing crowd. My girl was worth making them wait.

"Glad you could finally make it, Mr. Johnson." Mrs. Nieves said with a teasing smile.

"You know me, Mrs. Nieves, I'm a sucker for my girl." I grinned back.

"Get out of here before I decide to take back your diploma."

"Yes, ma'am."

I turned back after a step, "You're coming to the wedding, right?"

"I wouldn't miss it!" She called out and turned to shake the next student's hand.

I waved to the cheering crowd and walked down the other side of the stage to join my row but took a quick detour. Paige was already standing up, waiting for me. I picked her up and spun her in a tight circle before setting her down again and adjusting her stole and cords. I only allowed myself to give her one quick peck on the lips before strolling back to my spot.

The rest of the ceremony went by reasonably quickly, and then, before we knew it, we were moving our tassels to the opposite side as our family and friends cheered for us.

I was out of my seat and rushing to the last place I had seen my buddy, but she wasn't there. I felt my heart race and had to stop and breathe. She wasn't taken. She wasn't hurt. Another deep breath and I was calm enough to turn to the little red-headed guy that had been salutatorian.

"Hey, man, good speech! Do you know where my girl is?" I was practically hopping from foot to foot while staring out over the crowds of people. Height had its advantages.

He blushed and stammered, "P-Paige?"

"Yeah, man, Paige, my girl. Where did she run off to?"

"Uhhh…"

I was starting to wonder if I broke him when I felt a tap on my shoulder and spun around, just knowing it was my buddy. I picked her up, and her legs went around my waist. I carefully grabbed the back of her head. I still wasn't over the fact that she'd had a skull fracture and kiss her hungrily.

"I missed you," I growled against her lips.

She threw her head back and laughed. "It's been like an hour!"

"It's been way more than an hour!"

"Well, maybe an hour and a half then?" She asked sassily.

"Too long. Any amount of time is too long." I kissed her before she could respond and set her carefully on her feet. "Come on. You know my mom's getting antsy."

I linked our fingers together and led her around the stage and to where I last saw my parents, but of course, their seats were empty. I turned to look at Paige. "Maybe we should just go home? They could come visit us there?" I asked hopefully.

"No way! Your mom would kill you!"

I just grunted and spun around, still looking. But then, I finally had a bright idea.

"Here, you look." I picked her up and stood her on top of the chair, and held onto her hips to steady her. "Do you see them?"

"There they are! Your mom is talking to Jenna."

"Great, let's go so we can get home."

"We still have to go to dinner, you know. My uncle made reservations weeks ago." She teased.

We walked up to my parents and Jenna while I was still grumbling.

"He wants to leave, huh?" Jenna teased as she reached out her arms for a hug. Paige leaned into her, careful of the newborn that Jenna had cradled in her arms.

"Of course!"

"Hey!" I pouted and smiled when Paige was handed the tiny blue bundle.

Jenna ended up dropping out and getting her GED once she was too far along in her pregnancy to continue comfortably going to school every day. Her situation was another one that was affected by Paige's kidnapping ordeal. She had been jealous, and, yes, she had been hoping to get closer to me because she was desperate to find someone that would stand by her and support her. After the 'incident' she came to the hospital and confessed all, which wasn't much, just a lot of petty feelings that she hadn't acted on. Since then, she and Paige had become good friends. Funny how tragedy can bring so many people together.

She never did confess who the baby daddy was and refused to say even now. The baby's looks weren't any help in trying to figure it out since he looked exactly like Jenna with nearly white hair. Paige said she never got a good look at the guy she had been arguing with at the beginning of the school year, so that wasn't helpful. We figured we just wouldn't know unless she decided to tell us. I wanted to know mostly so I could kick the guy's ass since he knows he has a son but is refusing to acknowledge him. Looking at Paige holding a baby to her chest makes me wonder how anyone could refuse to be in his life.

I had to give myself a serious talk about not wanting to see Paige holding our baby right now. We had plans.

But first, dinner, then home to our apartment.

One Month Later

I HELD my wife in my arms as we slowly moved to Loving You by Seafret. I was man enough to admit that I may have teared up a little bit as we swayed to the words.

Even if I could rewrite the history
It's clear to see
That I'd still be

Loving you

OUR STORY WAS ALREADY TESTED, we wore the scars from the nightmare we faced, but together we came out on the other side stronger than before. If we had to face more drama, more trauma, we would do it together. Always together.

EPILOGUE ONE

4 Years Later

Paige

I was hot, tired, sweaty, and needed to get this over with *right now*.

I practiced taking big breaths in through my nose and slowly let it out through my mouth, but I was on the verge of saying fuck it and pushing the people in line in front of me out of the way.

I can do this! I can do this!

Inch by inch, the line moved forward, and finally, finally! my name was announced, and I took quick steps forward and shook hands without any idea whose hands they were. I was sure the smile I wore resembled more of a grimace.

I heard all of my family cheering and clapping for me and waved absently towards them and walked down the short stairs from the stage to the floor as quickly as was possible.

"I've got you, buddy." My husband swept me up in his arms and carried me swiftly away from my nursing graduation ceremony as I sighed in relief. "So," he started as my mother-in-law helpfully opened the door for us, and he nodded his thanks. "How long have you been in labor?"

"Hmmm… what?" I mumbled, pretending that I didn't know what he was talking about.

Jessica was tagging along behind us, giggling while she cuddled her two month old and her husband carried their three year old daughter. She might have done something similar when she didn't want to miss an award ceremony for an article she had written about the corruption in a local government in Texas that led to arrests of several high-profile individuals.

"Paige," he growled.

"Reid," I growled back.

"I swear to god if I didn't love you so much…"

"What, Reid? You'd do what?" I may have left out a small sniffle and bottom lip wobble to make him feel bad for being irritated with me.

He cuddled me closer and whispered into my hair. "Nothing, baby. I love you and never want you to change."

Good answer.

"But," he raised his voice to give me more hell for insisting I go to my graduation ceremony knowing I was so close to my due date. I really thought it would be fine. Sure, I had woken up with a bit of back pain, but I thought it was just more aches from carrying his ginormous baby. He sighed and dropped his shoulders. "Never mind. Let's just get you to the hospital."

All I could do was nod my head since another wave of pain swept over me. I tried to hold in my whimper, but he had to have felt my body tense up. He picked up the pace and was practically running for the SUV.

Once we all reached our cars, Reid yelled out that he'd meet them there and all but shoved me inside but carefully buckled me in, making sure the belt was securely below my huge belly.

"Reid," I whispered after he pulled out of the parking lot and headed in the direction of the nearest hospital.

"Yeah, baby? I wonder if I should take the freeway. But, no, the traffic gets kind of bad around this time. So it's probably better to take the side roads." He rambled to himself.

"Reid?" I called out again.

"Don't worry, buddy. We will be there soon." He reached over and took my hand, and I grasped it like it was my lifeline.

"Reid!" I shouted.

He nearly swerved off the road as I startled him.

"What? What is it? You're not feeling pressure, are you?" he asked frantically.

"No. But I'm not going to be able to eat once we get there. Can you pull into that fast food place and get me a burger?"

His jaw dropped. "Yeah, uh, baby? I don't think that's a good idea."

"But why?" I whined. I was hungry, and I didn't eat this morning because I was nervous.

He swallowed hard. "You know I don't like saying no to you, but…"

"Please, honey?" I gave him my saddest puppy eyes and tried the lip wobble again.

WHEN WE PULLED up to the hospital doors, I stuffed about five french fries in my mouth, groaning at the delicious taste of grease and salt. A nurse ran out and listened as Reid explained while I leisurely took one last sip of my sweet tea. By the time they came back with a wheelchair, I was standing next to the SUV, hunger satisfied and ready to do this thing.

Reid turned to glare at me, seeing I climbed out by myself, but I just smiled. And then I felt my stomach start to tighten back up, and just as I was grabbing my poor belly, I felt water pouring down my bare legs. "Oh damn. I hope that doesn't ruin my shoes. I really like these...ahhhh!" And there was the pain. It was so much worse than it had been while I was at the ceremony.

"Let's get you inside, sweetheart." The nurse quickly helped me into the wheelchair as Jason walked up.

"Here, give me your keys. You go up with Paige."

A freaked out looking Reid just tossed his keys and took off after the nurse as she started wheeling me inside.

"Is this your first?" She asked as if we were having a leisurely stroll through a fucking meadow.

"Yes," I growled out through clenched teeth.

"Oh, that is so wonderful! I bet you're excited!" She exclaimed as she pushed the button to the labor and delivery ward.

Reid quickly grabbed my fist before I could swing it at her.

I thought she might have caught the movement from the corner of her eye because she just smirked and stared straight ahead after that.

Getting settled into a room didn't take very long, and I was grateful for Reid's mom and Jessica coming in to help me get changed out of my graduation dress and into the hospital gown. Everyone was excited, and I was trying to be brave. I had sworn throughout this entire surprise pregnancy that I was going to do everything all natural, but by the time I was hooked up to the monitors, I was ready to beg for medicine.

The nurse assured me that I could have something just as soon as they checked my cervix, and I was doing my best to breathe through yet another contraction while the nurse had her fist up my crotch, but I nearly started crying when she pulled back and said, "Sorry sweetie, you're ready to push, there's no time for pain meds now."

"Reid!" I wailed.

"I'm right here. We'll do this together."

He turned white when I turned my head and looked at him. I wasn't sure what he saw on my face, but he swallowed quickly and said, "I'll help you while you do this. I'll do anything you need me to."

"Oh, no," I whispered.

"What's wrong?" He asked, panicked.

"I don't feel so good." I moaned.

The nurse was lightning fast and had a bin next to me in the next heartbeat as I lost the meal I had begged for.

"Oh dear, you must have eaten recently. We try to warn women not to do that if they are in labor."

I glared at Reid for allowing me to eat that shit.

The doctor came in smiling. "Are we ready to have a baby?" He called out and stood still while a couple of other nurses helped him put on gloves and took my bed apart, making me scoot my giant ass to the edge of the table. Before I knew it, my feet were in the air, and I had a roomful of people staring at my cooch and yelling at me to push.

I ROLLED my head to the side and watched as my gorgeous husband cuddled our baby boy to his chest and crooned to him. I couldn't hear what he was saying, but it made me smile.

It was finally quiet after all the staff, and our family members left.

My delivery was fast and frenzied, and I barely remembered the aftermath. I did remember the doctor getting into a conversation with my husband about the draft and how he was a fifth-round pick a few months ago. Reid had been chosen by the team he had been hoping for, and it just so happened to be the team that Jason had joined a year ago. Unlike Reid, Jason didn't wait to finish his bachelor's degree. He was ready to go straight to the NFL as soon as he was approached.

While the doctor talked Reid's ear off about how great of a football player he had been before he started medical school, how he could have gone pro if he really wanted to, I stared at my beautiful boy as the nurse cleaned and dressed him.

I never expected him. He was a surprise that worried and scared me when I had first found out I was pregnant. We had planned to wait several years until we were both established in our careers.

I had done what thousands of other women had done over the years - gotten sick and had to have antibiotics. There really needed to be commercials running 24/7 on TV, so women knew that antibiotics negate the effectiveness of birth control pills. When the OB/GYN had explained why I had gotten pregnant and how common it was, I didn't know whether to laugh or cry. But now, looking at my husband and my son, all I could do was smile.

EPILOGUE TWO

Another 4 years later

Paige

Years ago, I watched my first football game and was confused by the action. There was so much happening, and the energy from the spectators was overwhelming to my senses. Now here I was, four years into watching nearly every game as my husband played for the professional football team that had picked him during the draft in his senior year of college. There wasn't a rule or a play that I didn't know the meaning of. I took being a player's wife seriously.

At this game, in particular, every single member of our extended family surrounded me as we watched from the stands. There was rarely a moment of silence in the crowd as we watched our team playing for the ring and the trophy.

It was down to the last two minutes of the Super Bowl game. It was freezing cold outside with snow and ice on the ground, but not a single one of us felt the chill.

The score was 27-30. The other team had played to win and had made our guys work for every yard, every single first down. They had the top spot in the league for defense. It was a very good thing that our guys had the number one spot for offense.

The entire crowd groaned as Jason was sacked for the fifth time, and the ball went flying from his hands. We all collectively held our breaths to see who had captured the ball as, one by one, each player climbed off the dogpile. I could practically feel my uncle breathe a sigh of relief when Jason stood up and shook off the hit he had just taken from the other team's defensive lineman. And then my eyes immediately darted to the left of him when a loud roar from the crowd rang out across the stadium. Our team had managed to keep the ball.

"Is daddy going to win, mommy?" Little Porter asked from beside me as he munched on his third bag of popcorn.

"I sure hope so, baby," I told him as I hugged our three month old, Maggie, to my chest like a life preserver. I wasn't sure my heart would be able to take much more excitement.

"Daddy and Uncle Jason will win!" He declared and nodded his adorable little head.

Everyone in the stadium held their breaths as the two teams got into position again for another play. It was 3rd and 4. If they didn't make those 4 yards in this play, they would be going for a field goal. While that would put them at 27-33, those extra six points wouldn't be impossible for the opposing team to make in the one and a half minutes they'd have left in order to tie it up and cause the game to go into overtime. That is unless they also managed to get a field goal-then the game would be over.

This was Reid's and Jason's first Super Bowl, and the whole family was thrilled that they had done so well in their careers already. Together they were a nearly unstoppable team, and it showed. They had made the playoffs each year on the team, but this was the big game. Reid had been quiet for the last two weeks. He had stayed focused, going over plays, watching tapes of the other team. He was confident, but he was nervous as hell.

The ball snapped, and there was an outraged cry from all the fans as the ball slipped awkwardly from the center's hands and bounced until Jason threw his body on top of it, keeping it from the hands of the defense.

I sat back, scared to breathe. "Oh no," I mumbled. *Oh no, oh no. It can't end like this.*

A time-out was quickly called, the last one that our team had, and the group huddled together as the head coach ranted and waved his arms from the sidelines. After about a minute, the team walked away from the huddle. I expected to see Reid and Jason heading to the sidelines to let the special team take over for a field goal attempt, but my mouth dropped open as they got into position again for a final play.

I kept one eye on the clock, and one on the field as the stadium started chanting. A tear slipped from my eye as I realized they were chanting my husband's name - *Johnson! Johnson! Johnson!* Everyone knew that if we were going to win, it would be because of Jason's arm and Reid's hands.

The snap was made, and the ball flew out of the center's hands.

Reid

I HAD BEEN PLAYING football since I was seven years old. I learned quickly that nothing felt better than feeling that football in my hands. Catching it, running with it, making a touchdown with it. It became my dream at the age of 10 to become a professional football player, and from that moment on, nothing else mattered but getting there. My parents sat me down and made me understand what it would take to make that dream come true. I studied hard, got good grades so I would have a chance at a scholarship. I practiced hard so I would have a chance at being scouted.

It wasn't until I moved to that small town in Texas that I realized that I had another dream. Paige became more important to me than football. My love for the game was still there, and it never lost its shine. It's just that Paige and then the family we had started to make together edged it out for supremacy in my heart.

Winning the playoffs and gaining the spot as one of the two Super Bowl teams was one of the most memorable events in my life, but it still didn't compare to when I kissed Paige's sweet lips after saying 'I do'. Holding my babies after they were born could never mean less than stepping onto the field where I would be playing in my first Super Bowl game.

I wanted to win with every fiber of my being. I wanted to slip that ring on my finger and shout to the world that I did it, and I made my dream come true. But if I didn't get it this year? I would just try again next year. Because, at the end of the day, the only thing that mattered was tucking my babies into their beds and holding my wife close as I made love to her.

"Can we do it, man?"

I looked at Jason. He believed that with one more chance, we would have that last touchdown.

"The coach will have our asses," I warned.

"Let me worry about that," he said. "But, can we do it? I need you, man."

I put my head down and thought. If we tried and failed, the other team could win or tie us up for overtime. If we didn't try, the other team could win or tie us up for overtime. So what did we have to lose?

I nodded.

"Right!" He grinned and stepped back.

I glanced over to the sidelines and watched as coach threw his hands up, and then his face got hard with determination and nodded. He was backing us.

We got into position and flexed my fingers in my gloves. I ignored the taunts from the other team and focused everything on that spot up the field, the sweet spot. The one that Jason and I had won with since twelfth grade. Deep breath in. Deep breath out. The sweet spot.

The call was made, and the ball snapped with a flurry of bodies rushing and the deafening sound of pads colliding. I spun and dodged the hands that reached for me and darted to the left and then to the right, my eyes not leaving that magical spot on the field where I knew the ball was, even now, soaring towards. Ten steps...five steps, I turned and jumped, hands outstretched, and felt the ball glide right into my palms like it was meant to be there and it was home.

I dropped to the ground in the next fraction of a second, spun, and ran like the hounds of hell were on my ass. Just ten more yards, and I would be there. I felt a hand pull on my bicep and twisted my torso without pausing my steps. Three more yards, all I could see was the vivid color of the end zone and the line I needed to cross.

I felt a shove against my back and gripped the ball tighter as my feet flew over the goal line and landed on my side, skidding several feet to a stop.

I closed my eyes tight and let out a breath. We did it. We won the mother fucking Super Bowl.

I was yanked to my feet and felt Jason's arms coming around me as he shouted in my ear and thumped the top of my helmet. I couldn't do anything but stand there until the shock wore off and then grinned.

"We did it!"

"Hell, fucking, yeah, we did it!" Jason yelled back.

I looked up into the crowd where I knew our family was sitting. I couldn't see them, but I knew they were there. My girl and my babies. Jason's wife and little girl. Jessica's three kids and her husband that was no longer the assistant coach but instead the head coach for the Rocky Hills High football team. My parents, Paige's uncle, and his new wife. Even some of the good friends we had made along the way.

I lifted my fingers and brought them to my heart before pointing them to where I knew my buddy was.

The End

AKNOWLEDGMENTS

I want to take a minute to thank the people that have supported me from the beginning. Without you, your friendship, and your encouragement, this book may not exist.

To my readers...
Once again, thank you from the bottom of my heart for reading my words.
Please, if you will help me out by leaving a review I would be forever grateful!
Also, if you find a horrible error in my book please don't hesitate to email me so I can get it fixed immediately! I have tried to be diligent in my editing but I am only human and may have missed something.

ABOUT THE AUTHOR

R. Sullins is an extremely avid reader. When she's not writing you will probably be able to find her reading a book. No matter what genre you find her immersed in, there is always one thing that her favorite stories have in common...you will never, ever find her reading any book with cheating. So rest assured! She will never write one either.

A bit of drama, a dash of spice, a little bit of innocence, and a large dab of alpha is what makes up the recipe for her stories. Enjoy!

ALSO BY ME

The Hunter series

A paranormal romance/urban fantasy

Hunter's Blood - The Hunter series book 1

My name is Ivy Moore.

This morning I woke up a 21-year-old overworked waitress, sister, and not much else.

6 years ago I watched my mother walk away while I was trapped in the mangled car that held my crippled twin sister and the body of my dead father.

My hatred for her ran deep into my bones.

It wasn't until I was attacked by monsters that were attracted to my blood that I began to understand.

With the help of the local arrogant vampire lord, I learned all about my heritage, about vampires and revenants, about what it was like to live again. About learning to love.

While Crispin spent his nights training me to be a deadly killer, someone else was creating an army.

I was a Hunter.

And someone wanted me for my blood.

Approximately 73k words

Important Note: This is the first book in a series, please be aware that it ends in an HFN but the second book picks right up where the first left off.

Warning: This book has blood and gore that may offend or disturb sensitive readers. Due to sexual content, this book is not intended for anyone below 18

Link: Hunter's Blood

Hunter's Promise - The Hunter series book 2

Ivy Moore defined herself as a woman who was responsible for taking care of her sister. She spent years paying for an accident that was never her fault. Until the night she was attacked by monsters and was rescued by the powerful vampire king, Crispin Decius. Through his help, she discovered that she was strong, deadly, a Hunter.

Now she is facing something far worse than just the monsters that she was born to destroy. The insane vampire, the one that was building an army of monsters fed on Hunter's blood, is in hiding, but she isn't through tormenting Ivy. She does the unthinkable in the name of vengeance, and the Hunter will face a challenge that has the potential to break her.

Ivy's life has changed drastically since knowing that vampires exist, but there was no way to prepare for how many more changes were to come.

Approximately 73k words

This is book two in the Hunter Series. This NOT a standalone. Book one is Hunter's Blood

warning this book contains graphic violence and sexual scenes that are not appropriate for readers under 18. Please read responsibly.

Link: Hunter's Promise

Jared - The Hunter series book 2.5 (coming soon)

Hunter's Forever - The Hunter series book 3 (coming soon)

Stand Alones

The Darkness Within - PNR (coming soon)

Running Home - Contemporary YA (coming soon)

Those Who Whisper - Contemporary Ghost story (coming soon)

Printed in Great Britain
by Amazon